THE FIRE
WHEN IT COMES

By Parke Godwin

Beloved Exile
The Fire When It Comes
A Cold Blue Light (WITH MARVIN KAYE)
Wintermind (WITH MARVIN KAYE)
Firelord
The Masters of Solitude (WITH MARVIN KAYE)
A Memory of Lions
Darker Places

THE FIRE
WHEN IT COMES

PARKE GODWIN

DOUBLEDAY & COMPANY, INC.
GARDEN CITY, NEW YORK
1984

PZ
637
D9F4

ACKNOWLEDGMENTS

Introduction copyright © 1984 by Marvin Kaye.

"The Fire When It Comes" copyright © 1981 by Mercury Press. First appeared in *The Magazine of Fantasy and Science Fiction*, May 1981.

"The Lady of Finnigan's Hearth" copyright © 1977 by Ultimate Publishing Co. First appeared in *Fantastic*, September 1977.

"Unsigned Original" copyright © 1975 by Pinnacle Books, Inc. First appeared in *Brother Theodore's Chamber of Horrors*, edited by Marvin Kaye (Pinnacle Books, 1975).

"Stroke of Mercy" copyright © 1981 by TZ Publications. First appeared in *Twilight Zone Magazine*, September 1981.

"The Little Things" copyright © 1981 by Montcalm Publishing Corp. First appeared in *Gallery*, July 1981.

"Up Yours, Federico" copyright © 1981 by Ultimate Publishing Co. First appeared in *Fantastic*, November 1981.

"The Last Rainbow" copyright © 1978 by Ultimate Publishing Co. First appeared in *Fantastic*, July 1978.

"The Second Day of Genius" copyright © 1984. By arrangement with the author.

"Influencing the Hell Out of Time and Teresa Golowitz" copyright © 1982 by TZ Publications. First appeared in *Twilight Zone Magazine*, January 1982.

Library of Congress Cataloging in Publication Data

Godwin, Parke.
The Fire When It Comes.

1. Fantastic fiction, American. I. Title.
PS3557.O316F49 1984   813'.54

CONTENTS

INTRODUCTION
by Marvin Kaye

Parke Godwin and I are in love.

We adore old films and competent literature and fine food and drink, and we're positively passionate about music. True, these days Parke stays busy at the typewriter, but there was a time when his fingers were just as comfortable striking the keys of a piano. I love to sing, and both of us are frustrated composers. Indeed, when we collaborated on *The Masters of Solitude*, *Wintermind* and *A Cold Blue Light*, we were more apt to discuss our effects in musical terms than literary. ("Marv, here's where we want a single oboe, not the full Tchaikovskian strings.")

But any attempt to analyze the special bond that shapes our friendship and our joint writings must ultimately explore the emotional attachment Parke and I have for the world of the theatre . . . and spell that, please, with an *re* and let all modish proofreaders be damned!

How now, Tubal, what news from Genoa?

Those were the first words Parke spoke to me, and they were written by Shakespeare. Since then, Parke and I have shared good talk in Manhattan and on trips to the Georgetown of his youth and my own native Pennsylvania. The blarney started on a winter evening in the late 1960s at a West Side Manhattan YMCA where a showcase production of *The Merchant of Venice* was rehearsing. Parke played Shylock, I was everyone else. Practically. I had to change costumes and makeup three times because I had three roles: Old Gobbo, Tubal and the Duke of Venice. The first time I officially met Parke was when he opened his mouth and addressed me as Shylock's countryman, Tubal, Scene 31, which is theatrical shorthand for Act III, Scene One.

I suspect Parke shared my opinion of most of the cast: good people, but few of them besides us trained in Shakespearean acting technique. At any rate, I felt enormous admiration for this white-haired, potbellied old gaffer Godwin, who looked to me about as old as Methuselah's wetnurse. By dress rehearsal week in an ice-cold dressing room on the Lower East Side, Parke and I gabbed incessantly as we smeared on the cold cream and greasepaint. We discovered our mutual interest in theatre, music, film, brandy, beer . . . and science-fantasy.

Several months later, I directed a pair of plays by Ray Bradbury at Lincoln Center. Because I needed a good character actor for the role of the Old Man in the second script, *A Clear View of an Irish Mist*, I phoned that "old fellow" who played Shylock.

Parke agreed to be in the cast. A few nights later, he strode into the rehearsal studio: trim (he'd lost about fifteen pounds), lean, vital, a fortyish man with prematurely-white hair. I felt beamish, decrepit and decidedly rotund.

That's the way he's affected me ever since.

Up till the early seventies Parke and I mostly met on stage. He was out of the city doing touring productions, and for reasons that any union actor understands, started calling himself Pete. Nowadays, he'll tell you that his friends still call him Pete, but I don't—somebody's got to keep the bum humble.

Then something happened to Parke and me to wean us away from theatre.

We discovered we're really writers.

I sold my first novel in the early 1970s, a murder mystery with a scene backstage at the same theatre where Parke and I first met. Other contracts followed.

One afternoon, Parke stopped by with a partial manuscript of a book he said he was trying to write. He asked if I'd mind reading it, but his attitude suggested he already regarded his labors as folly. It gave me a sinking sensation. I was sure I was about to wade through a quantity of bovine effluent, and I was also certain that Parke cared a hell of a lot more than his casual manner seemed to suggest.

I didn't know that Parke once was a promising writer, long before he switched to acting. But I only had to read the first few pages of his manuscript to realize that this was no abortive first try by a tyro, but rather the work of a consummate storyteller.

That night, I devoured sixty pages—all that was then ready—of *Darker Places*, one of the most harrowing horror stories I've ever read. I called Parke up next day and demanded more.

More pages came, and more, and soon the book was finished and with enviable ease, Parke sold it to the colorful Pat O'Connor, then at Curtis. Several years afterward, Parke did a partial rewrite and resold *Darker Places* to Playboy Press, whose paper edition still may be tracked down by aficionados of the macabre.

A Memory of Lions, recently rereleased by Berkley, followed. It is a brilliant historical novel with strong overtones of mystery and terror. It also persuaded me to approach Parke and suggest that we collaborate on a vast philosophic epic that I'd been wrestling with conceptually for years. Parke said he might be interested if he could add certain dimensions to the plot, and when we got into the nuts-and-bolts of it, we realized that in some ways we'd both been trying to write the same book for years. Eventually our labors were rewarded with the steadily growing appreciation of *The Masters of Solitude*, which may be the best-circulated "cult classic" in the genre.

Somehow, in between working on the sequel to *Masters* and our 1983 haunted-house novel, *A Cold Blue Light*, Parke also managed to write his important Arthurian novel, *Firelord*, and its soon-to-be-released Guineverian sequel, *Beloved Exile*.

We've never collaborated to the extent that we write in the same room . . . we'd probably throttle one another if we tried. But we have marvelous plot conferences, steeped in Martell or Glenmorangie (or during leaner seasons, Colt 45). We divide up the work so that each does the first draft of those sections with which we individually feel most comfortable. Thus, Parke did the primary writing of the coven and battle scenes in *Masters*, while I handled the Singer and City sections. Once our books reach final stage, Parke and I haggle over minute points and word choices like Talmudic students engaged in *pilpul*. We defend our choices staunchly enough, but never quarrel. Indeed, the only time I ever got mad at Parke was when he changed the word "canvas" to "sail" in one stanza of the "Ballad of the Wintermind" without telling me . . . and typically, I was only aggrieved because I'd composed a melody in my mind for the ballad and I couldn't really be comfortable with a quarter note when "canvas" required eighth notes.

Our genuine admiration and friendship for each other is perhaps remarkable, considering the contrast in our natures. If we were like our own characters, Parke would come closest to Arin or Garick, while I'd be Singer. Parke's tallish, I'm undersized; he's open and direct, I'm introspective and convoluted (Parke calls it "kinky"); he's mad for earthy brunettes, I'm partial to ethereal blondes; he likes Martell, I prefer Hennessy; he adores *Watership Down* and Ursula LeGuin and has no patience for Tolkien, I'm exactly the opposite; he prefers working longhand, I compose directly at the keyboard. Most drastic of all, he smokes and I'm allergic to it, and Parke wakes cheerfully at dawn whereas I'm apt to bite anyone who breathes too loud a block away from my bed.

And yet Parke and I are inordinately fond of Indian food, late Sibelius and beer, so I guess there actually is a basis for the marriage.

The American fiction market has long been a vast wasteland. Fortunately, Parke and I have another great asset in common: that treasure of a Doubleday editor named Pat LoBrutto. Pat made it possible for me to see my shorter fiction in hardcover, and now he extends the same courtesy to Parke.

And no wonder. In the following pages, the reader will encounter a storehouse of human drama refracted by the Funhouse mirror of the fantasy genre. There is the richly compassionate comedy of "The Lady of Finnigan's Hearth"—pretheatre Godwin and would you believe I had to talk him out of consigning the manuscript to the wastebasket? There are sly urbanities such as "Unsigned Original" or "The Second Day of Genius"—stories reminiscent of, and quite equal to certain tales of John Collier and Charles Beaumont. There's the wonderfully wise you-have-to-live-it-to-know philosophy of "Influencing the Hell Out of Time and Teresa Golowitz," the Celtic twilight (plus contemporary weltschmerz) of "The Last Rainbow" and that masterful tour de force of horror, "Stroke of Mercy." All told in language of stunning poignancy and beauty.

"The Fire When It Comes" deserves the place of honor in this collection. Quite a few years ago, Parke showed me the first five thousand or so words of it. I was quite taken by the fragment, but he never followed through on the project. Then, some time in the early 1980s, I told Parke I'd like to buy something by him for my Nelson Doubleday anthology, *Ghosts*.

Parke resurrected the partial manuscript of "Fire" and in a re-markably short time, submitted it to me. I was overwhelmed by it: something of an upbeat variation, on Oliver Onions' *The Beckoning Fair One*, "Fire" is one of the finest ghost stories in the English language. Parke's acting teachers drilled into him the necessity of playing against the emotion—in a dramatic role, look for the com-edy, and vice versa. So in "Fire," Parke paradoxically is chiefly concerned with the quality and texture of being alive. Indeed, all of Parke's characters passionately love life. They may bleed or belly-ache, cry or laugh, but they are committed to the only game there is.

"The Fire When It Comes" never made it into my anthology. A gaggle of editorial nervous nellies worried that the sexual content of the story (strictly PG) might offend the nation's librarians. So Parke sent the tale to Ed Ferman at *The Magazine of Fantasy and Science Fiction*. Ed published it in the lead slot for the issue in which "Fire" appeared and the tale went on to win as best novella for 1982 at the World Fantasy Convention in New Haven. When Parke and I heard them call his name, we hugged each other hard enough to break ribs and I thought of a line from *Man of La Mancha:* "And virtue shall triumph at last."

Now Parke has a bust of H. P. Lovecraft jauntily perched on one of his shelves. He hopes he'll win another so he can own a unique set of bookends. I'm betting that he will.

—Manhattan, 1983

I could almost believe in God, though He hasn't called lately.
—Gayla Damon, "The Fire When It Comes"

THE FIRE
WHEN IT COMES

THE FIRE
WHEN IT COMES

For Betty H.—wherever

Got to wake up soon.

I've been sick a long time, I mean really sick. Hard to remember why or how long, but it feels like that time I had a 103 fever for a week. Sleep wasn't rest but endless, meaningless movement, and I'd wake up to change my sweaty night dress for a clean one, which would be soaked by sunup.

But this boring, weary dream has gone on for ages. I'm walking up and down the apartment trying to find the door. The furniture isn't mine. People come and go, replaced by others with even tackier sofas in colors loud enough to keep them awake, and I flutter around and past them on my own silly route as if I'd lost an earring and had to find it before I could get on with life. None of it's very real, murky as *cinéma-vérité* shot in a broom closet. I have to strain to recognize the apartment, and the sound track just mumbles. No feeling at all.

Just that it's gone on so long.

All right, enough of this. Lying around sick and fragile is romantic as hell, but I have to get it together, drop the needle on the world again and let it play. I'm—

Hell, I am out of it, can't even remember my name, but there's a twinge of pain in trying. Never mind, start with simple things. Move your hand, spider your fingers out from under the covers. Rub your face, open your eyes.

That hasn't worked the last thousand times. I can't wake up, and in a minute the stupid dream will start again with a new cast and no script, and I'll be loping up and down after that earring or the lost door. Hell, yes. Here it comes. Again.

No. It's different this time. I'd almost swear I was awake, standing near the balcony door with the whole long view of my apartment stretching out before me: living room, pullman kitchen, the bedroom, bathroom like an afterthought in the rear. For the first time, it's clear daylight and the apartment is bare. Sounds are painfully sharp. The door screams open and shuts like thunder.

A boy and a girl.

She's twenty-two at the outside, he's not much older. He looks sweet, happy and maybe a little scared. Nice face, the kind of sensitive expression you look at twice. The girl's mouth is firmer. Small and blonde and compact. I know that expression, tentative only for a moment before she begins to measure my apartment for possibilities, making it hers.

"Really a lot of room," she says. "I could do things with this place if we had the money."

My God, they're so *loud*. The boy drifts toward me while she bangs cupboard doors, checks out the bathroom, flushes the toilet.

"The john works. No plumbing problems."

"Al, come here. Look, a balcony."

"Wow, Lowen, is that for real?"

Of course it's real, love. Open the door, take a look and then get the hell out of my dreams.

"Let's look, Al." He invites the girl with one hand and opens the balcony door. He's in love with her and doesn't quite know how to handle it all yet. They wander out onto my tiny balcony and look down at Seventy-seventh Street and out over the river, where a garbage scow is gliding upstream. It's a lovely day. Jesus, how long since I've seen the sun? Kids are romping in the playground across Riverside Drive. Lowen and Al stand close together. When he pulls her to him, her hand slips up over his shoulder. The gold ring looks new.

"Can we afford it, Lowen?"

"We can if you want it."

"If? I never wanted anything so much in my life."

They hold each other and talk money as if it were a novelty, mentioning a rent way over what I pay. The frigging landlord would love to hang that price tag on this place. Lowen points to the drainpipe collar bedded in a patch of cement, monument to my epic battle with that bastard to clear the drain and anchor it so every rain didn't turn my balcony into a small lake. Lowen's pointing to letters scratched in the cement.

"GAYLA."

That's right, that's me. I remember now.

They look through the apartment again, excited now that they think they want it. Yes, if they're careful with their budget, if they get that cash wedding present from Aunt Somebody, they can work it. I feel very odd; something is funny here. They're too real. The dream is about them now.

Hey, wait a minute, you two.

The door bangs shut after them.

Hey, wait!

I run out onto the balcony and call to them in the street, and for the first time in this fever dream, I'm conscious of arms and legs that I still can't feel, and a fear growing out of a clearing memory.

Hey, hello. It's me, Gayla Damon.

Lowen turns and tilts his head as if he heard me, or perhaps for one more look at where he's going to live with Al-short-for-Alice. I can't tell from his smile, but I lean to it like a fire in winter, out over the low stone parapet—and then, oh Christ, I remember. For one terrible, sufficient flash, the memory flicks a light switch.

If I could cry or be sick, I'd do that. If I screamed loud enough to crack the asphalt on West End Avenue, nobody would hear. But I let it out anyway, and my scream fills the world as Lowen and Al stroll away toward Riverside Drive.

As if they could actually see me hunched over the balcony edge, head shaking back and forth in despair. They could will their real bodies to stop, real eyes lift again to a real, vacant balcony.

Because they're real. I'm not. Not sick or dreaming, just not.

You died, Gayla baby. You're dead.

The last couple of days have been bad. Panic, running back and forth, scared to death or life, I don't know which, trying to find a way out without knowing where to go or why. I know I died; God, am I sure of that, but not how or how to get out.

There's no fucking door! Lowen and Al sail in and out unloading their junk, but when I try to find the door, it's Not, like me. I'm stuck here. I guess that's what frightens all of us, because you can't imagine Not. I never bought the MGM version of heaven. For me, being dead was simply not being, zero, zilch, something you can't imagine.

The closest you can come is when a dentist knocks you out with Pentothal or how you felt two years before you were born.

No. I don't end, you say. Not me, not the center of the universe. And yet it's happened and I'm stuck with it, no way out, trying to hack the whole thing at once, skittering back and forth from the bedroom to the living room, through the kitchen with its new cream paint, crawling like cigarette smoke in the drapes, beating my nothing-fists against the wall sometimes, collapsing out of habit and exhaustion into a chair or bed I can't feel under me, wearing myself out with the only sensations left, exhaustion and terror.

I'm not dead. I can't be dead, because if I am, why am I still here. Let me out!

To go where, honey?

There's a kind of time again. Al's pinned up a Japanese art calendar in the kitchen, very posh. This month it's a samurai warrior drawing his sword; either that or playing with himself. I can't see it that well, but the date is much too clear. 1981. No wonder the rent's gone up. Seven years since I—

No, that word is a downer. Exited is better. Just how is still a big fat blank wrapped in confusion. All I remember is my name and a few silly details about the apartment. No past, no memory to splice the little snippets of film that flash by too swiftly to catch. Not that it matters, but where's my body? Was I buried or burned, scattered or canned in memoriam in some mausoleum? Was there a husband, a lover? What kind of life did I have?

When I think hard, there's the phantom pain of someone gone, someone who hurt me. That memory is vaguely connected with another of crying into the phone, very drunk. I can't quite remember, just how it made me feel. Got to organize and think. I've worn myself out running scared, and still no answers. The only clear thought is an odd little thing; there must have been a lot of life in me to be kept so close to it.

Don't ask me about death. The rules are all new. I might be the first of the breed. It's still me, but unable to breathe or sleep or get hungry. Just energy that can still run down from overuse, and when that happens, Lowen and Al grow faint.

Everything we do takes energy. A step, a breath, lifting an arm. Because it takes so little, we never notice until we're sick with something like a raging case of flu. That's when we're reminded of the accounting department. Take a step and pant. Take another and stop to rest. Try to walk faster and feel your body straining to function on a fraction of its usual energy. That's all there is to me now, energy, and not much of that. I have to conserve, just float here by Al's painfully correct window drapes and think.

Does anyone know I'm here? I mean, Anyone?

A few more days. Al and Lowen are all moved in. Al's decor works very hard at being House Beautiful, an almost militant graciousness. Style with clenched teeth. And all her china matches; hell yes, it would. But let's face it: whatever's happening to me is because of them. When they're close, I get a hint of solid objects around me, as if I could reach out and touch tables and chairs or Lowen, but touching life costs me energy. The degree of nearness determines how much of my pitiful little charge is spent. Like being alive in a way. Living costs. I learned that somewhere.

Just got the hell scared out of me. Al has a mirror in the bedroom, a big antique affair. Sometimes when she brushes her hair, I stand behind her, aching out of habit to get that brush into my own mop. Tonight as I watched, I saw myself behind her.

I actually jumped with fright, but Al just went on pumping away with the brush while I peered over her head at Gayla Damon. Thirty-three—I remember that now—and beginning to look it. Thank God that won't bother me anymore. Yes, I was tall. Brownish black hair not too well cut. Thin face, strong chin, eyes large and expressive. They were my best feature, they broadcast every feeling I ever had. Lines starting around my mouth. Not a hard mouth but beginning to turn down around the edges, a little tired. Hardness would have helped, I guess. Some of Natalie Bond's brass balls.

Nattie Bond: a name, another memory.

No, it's gone, but there was a kind of pain with it. I stared at the mirror. Cruddy old black sweater and jeans: was I wearing them? You'd think I could check out in something better. Hey, brown eyes, how did they do you for the curtain call? Touch of pancake, I hope. You always looked dead without it. Oh shit . . .

A little crying helps. Even dry it's something.

I watch Lowen more and more, turning to him as a flower follows the sun, beginning to learn why I respond to him. Lowen's a listener and a watcher. He can be animated when he's feeling good or way down if he's not. Tired, depressed or angry, his brown eyes go almost black. Not terribly aggressive, but he does sense and respond to the life going on around him.

He likes the apartment and being quiet in it. He smokes, too, not much but enough to bother Al. They've worked out a compromise: anywhere but the bedroom. So, sometimes, I get a surprise visit in the living room when Lowen wakes up and wants a smoke. He sits for a few minutes in the dark, cigarette a bright arc from his mouth to the ashtray. I can't tell, but sometimes it seems he's listening to pure silence. He turns his head this way and that—toward me sometimes—and I feel weird; like he was sifting the molecules of silence, sensing a weight in them. Sometimes in the evening when he and Al are fixing dinner, Lowen will raise his head in that listening way.

It's a long-shot hope, but I wonder if he can feel *me*.

Why has he brought me back to time and space and caring? All these years there's been only blurred shadows and voices faint as a radio in the next room. Real light and sound and thought came only when he walked in. When Lowen's near, I perk up and glow; when he leaves, I fade to drift, disinterested, by the balcony door.

Lowen Sheppard: twenty-four at most, gentle, unconsciously graceful, awkward only when he tries to be more mature than he is. Don't work at it, lover, it'll come. Soft, straight brown hair that he forgets to cut until Al reminds him, which is often. She's great on detail, lives by it. Faces this apartment like a cage of lions to be tamed, a little scared of it all. Perhaps it's the best she ever had.

Lowen seems used to this much or maybe better. Mister nice guy, not my type at all, and yet I'm bound to him by a kind of fascination, bound without being able to touch his hair or speak to him. And it's no use wondering why, I'm learning that, too. Like that old Bergman flick where Death comes to collect Max Von Sydow. Max says, "Tell me what eternity is like." And Death says, "Who knows? I just work here."

Don't call us. We'll call you.

Well, dammit, *someone* is going to know I'm here. If I can think, I can do, and I'm not going to sit here forever just around the corner from life. Lowen and Al are my world now, the only script left to work with. I'm a part of their lives like a wart on the thigh, somewhere between God and a voyeur.

Wait, a memory just . . . no. Gone too quick again.

If I could touch Lowen somehow. Let him know.

Lowen and Al are settled in, place for everything and everything in its place, and Al daring it to get out of line. Lowen works full-time, and Al must do some part-time gig. She goes out in the early afternoon. The lights dim then. Just as well; I don't like what she's done with my apartment. Everything shrieks its price at you, but somehow Al's not comfortable with it. Maybe she never will be. That mouth is awful tight. She wanted to keep plastic covers over the sofa and chairs, the kind that go *crunkle* when you sit on them and make you feel like you're living in a commercial. But Lowen put his foot down on that.

"But, Al, they're to use, not just to look at."

"I know, but they're so nice and new."

"Look, I wear a rubber when we make love. I don't need them on the furniture."

She actually blushed. "Really, Lowen."

Son of a—she makes him—? Do guys still wear those things? Whatever happened to the sexual revolution?

It's indicative of their upbringing the way each eats, too. Al sits erect at the table and does the full choreography with her knife and fork, as if disapproving Momma was watching her all the time. Cut the meat, lay the knife down, cross the fork to her right hand, spear, chew, swallow, and the whole thing over again. Left hand demurely in her lap.

Lowen leans slightly into his plate, what-the-hell elbows on the table. More often than not, he uses the fork in his left hand, placing things on it with his knife. The way he handles them both, he's definitely lived in England or Europe. Not born there, though. The fall of his speech has a hint of softness and mid-South nasal. Virginia or Maryland. Baltimore, maybe.

Perhaps it's just plain jealousy that puts me off Alice. She's alive. She can reach out and touch, hold, kiss what I can only look at. She's the strength in this marriage, the one who'll make it work. Lowen's softer, easier, with that careless assurance that comes from never having to worry about the rent or good clothes. He's been given to; Al's had to grab and fight. Now he's got a job and trying to cut it on his own for the first time. That's scary, but Al helps. She does a pretty fair job of supporting Lowen without letting him notice it too much.

She has her problems, but Lowen comes first. She gets home just before him, zips out to get fresh flowers for the table. A quick shower and a spritz of perfume, another swift agony at the mirror. And then Lowen is home and sitting down to dinner, telling her about the day. And Al listens, not so much to the words but the easy, charming sound, the quality she loves in him, as if she could learn it

for herself. She's from New York, probably the Bronx. I remember
the accent somehow. Petite and pretty, but she doesn't believe it no
matter how much attention Lowen gives her. Spends a lot of time at
the mirror when he's gone, not admiring but wondering. What does
she really look like? What type is she, what kind of image does she,
should she, project, and can she do it? Lipstick: this shade or that?
So she fiddles and narrows her eyes, scrutinizing the goods, hopes
for the advertised magic of Maybelline and ends up pretty much the
same: more attractive than she thinks, not liking what she sees.

Except she doesn't see. She's carried it around all her life, too
busy, too nervous and insecure to know what she's got. Stripped
down for a bath, Al looks like she never had a pimple or a pound of
fat in her life, but I swear she'll find something wrong, something
not to like.

Don't slop that goo on your face, girl. You're great already. God, I
only wish I had your skin. The crap I had to put on and take off every
night, playing parts like—

Parts like . . .

My God, I remember!

I was an actress. That's what I remember in quick flashes of hard
light. The pictures whiz by like fast cars, but they're slowing down:
stage sets, snatches of dialogue, dim faces in the front rows. Bill
Wrenn giving me a piece of business to work out. Fragments of me
like a painting on shattered glass. I grope for the pieces, fitting them
together one by one.

Bill Wrenn: there's a warm feeling when I think of him, a trusting.
Where did I meet him? Yes, it's coming back.

Bill directed that first season at Lexington Rep. Gentle and patient with a weariness that no longer expected any goodies from life,
he always reminded me of a harried sheepdog with too many sheep
to hustle. Forty years old, two marriages and struck out both times,
not about to fall hard again.

But he did for me. I made it easy for him. We were out of the same
mold, Bill and I. He sensed my insecurity as a woman and found
ways to make it work for me onstage, found parts in me I'd never
dream of playing. With most men, my whole thing began in bed and
usually ended there. Bill and I didn't hurry; there was a love first. We
enjoyed and respected each other's work, and theater was a church
for us. We'd rehash each performance, sometimes staying up all
night to put an extra smidge of polish on business or timing, to get a
better laugh, to make something good just a hair better. We started

with a love of something beyond us that grew toward each other, so that bed, when it came, was natural and easy as it was gorgeous.

I made him love me, my one genuine conquest. We even talked about getting married—carefully skirting around a lot of if's. I seem to remember him asking me one night in Lexington. I *think* he asked then; there's a thick haze of vodka and grass over that night. Did I say yes? Not likely; by that time the old habits were setting in.

It was too good with Bill. That's not funny. Perfection, happiness, these are frightening things. Very few of us can live with them. After a while, I began to resent Bill. I mean, who the hell was he to take up so much of my life? I began to pick at him, finding things not to like, irritating habits like the nervous way he cleared his throat or dug in his ear when he was thinking out some stage problem; the way he picked his feet in bed and usually left the bathroom a mess. Just bitchiness. I even overreacted when he gave me notes after a performance. All bullshit and panic; just looking for a way out. How dare you love me, Bill Wrenn? Who asked you? Where did I get that way, where did it begin?

When Nick Charreau came into the company, he was tailor-made for me.

He was alone onstage the first time I saw him, a new cast replacement going through his blocking with the stage manager. Everything his predecessor did, Nick adjusted to show himself in a better light. He wasn't a better actor, but so completely, insolently sure of himself that he could pull off anything and make it look good, even a bad choice. Totally self-centered: if there were critics in the house, Nick lit up like a sign, otherwise it was just another working night in the sticks.

Nick was a lot better-looking than Bill and eighteen years younger. Even-featured with a sharp, cool, detached expression. Eyes that looked right through you. He could tell me things wrong with myself that would earn Bill Wrenn a reaming-out, but I took it from Nick. He didn't get close or involved all the way down. Perhaps that's why I chose him, out of cowardice. He wouldn't ever ask me to be a person.

When he finished the blocking session, I came down to lean on the stage apron. "You play that far back, you'll upstage everyone else in the scene."

"It's my scene. I'm beautifully lit up there." Nick's smile was friendly with just the right soupçon of cockiness. A little above us all, just enough to tickle my own self-doubt and make me want to take him on. I can handle you, mister. You're not so tough.

But he was. There was always part of Nick I couldn't reach or satisfy. I started out challenged, piqued, to cut him down to size in bed and ended up happy if he'd just smile at me.

Looking over Al's shoulder in the mirror, I know it's not what we're born but what we're made into. The game is called Hurt me, I haven't suffered enough. I needed a son of a bitch like Nick. You don't think I'd go around deserving someone like Bill, do you?

Call that weird, Alice? You're the same song, different verse. You have that wary, born-owing-money look yourself. You handle it better than I did—you knew a good man when you saw one—but you still feel like a loser.

The fights with Bill grew large, bitter and frequent. He knew what was happening and it hurt him. And one night we split.

"When will you grow up, Gayla?"

"Bill, don't make it harder than it has to be. Just wish me luck."

Dogged, tired, plopping fresh ice cubes into his drink. "I care about you. About you, Gayla. That makes it hard. Nick's twenty-two and about an inch deep. He'll split in six months and you'll be out in the cold. When will you learn, Gay? It's not a game, it's not a great big candy store. It's people."

"I'm sorry, Bill."

"Honey," he sighed, "you sure are."

I still hovered, somehow needing his blessing. "Please? Wish me luck?"

Bill raised his glass, not looking up. "Sure, Gay. With Nick you'll need it."

"What's that mean?"

"Nothing, forget it."

"No, you don't just say things like that."

"Sorry, I'm all out of graciousness."

"What did you mean I'll need it?"

Bill paused to take a swallow of his drink. "Come on, Gay. You're not blind."

"Other women? So what."

"Other anybody."

"Oh boy, you're—"

"Nick swings both ways."

"That's a lie!"

"He'd screw a light socket if it helped him to a part."

That was the nastiest thing Bill ever said about anyone. I felt angry and at the same time gratified that he made it easier to walk out mad. "Good-bye, Bill."

And then he looked up at me, showing what was hidden before. Bill Wrenn was crying. Crying for me, the only person in this fucking world who ever did. All the pain, anger, loss, welling up in those sad sheepdog eyes. I could have put my arms around him and stayed . . . no, wait, the picture's changing. I'm here in the apartment. *Get him out of here, Nick*—

No, it goes too fast or I will it to go. I can't, won't remember that yet because it hurts too much, and like a child I reach, cry out for the one thing I could always trust.

Bill-l-l—

Not a scream, just the memory of sound.

Lowen looks up from his book, puzzled. "Al? You call me?"

No answer. It's late, she's asleep.

Once more Lowen seems to listen, feeling the air and the silence, separating its texture with his senses. Searching. Then he goes back to his book, but doesn't really try to read.

He heard me. He heard *me*. I can reach him.

Sooner or later he'll know I'm here. Bust my hump or break my heart, I'll do it. Somehow. I've got to live, Baby. Even dead it's all I know how to do.

I've hit a new low, watched Lowen and Al make love. At first I avoided it, but gradually the prospect drew me as hunger draws you to a kitchen; hunger no longer a poignant memory but sharp need that grows with my strength.

I've never watched lovemaking before. Porn, yes, but that's for laughs, a nowhere fantasy. One of the character men in Lexington had a library of films we used to dig sometimes after a show, hooting at their ineptitude. They could make you laugh or even horny now and then, but none of them ever dealt with reality. Porn removes you from the act, puts it at a safe distance.

Real sex is awkward, banal and somehow very touching to watch. It's all the things we are and want: involvement, commitment, warmth, passion, clumsiness, generosity or selfishness, giving and receiving or holding back, all stained with the colors of openness or fear, lovely—and very vulnerable. All that, and yet the words are inadequate; you can't get any of that from watching. Like the man said, you had to be there.

Rogers and Astaire these two are not. It's all pretty straight missionary and more of an express than a local. Lowen does certain things and Al tries a few herself, sort of at arm's length and without much freedom. I don't think Lowen's had much experience, and Al, though she needs sex, probably learned somewhere that she oughtn't like it all that much. She's the new generation; she's heard it's her right and prerogative, but the no-no was bred in early, so she compromises by not enjoying it, by making it uphill for both of them. She inhibits Lowen without meaning to. He has to wait so long for her to relax and then work so hard to get her going. And of course at the best moment, like an insurance commercial in the middle of a cavalry charge, he has to stop and put on that stupid rubber.

I wonder if Al's Catholic, she never heard of a diaphragm? Or maybe it's money. That's not so far out. Maybe she's uptight about getting pregnant because she remembers how it was to grow up poor. Maybe it's a lot of things adding up to tense ambivalence, wondering why the bells don't ring and the earth shake like she read in *Cosmopolitan.* I seem to remember that trip.

She doesn't give herself much time to relish it afterward, either. Kiss-kiss-bang-bang, then zip with the Kleenex and pit-pat into the shower as if someone might catch them. Maybe that's the way it was before they married, a habit that set before either of them realized it.

But I've touched Lowen. God, yes, for one galvanized split second I felt his body against me. I paid for it, but it had to be.

It was after they made love and Al did her sprint from bed through the shower and into her nightie-cocoon. Lowen went into the bathroom then. I heard the shower running and drifted in after him.

His body looked marvelous; smooth light olive against Al's blue flower-patterned bath curtains, the soap lather standing out sharp white against the last of his summer tan. Not too muscular; supple like Nick. It'll be a while before he has to worry about weight.

Lowen soaped and rinsed, and I enjoyed the shape of his chest and shoulders when he raised his arms over his head.

You're beautiful, Mr. Sheppard.

I had to do it then. I moved in and kissed him, *felt* his chest, stomach, the bulge of his cock against the memory of my pelvis. Only a second, a moment when I had to hold him.

The sensation that shivered through me was like a sudden electric shock. I pulled back, frightened and hurt, hovering in the shower curtain. Lowen jerked, grabbing for the towel rack, taut, scared as myself. Then, slowly, the fear faded and I saw that listening, probing attitude in the lift of his head before the instinctive fear returned. Lowen snapped the water off, stumbled out of the tub and just sat down on the john, dripping and shaking. He sat there for minutes, watching the water drying on his skin, runneling down the sides of the tub. Once he put a hand to his lips. They moved, forming a word I couldn't hear.

You felt me, damn you. You know I'm here. If I could just talk to you.

But the exhaustion and pain ebbed me. We slumped at opposite ends of the small bathroom, Lowen staring through me, not hearing the sob, the agony of the pictures that flashed into life. Touching him, I remember. After the shock of life comes the memory, filling me out by one more jagged fragment, measuring me in pain.

Al, Al, frowning at your mirror, wondering what magic you lack— I should have your problem. The guys probably lined up around the block when you were in school. Not for Gayla Damon; hell, that wasn't even my real name, not for a long, hard time. First there was big, fat Gail Danowski from the Bronx, like you, and at seventeen what you men prayed for and likely never got, I couldn't give away.

Why do I have to remember that? Please, I tried so hard to get away from it. My father who worked for the city as a sandhog, my dumpy mother with her permanent look of washed-out disgust, both of them fresh off the boat in 1938. My sister Sasha, who got married at seventeen to get away from them. Big change: all Zosh did after that was have kids for that beer-drinking slob husband of hers. Jesus, Charlie disgusted me. Sunday afternoons he'd come over and watch football with my father, swill beer and stuff potato chips. Every once in a while he'd let out a huge belch, then sigh and pat his pot gut like he was so goddam pleased with himself. For years, while Zosh's teeth went and her skin faded to chalk delivering five kids.

And me growing up in the middle of it, waiting for the big event of the day in the South Bronx, the Good Humor truck out on the street.

"Mommy, Mommy, the goojoomer's here! C'n I have a dime for the goojoomer?"

"Y'fadda din leave me no money."

Urgent jingling from the Good Humor, ready to leave and take excitement with it. "Mommy!"

"Geddouda here. I ain't got no dime, now shaddup."

I used to think about that a lot: a lousy dime. So little and so much to a kid. Go to hell, Momma. Not for the dime, but for a whole beauty you never had and never missed. You weren't going to keep me from it.

It wasn't much better in high school. I was embarrassed to undress for gym because of the holes in my underwear. And the stains sometimes because I had to use Momma's Kotex and she didn't care if she ran out. I could have used Tampax; virgin or not, I was a big, healthy ox like her and Zosh. I could have conceived an army. When Momma found the Tampax I bought, she slapped me halfway across the room.

"What's this, hah? *Hah?* I ain't got enough trouble, you started already? You sneakin around, you little bitch?"

No such luck, Momma. They didn't want me. The closest I got to boys was talking about them. Sitting in a coffee shop over the debris of my cheap, starchy lunch, the table a garbage dump of bread crusts, spilled sugar and straw wrappers, shredding food bits and paper ends like our envious gossip dissected the girls we knew and the boys we wanted to know.

I never had any sense about men or myself. That happens when you're five foot seven in high school and still growing. A sequoia in a daisy bed, lumpy and lumbering, addicted to food, my refuge when I lost the courage for school dances. I fled home to the icebox and stayed there, eating myself out of my clothes, smearing my acne with Vis-o-Hex, or huddled for hours in a movie, seeing it twice over to pretend I was Hepburn or Bacall, slim, brittle and clever. Or Judith Anderson tearing hell out of *Medea.* I read the play and practiced the lines at my mirror with stiff approximations of her gestures.

But it was *A Streetcar Named Desire* that changed my life. I hardly spoke for days after seeing it. The play stabbed me deep and sparked something that was going to be. I bought more plays and devoured them. Fewer trips to the movies now and more downtown to Broadway and the Village. Live theater, not unreeling on a spool, but happening the moment I saw it.

I was still a lump, still a hundred and fifty pounds of un-lusted-after virgin bohunk, and nobody was going to star Gail Danowski in anything but lunch. I walked alone with my dreams while the hungers grew.

You can go a little mad with loneliness, past caring. Virginity? I couldn't give it away, Momma; so I threw it away. No big Zanuck production, just a boy and a party I can't picture too clearly. We were drinking and wrestling, and I thought, all right, why not? Just once I'm gonna grab a little happiness even if it's just getting laid, what am I saving it for? But I had to get drunk before he fumbled at me. If there was pain or pleasure, I barely felt them, only knew that at last I tasted life where it sprang from the fountain. A meager cup, the cut version, the boy pulling at his clothes afterward, distant, disgusted.

"Shit, whyn't you tell me, Gail?"

Tell you what, lover? That I was a virgin, that by accident you were the first? Is that a guilt trip? Whatever I lost, don't mourn it. Cry for the other things we lose in parked cars and motel beds because we're too drunk or there's too much guilt or fear for beauty. It was the beauty I missed. Be first any time, score up a hundred stiff, clumsy girls, say the silly words, break a hundred promises, brag about it afterward. But leave something of yourself, something of beauty. Only that and you part with a blessing.

He didn't.

The next morning, hung over and miserable, I looked at that frazzled thing in the mirror, had clean through and down to rock bottom, and knew from here on out I'd have to be me or just another Zosh. That day I started to build Gayla Damon.

I graduated an inch taller and thirty pounds lighter, did hard one-week stock as an apprentice. Seventeen hours a day of walk-ons, painting scenery, fencing and dance classes. Diction: practicing for hours with a cork between my teeth—

"Baby, the word is dance. DAAnce, hear the A? Not de-e-ance. Open your mouth and *use* it when you speak."

—Letting my hair grow and moving down to Manhattan, always running away from that lump in the mirror. I never outran her. She was always there, worrying out of my eyes at a thousand auditions, patting my stomach and thighs, searching a hundred dressing room mirrors, plastering pancake on imagined blemishes, grabbing any man's hand because it was there. The years just went, hurrying by like strangers on a street, trailing bits of memory like broken china from a dusty box: buses, planes, snatches of rehearsal, stock, repertory, old reviews.

Miss Damon's talent is raw but unmistakable. When she's right, she *is* theater, vivid, filled with primordial energy that can burn or chill. If she can learn to control . . . she was superbly cast as . . .

—a self-driven horse record-time sprinting from nowhere to noplace. Life? I lived it from eight to eleven o'clock every night and two matinees a week. For three hours each night, I loved, hated, sang, sorrowed enough for three lifetimes. Good houses, bad houses, they all got the best of me because my work had a love behind it. The rest was only fill and who cared? Season after season of repertory, a dozen cities, a dozen summer towns barely glimpsed from opening night to closing, a blur of men and a lot of beds, flush or broke, it didn't matter.

Zosh caught a show once when I was playing in Westchester. Poor Zosh: pasty and fat as Momma by then, busting out of her dresses and her teeth shot. She came hesitantly into my dressing room, wondering if someone might throw her out. The first stage play she ever saw. She didn't know really what to make of it.

"Oh, it was great and all. You look good, Gail. God, you really got some figure now, what size you wear? I never knew about plays. You know me'n school, I always got my girlfriend to write my reports."

She barely sipped the scotch I poured her. "Charlie never buys nothin but beer." I wanted to take her out for a good dinner, but no, she had a sitter at home and it was expensive, and Charlie would yell if she came home too late when he was out bowling.

"Let the dumb fuck yell. You're entitled once in a while."

"Hey, you really gettin a mouth on you, Gail."

"Speaking of that, doesn't Charlie ever look at yours? Doesn't he know you need a dentist?"

"Well, you know how it is. The kids take it out of you."

I gave Zosh a hundred dollars to get her teeth fixed. She wrote that she spent it on the house and kids. *There was the gas bill and Christmas. You cant complain theres nobody on the other end of the phone. Haha. My friends all want to know when your on TV.*

Are you still around, Zosh? Not that it matters. They buried you years ago. No one was going to do that to me.

And then suddenly I was thirty, that big, scary number. Working harder, running harder without knowing where, doing the where-did-it-all-go bit now and then (while the lights caught her best, most expressive angle). Where are you now, Bill? You must be pushing fifty. Still a great lay, I hope. Did you find someone like me or just the opposite? I wouldn't blame you.

And how about you, Nick?

He'll split in six months. You'll be out in the cold.

When Bill said that, I remember thinking, hell, he's right. I'm thirty-two and after that comes thirty-three. Fourteen years, seven dollars in the bank, and where the hell am I?

But I was hung up on Nick's eyes and Nick's body and trying to please him. Perhaps there were other, unspoken things that have nothing to do with loving or sex. You get used very early to not liking yourself. You know you're a fraud, someday they'll all know. The Lump hiding inside your dieted figure and with-it clothes knows you haven't changed, no matter what. The Lump doesn't want to like you. How can she tolerate anyone who does? No, she'll sniff out someone who'll keep her in her lowly place.

Crimes and insanities. Hurting Bill was a very countable sin, but I knew what I needed. So it was Nick, not Bill, who moved in here with me.

And where are you this dark night, Nick? Did you make the big time? I hope so. You're almost thirty now. That's getting on for what you had to sell. Your kind of act has a short run.

My mind wanders like that when Lowen's not around.

Energy builds again, the lights fade up. I drift out onto the balcony, feeling that weight of depression it always brings. My sense of color is dimmed because the kids are asleep. Seventy-seventh Street is a still shot in black and white. Not a soul, not even a late cab whispering up Riverside Drive.

Hey, look! There's a meteor, a falling star. Make a wish: be happy, Bill Wrenn.

And listen! A clock tower. Even with Lowen asleep, I can hear it. Two-three-four o'clock. Definitely, I'm getting stronger. More and more I can feel and sometimes see my legs when I walk, less like floating in a current. I move back through the apartment to hover over Lowen as he sleeps. Wanting. Wondering.

After all this time, why should it be Lowen who wakes me? He felt me in that shower, and we both wonder how, why? Nothing's clear but that I can touch life again with him. If that's wrong, I didn't write the script. Name any form of life you want. A cold germ is just a bug trying to make a living in the only way it knows, in a place it doesn't understand, and it only takes a little out of the place trying. That's

me, that's all of us. I'll take what I need to live. If there's air to
breathe, don't tell me I can't. That's academic.

Al sleeps tiny and still beside Lowen, hardly a bump under the
covers. It must be wonderful to sleep like that. I could never stay out
more than two hours at a time. No, wait: here she comes up out of it
with a sigh and turnover that barely whispers the covers. She slides
out of bed and pit-pats to the bathroom. Bladder the size of an
acorn, up three times a night like I was.

When the john flushes, Lowen stirs and mumbles, flops over and
sinks again. The bathroom door creaks, Al slips back in beside him.
She doesn't settle down yet, but rests on one elbow, a momentary
vigil over Lowen, a secret protecting. I'll bet he doesn't know she
watches him like that. Then she slides under the covers very close,
one arm over him, fingers spread lightly on his skin where his
pajama top is unbuttoned.

To lie beside Lowen like that, to touch him simply by willing it. If
that were my hand resting on his skin. What wouldn't I give for that?

The idea is sudden and frightening. Why not?

If I could get inside Al, stretch out my arm through hers, wear it
like a glove; just for a moment move one real finger over Lowen's
skin. It couldn't hurt her, and I need it so.

I wait for Al to fall asleep, scared of the whole notion. It could
hurt. It hurt to touch Lowen before. Maybe it's against some natural
law. They're flesh, I'm a memory. Lots of maybes but I have to try.
Slow and scared, I drift down over Al and will what shape there is to
me into the attitude of her body. There's no shock when I touch her,
but a definite sensation like dipping into swift-running water. So
weird, I pull away and have to build up my nerve to try again,
settling like a sinking ship as the current of Al's healthy young life
surges and tingles around me, and her chest rises and falls like a
warm blanket over cozy sleep. My breasts nestle into hers, my arm
stretching slowly to fill out the slim contour of her shoulder, elbow,
wrist. It's hard and slow, like half-frozen syrup oozing through a
hose. My fingers struggle one by one into hers.

So tired. Got to rest.

But I feel life, I *feel* it, humming and bubbling all around me.
Jesus, I must have sounded like a steel mill inside, the way I drove
myself. The power, such a wonder. Why did I waste so much time
feeling miserable?

The electric clock glows at 5:03. More minutes pass while each
finger tests itself in Al's, and then I try to move one on Lowen's skin.

The shock curdles me. I cringe away from it, shriveling back up Al's arm, all of me a shaky little ball in her middle. Just as in the shower, I felt skin against skin, even the tiny moisture of pores, but it drains me as if I've run five miles.

Rest and try again. Slow, so slow, so hard, but my fingers creep forward into Al's again. Same thing: the instant I let myself feel with Al's flesh, there's a bright shock and energy drains. If that's not enough, those delicate fingers weigh ten pounds each. I push, poop out, rest, try again, the hardest battle of my life, let alone death, and all in dogged silence broken only by their breathing and the muted whir of the clock.

6:32. The dark bedroom grays up to morning. I can see Lowen's face clearly now: very young, crumpled with sleep. He can't hear my soundless, exhausted panting like the heartbeat of a hummingbird.

6:48. Twelve minutes before the clock beeps the beginning of their day, one finger, one slender thread binding me to Lowen . . . moves. Again. I go dizzy with the sensation but hang on, pouring the last of my strength into one huge effort. The small hand flexes all five fingers like a crab, sliding over the sparse hair on Lowen's chest. A flash-frame of Bill, of Nick, and a thrill of victory.

Hi, baby. I made it.

Then Al stirs, moves *don't, please, wait!* and flips over on her other side, unconcerned as a pancake. I let go, used up, drifting out to nowhere again, barely conscious of space or objects, too burned out even to feel frustrated after all that work.

But I did it. I know the way now. I'll be back.

Night after night I kept at it, fitting to Al's body, learning how to move her fingers without burning myself out. Stronger and surer, until I could move the whole hand and then the arm, and even if Lowen pressed the hand to his mouth or nestled his cheek against it, I could hold on.

And then I blew it, the story of my life. Klutz-woman strikes again. I tried to get in when they were making love.

I said before they're not too dexterous in bed. Al gets uptight from the start, and I can see her lying there, eyes tight shut over Lowen's shoulder, hoping he'll come soon and get it over with. Not always; sometimes she wants it as much as him, but the old hang-ups are always there. She holds back, so he holds back. It's usually one-sided and finished soon.

But that evening everything seemed perfect. They had a light supper, several drinks rather than the usual one, and Lowen didn't spare the vodka. They just naturally segued to the bedroom, not rushed or nervous, undressing each other slowly, enjoyably, melting into each other's arms. Al brought in a candle from the supper table. Nice touch: Nick and I used to do that. They lie there caressing each other, murmuring drowsily. Lowen looks gorgeous in the soft glow, Al like a little Dresden doll. And me—poor, pathetic afterthought— watching it all and yearning.

Jesus, Al, act like you're alive. That's a man. Take hold of him.

Damn, it was too much. The hell with consequences. I draped myself over Al with the ease of practice, stretched my arms and legs along hers. Foolhardy, yes, but at last *my* arms went around Lowen, smoothing, then clawing down his back.

Love me, baby. Love all of me.

My mouth opened hungrily under his, licking his lips and then nipping at them. I writhed Al's slim body under his, pushed her hands to explore him from shoulders to thighs. I never had much trouble in bed. If the guy had anything going and didn't run through it like a fire drill, I could come half a dozen times, little ones and big ones, before he got there.

With Lowen it was like all the best orgasms I ever had. The moment before you start to go, you want to hold back, prolong it, but you can't. I was dependent on Al's chemistry now. Her body was strangely stiff as I hauled her over on top of Lowen. Something new for her. She went taut, resisting it.

"Lowen, wait."

He can't wait, though I'm the only one who sees the irony and the lie. Lowen is coming, I certainly want to, but Al is out of it. I want to *scream* at her, though I should have guessed it long before this. She always times her cries with his, as if they came together.

But it's a lie. She's faking it. She's learned that much.

My God, you're alive, the greatest gift anyone ever got. Does a past tense like me have to show you how?

With a strength like life itself, I churned her up and down on Lowen, hard, burning myself out to tear Al's careful controls from her emotions. She moaned, fighting me, afraid.

"Lowen, stop. Please stop."

You don't fake tonight, kid.

"Stop!"

No way. Go . . . *go!*

Lowen gripped her spasmodically, and I felt his hips tremble under mine/hers. He couldn't hold back any longer. With the last ounce of my will, I bent Al's body down over his, mouth to mouth.

"Now, Lowen. Now!"

Not Al's voice but mine, the first time I've heard it in seven years. Deeper, throatier than Al's. In the middle of coming, an alien bewilderment flooded Lowen's expression. Al stiffened like she was shot. With a cry of bleak terror, she tore herself loose and leaped clear off the bed, clawing for the lamp switch, big-eyed and terrified in the hard light.

"Oh God. Oh Jesus, what's happening?"

Confused, a little out of it himself now, Lowen sat up to stare back at her. "Al, what's the matter?"

She shuddered. "It's not me."

"What?"

"It's not *me*." She snatched up her bathrobe like the last haven in the world. Lowen reached for her instinctively, comforting.

"It's all right, honey, it's—"

"No. It's like something hot inside me."

He went on soothing her, but he knew. I could see that in his eyes as he pulled Al down beside him. He knew: the last thing I saw, because the lights were going down for me, their last spill playing over memory fragments before fading. A confused montage: Nick putting on his jacket, me fumbling for the phone, then pulling at the balcony door, and the darkness and the silence then were like dying again.

I've had some hangovers in my time, mornings of agony after a messy, screaming drunk. Coming back to queasy consciousness while the night's party repeats in your mind like a stupid film loop, and you wonder, in a foggy way, if you really spilled that drink on somebody, and—oh no—you couldn't have said *that* to him, and if you're going to be sick right then or later.

Then the smog clears and you remember. Yeah. You spilled it and did it and you sure as hell said it, and the five best bloody marys in the world won't help.

I blew it good this time, a real production number. Now they both know I'm here.

December 23. I know the date because Al's carefully crossed the days off her calendar where she never bothered before. I've been turned off for days. Almost Christmas, but you'd never know it around here. No holly, no tree, just a few cards opened and dropped on the little teakwood desk where they keep their bills. When Lowen brushes one aside, I can see a thin line of dust. Al hasn't been cleaning.

The kitchen is cluttered. The morning's dishes are still in the sink. Three cardboard boxes stand on the floor, each half full of wrapped dishes and utensils.

So that's it. They're moving. A moment of panic: where do I go from here, them? All right, it was my fault, but . . . don't go, Lowen. I'm not wild about this script myself, but don't ask me to turn out the lights and die again. Because I won't.

There's a miasma of oppression and apprehension all through the apartment. Al's mouth is tighter, her eyes frightened. Lowen comes out into the living room, reluctant and dutiful. Furtively he tests the air as if to feel me in it. He sits down in his usual chair. 3:13 by the miniature grandfather clock on the bookcase. The lights and sound come up slowly with Lowen's nearness. He's home early this afternoon.

Al brings out the Waterford sherry set and puts it on the coffee table. She sits down, waiting with Lowen. The whole scene reminds me of actors taking places before the curtain rises, Al poised tensely on the sofa, revolving her sherry glass in white fingers, Lowen distant, into his own thoughts. The sound is still lousy.

". . . feel silly," Lowen ventures. ". . . all this way . . . time off from . . . just to . . ."

"No! . . . live here like this, not with . . ." Al is really shook; takes a cigarette from Lowen's pack on the coffee table and smokes it in quick, inexpert puffs. "You say you can feel her?"

Lowen nods, unhappy. He doesn't like any of this. "I loved this place from the first day."

"Lowen, answer me. Please."

"Yes."

"Where?"

"Somewhere close. Always close to me."

Al stubs out the cigarette. "And we sure know it's *she*, don't we?"

"Al—"

"Oh hell! I loved this place, too, but this is crazy. I'm *scared*, Lowen. How long have you known?"

"Almost from the start."

"And you never told me."

"Why?" Lowen looks up at her. "I'm not a medium; nothing like this ever happened before. It was weird at first, but then I began to feel that she was just *here*—"

"What!"

"—and part of things like the walls. I didn't even know it was a woman at first."

"Until that time in the shower," Al finishes for him. "Bitch."

Thanks a lot, kid. At least I know what to do with him.

"Look, Al, I can't tell you how I know, but I don't think she means any harm."

Al gulps down her sherry and fills the glass. "The—hell—she—doesn't. I'm not into church anymore. Even if I were, I wouldn't go running for the holy water every time a floor creaked, but don't tell me she doesn't mean anything, Lowen. You know what I'm talking about." Her hands dry-wash each other jerkily. "I mean that night, the way we made love. I—always wanted to make love to you like that. That . . . free."

The best you ever had, love.

Al gets up and paces, nervous. "All right, I've got these god-damned problems. You get taught certain things are wrong. If it's not for babies, it's wrong. It's wrong to use contraceptives, but we can't afford a baby, and—I don't know, Lowen. The world is crazy. But that night, it wasn't me. Not even my voice."

"No, it wasn't."

"All right." Her voice quavers a little as she sits back down. "I loved this place, too. But even if I'd been screwing since I was six, I couldn't live with that."

Lowen must be way down, depressed, because my energy is wavering with his, and sound fades in and out. There's a muffled knock at the door. Lowen opens it to a bald little man like a wizened guru in a heavy, fur-collared overcoat.

Wait, I know this guy. It's that little weasel Hirajian, from Riverside Realty. He rented me this place. Hirajian settles himself in a chair, briefcase on his knee, declining the sherry Al offers. He doesn't look too happy about being here, but the self-satisfied little bastard doesn't miss Al's legs, which make mine look bush-league in retrospect.

I can't catch everything but Hirajian's puzzled by something Al's saying. No problem about the lease, he allows, apartments rent in two days now, but she's apparently thrown him a curve.

Al now: ". . . not exactly our wish, but . . . ."

"Unusual request . . . never anything . . . ."

Now Al is flat and clear: "Did you find out?"

Hirajian opens his briefcase and brings out a sheet of paper while I strain at his through-the-wall mumble.

"Don't know why . . . however, the tenants . . . before you . . ." He runs through a string of names until I make the connection. The tenants who came after me, all those damned extras who wandered through my dreams before Lowen.

Lowen stops him suddenly. He's not as depressed as Al; there's an eagerness in the question. "Did anyone die here?"

"Die?"

"It's very important?" Al says.

Hirajian looks like an undertaker's assistant now, all professional solemnity and reluctance. "As a matter of fact, yes. I was getting to that. In 1974, a Miss Danowski."

Lowen's head snaps up. "First name?"

"Gail."

"Anyone named Gayla? Someone cut the name Gayla in the cement on the balcony."

"That was the Danowski woman. Gayla Damon was her stage name. She was an actress. I remember because she put that name on the lease and had to do it again with her legal signature."

"Gayla."

"You knew her, Mr. Sheppard?"

"Gayla Damon. I should, it's awfully familiar, but—"

"Single?" Al asks. "What sort of person was she?"

Hirajian cracks his prim little smile like a housewife leaning over a back fence to gossip. "Yes and no, you know show people. Her boyfriend moved in with her. I know it's the fashion nowadays, but *we*"—evidently Riverside and God—"don't approve of it."

There's enough energy to laugh, and I wish you could hear me, you little second-string satyr. You made a pass when you showed me this place. I remember: I was wearing that new tan suit from Bergdorf's, and I couldn't split fast enough. But it was the best place yet for the money, so I took it.

Dammit, how did I die? What happened? Don't fade out, weasel. Project, let me hear you.

Al sets down her sherry glass. "We just can't stay here. It's impossible."

Don't go, Lowen. You're all I have, all there is. I won't touch Al, I promise never again. But don't go.

Of course there were promises, Nick. There's always a promise. No one has to spell it out.

I said that once. I'm starting to remember.

While Hirajian patters on, Lowen's lost in some thought. There's something in his eyes I've never seen before. A concern, a caring.

"You mean he didn't come back even when he heard Gayla was dead?"

I love the way he says my name. Like a song, new strength.

"No end of legal trouble," Hirajian clucks. "We couldn't locate him or any family at first. A Mr. . . . yes, a Mr. Wrenn came and made all the arrangements. An old boyfriend, I suppose."

You did that for me, Bill? You came back and helped me out. Boy, what I had and threw away. Sand through my fingers.

"Gayla. Gayla Damon." I grow stronger as Lowen repeats my name, stronger yet as he rises and takes a step toward the balcony door. I could touch him, but I don't dare now. "Yes. Just the name I forgot. It's hard to believe, but it's the only thing I can believe."

Such a queer, tender look. Al reads it, too. "What, Lowen?"

He strides quickly away to the bedroom, and the lights dim a little. Then he's back with a folded paper, so deep in some thought that Al just stares at him and Hirajian is completely lost.

"The things we learn about life," Lowen says. "An English professor of mine said once that life is too random for art; that's why art is structured. Mr. Hirajian, you said no one else ever complained of disturbances in this apartment. I'm not a medium, can't even predict the weather. But I'm beginning to understand a little of this."

Will you tell me, for Christ's sake?

He hands the paper to Al. It looks like an old theater program. "You see, Mr. Hirajian, she's still here."

He has to say it again, delicately as possible. Hirajian pooh-pooh's the whole notion. "Oh really, now, you can't be sure of something like that."

"We know," Al says in a hard voice. "We haven't told you everything. She, it, something's here, and it's destructive."

"No, I don't think so." Lowen nods to the program. I can't see it too well. "Eagle Lake Playhouse, 1974. I saw her work."

You couldn't have. You were only—

"She played Gwendolyn in *Becket.* That's her autograph by her name."

Where the hell is Eagle Lake? Wait a minute. Wait—a—minute. I'm remembering.

"My father was taking me back to school. I spent my whole life in boarding schools all the way through college. Dad thought for our last night together, he'd take me to an uplifting play and save himself making conversation. My parents were very efficient that way.

"Gayla only had one scene, but she was so open, so completely translucent that I couldn't take my eyes off her."

I did play Eagle Lake, and there's a faint memory of some double-breasted country-club type coming back for an autograph for his kid.

"I still remember, she had a line that went: 'My lord cares for nothing in this world, does he?' She turned to Becket then, and you could see a *line* in that turn, a power that reached the other actor and came out to the audience. The other actors were good, but Gayla lit up the stage with something—unbearably human."

Damn right. I was gangbusters in that role. And you saw me? I could almost believe in God now, though He hasn't called lately.

"I was sixteen, and I thought I was the only one in the world who could be so lonely. She showed me we're all alike in that. All our feelings touch. Next day I hitchhiked all the way back to the theater from school . . ." Lowen trails off, looking at Al and the apartment. "And this was her place. She wasn't very old. How did she die?"

"Depressing," Hirajian admits. "Very ugly and depressing, but then suicide always is."

What!

"But as regards your moving out just because—"

The hell I did, no fucking *way*, mister. No. No. NO! I won't listen to any more. Don't believe him, Lowen.

Lowen's on his feet, head tilted in that listening attitude. Al puts down her glass, pale and tense. "What is it?"

"She's here now. She's angry."

"How do you know?"

"Don't ask me how, dammit. I know. She's here."

No, Lowen. On the worst, weakest day of my life, I couldn't do that. Listen. Hear me. Please.

Then Al's up, frightened and desperate. "Go away, whoever you are. For the love of God, go away."

I barely hear her, flinging myself away from them out onto the balcony, silent mouth screaming at the frustration and stupid injustice of it. A lie, a lie, and Lowen is leaving, sending me back to nothing and darkness. But the strength is growing, born of rage and terror. Lowen. Lowen. Lowen. Hear me. I didn't. *Hear me.*

"Lowen, don't!"

I hear Al's voice, then the sudden, sharp sound of the balcony door wrenching open. And as I turn to Lowen, the whole uncut film starts to roll. And, oh Jesus, I remember.

Eagle Lake. That's where it ended, Lowen. Not here, no matter what they tell you. That's where all the years, parts, buses, beds, the whole game came to an end. When I found that none of it worked anymore. Maybe I was growing up a little at last, looking for the *me* in all of it.

Funny, I wasn't even going to audition for stock that summer. Bill called me to do a couple of roles at Eagle Lake, and Nick urged me to go. It was a good season, closing with *A Streetcar Named Desire.* The owner, Ermise Stour, jobbed in Natalie Bond for Blanche Du Bois, and I was to be her understudy. Nattie's name wasn't smash movie box office anymore, but still big enough for stock and star-package houses. She'd be Erm's insurance to make up whatever they lost on the rest of the season.

Erm, you tough old bag. You were going to sell that broken-down theater after every season. I'll bet you're still there, chain-smoking over a bottle of Chivas and babying that ratty poodle.

Ermise lived in a rambling ex-hotel with a huge fireplace in the lounge. We had all our opening-night parties there with a big blaze going because Eagle Lake never warmed up or dried out even in August.

At the opening party for *Becket,* all of us were too keyed up to get drunk, running on adrenaline from the show, slopping drinks and stuffing sandwiches, fending off the local reviewers, horny boy scouts with a course in journalism.

Dinner? No thanks. I've got a horrible week coming up, and it's all I can do to shower and fall into bed. Bill, let's get *out* of here. Thanks, you're a jewel, I needed a refill. Gimme your sweater. Jesus, doesn't it ever get warm in this place? You could age beef in our dressing room.

Nick was down for a few days the week before. Bill rather pointedly made himself scarce. He was still in love with me. That must have hurt, working with me day after day, keeping it inside, and I didn't help matters by dragging Nick everywhere like a prize bull: hey, look what I got! Smart girl, Gayla. With a year's study, you could be an idiot.

But Nick was gone, and we'd managed to get *Becket* open despite failing energy, colds, frayed nerves and lousy weather. It was good just to stand with Bill against the porch railing, watching moths bat themselves silly against the overhead light. Bill was always guarded when we were alone now. I kept it light and friendly, asked about his preparations for *Streetcar*. He sighed with an Old Testament flavor of doom.

"Don't ask. Erm had to cut the set budget, first read-through is tomorrow morning, and Nattie's plane won't get in until one. I'm going to be up all night and I'll still only be about five pages ahead of you people on blocking."

"Why's she late?"

"Who the hell knows? Business with her agent or something. You'll have to read in for her."

Good. One more precious rehearsal on my Blanche, one more time to read those beautiful words and perhaps find one more color in them before Natalie Bond froze it all in star glitter. That was all I had to look forward to now. The fatigue, the wet summer, lousy houses, all of it accumulated to a desolation I couldn't shrug off. I had a small part in *Streetcar,* but understudying Natalie Bond meant watching her do my role, never to touch the magic myself. Maybe her plane could crash—just a little—but even then, what? Somehow even the thought of Nick depressed me. Back in New York he'd get in to see the right agents where I couldn't, landing commercials, lining up this, grabbing that, always smarter at business than me.

That night before the party I sat on my bed, staring glumly at the yellow-green wallpaper and my battered Samsonite luggage, and thought, *I'm tired of you. Something's gone. There's gotta be more than this.* And I curled up in my old gray bathrobe, wallowing in self-pity. Nick, you want to get married? Bring me the towel and wash my back? Baby me a little when I feel rotten, like now? There's a big empty place in me wants to be pregnant with more than a part. Tired, negative, I knew Nick would never marry me. I was kidding myself.

So it was good to have Bill there on the porch for a minute. I leaned against him and he put an arm around me. We should have gone to bed and let it be beautiful one more time. It would have been the last.

"Tired, Gay?"

"I want to go home."

Except I never in my whole life found where it was.

Natalie Bond came and conquered. She knew her lines pretty well going in and crammed the rest with me in her room or the restaurant down our street. No one recognized her at first with her hair done just the right shade of fading dishwater blond for Blanche, most of her thin face hidden behind a huge pair of prescription sunglasses. She was nearsighted to blindness; some of her intensity on film must have come from trying to feel out the blocking by braille. But a pro she was. She soaked up Bill's direction, drove herself and us, and I saw the ruthless energy that made Nattie a star.

I saw other things, too. Nattie hadn't been on a live stage for a lot of years. She missed values left and right in Blanche, and didn't have time to pick them up on a two-week stock schedule. Film is a director's medium. He can put your attention where he wants with the camera. Stage work takes a whole different set of muscles, and hers were flabby, unused to sustaining an action or mood for two and a half hours.

But for the first time that season, we were nearly sold out at the box office. Erm was impressed. Bill wasn't.

"They're coming to see a star. She could fart her way through Blanche and they'll still say she's wonderful."

Maybe, but life wasn't all skittles for Nattie. She had two children in expensive schools and got endless phone calls from her manager in California about taxes.

"I gotta work, honey," she told me over black coffee and dry toast. "The wolf's got my ass in his chops already."

She meant it. Another phone call, and that same afternoon between lunch and rehearsal call, Nattie Bond was gone, and I was sitting in Ermise's living room again while Erm swore back and forth across the worn carpet, waving her drink like a weapon, and Bill tried to look bereaved. He always wanted me for Blanche. He had me now.

"Fucked me from the word go." Ermise sprayed ashes over the rug and her poodle. "She knew this when she signed and never said a goddam word."

The facts filtered through my rosy haze. Natalie's agent had a picture deal on the Coast so close to signing that it was worth it to let Ermise sue. They'd just buy up her contract—if she could be in Los Angeles tomorrow.

Ermise hurled her cigarette into the trash-filled fireplace, gulped the last of her drink and turned a mental page. Nattie was one problem, the show another. "You ready to go, Gayla?"

"In my sleep, love."

I was already readjusting the role to the Blanche in my ear and not as sorry for the box office as Erm. Screw 'em all, they were going to see ten times the Blanche Nattie Bond could give them on the best day she ever worked.

"Bill wants me to give you a raise," Ermise said. "Wish I could, Gay, but things are tight."

I pulled the worn script out of my jeans, grinning like a fool back at Bill, who couldn't hide his glee anymore. "Just pay on time, Erm. Keep out of my hair and don't clutter up my stage. Bill, let's go to work."

From my first rehearsal, the play convulsed and became a different animal. The whole cast had to shift gears for me, but no longer suffused by Nattie's hard light, they began to find themselves and glimmer with life. I ate and slept with the script while Blanche came sure and clear. Hell, I'd been rehearsing her for fourteen years. It wasn't hard to identify with the hunger for love half appeased in bed-hopping and sexual junk food and what that does to a woman. The blurred, darkening picture of a girl waiting in her best dress to go to the dance of life with someone who never came.

Play Blanche? Hell, I *was* Blanche. And Stella with her stupid hots for Stanley, Roxane on her silly balcony, loving the wrong guy in the dark for the wrong reasons. I was Ophelia, fucked up and used and never knowing why or how; Alice falling on her butt through the Looking Glass, hunting for a crown on the eighth row that some son of a bitch sawed clean off the board. Man, I was all of them, the whole reamed-out world looking up at God and wondering where it all went with nothing to show. I paid my dues.

Then, just as it seemed to be coming together, it went flat, deader than I am now. But out of that death came a beautiful, risky answer.

Blanche Du Bois is a bitch of a role and demands a powerhouse actress. That's the problem. Like the aura that surrounds Hamlet, the role accumulates a lot of star-shtick and something very subtle can get lost. I determined to strip away the layers of gloss and find what was there to begin with.

"The part's a trap, Bill. All those fluttery, curlicued lines reach out and beg you to *act* them. And you wind up with dazzle again, a concert performance."

"Cadenzas," he agreed with me. "The old Williams poetry."

"Right! Cadenzas, scales. No, by God! I've played the Deep South. There's a smothered quality to those women that gets lost

that way. The script describes her as a moth. Moths don't dazzle.
They don't glitter."

"Remember that night on the porch," Bill said thoughtfully.
"They don't glitter, but they do need the light."

And that was it. Blanche aspired to the things she painted with
foolish words. A dream of glitter seen by a nearsighted person by a
failing candle. The lines are ornate, but just possibly Blanche is not
quite as intelligent as she's been played.

A long artistic chance, but they're the only ones worth taking. If
you don't have the guts to be wrong, take up accounting.

So my Blanche emerged a very pathetic woman, a little grotesque
as such women are, not only desperate for love but logical in her
hopes for Mitch. For all of Belle Reeve and the inbred magnolias,
she's not that far above him. Bill gave me my head, knowing that by
finding my own Blanche, even being wrong for a while, I'd find the
play's as well. On my terms and with my own reality.

I had three lovely labor-pained days of seeing her come alive. On
the third day, I was sitting in a corner of the stage with coffee and a
sandwich, digging at the script while the others lunched. When Sally
Kent walked in, I snapped at her.

"Where's the rest? It's two o'clock. Let's go."

"They want you over at the office, Gay."

"What the hell for? I don't have time. Where's Bill?"

"At the office," Sally admitted reluctantly. "Natalie Bond is here.
She's back in the show."

The kiss of death. Even as I shook my head, no, Erm wouldn't do
this to me, I knew she would.

Ermise hunched in a chair by the fireplace, bitter with what she
had to do, trying not to antagonize Bill any further. He poised on
the sofa, seething like a malevolent cat.

"Nattie will do the show after all," Ermise said. "I have to put her
back in, Gay."

I couldn't speak at first; sick, quivering on my feet with that
horrible end-of-the-rope hollowness in my stomach. No place to go
from here. No place . . .

"When we pulled her name off the advertising, we lost more than
a third of our reservations." Erm snorted. "I don't like it. I don't like
her right now, but she's the only thing'll keep my theater open."

Bill's comment cut with the hard edge of disgust. "You know what
this does to the cast, don't you? They've readjusted once. Now they
have to do it again and open in two days. They were coming beauti-

fully, they were an ensemble with Gayla. Now they're the tail end of a star vehicle."

Bill knew it was already lost, but he was doing this for me.

Ermise shook her head. "Gay, honey, I can't afford it, but I'm gonna raise you retroactive to the first week of your contract." Her hands fluttered in an uncharacteristically helpless gesture. "I owe you that. And you'll go back in as Eunice. But next season—"

I found my voice. It was strange, old. "Don't do this to me. This role, it's mine, I earned it. She'll ruin it."

"Don't look at me," Bill snapped to Ermise. "She's right."

Ermise went defensive. "I don't care who's right. You're all for Gay. Fine, but I can't run a theater that way. Lucky to break even as it is. Nattie's back, she plays and that's the end of it. Gay's contract reads 'as cast.' She's Eunice. What else can I say?"

I showed her what else. I ripped the *Streetcar* script in four parts and threw them in the fireplace. "You can say good-bye, Ermise. Then you can take your raise and shove it." I was already lurching toward the door, voice breaking. "Then you can put someone in my roles, because I'm leaving."

I meant it. Without Blanche, there was no reason to stay another minute. Finished. Done.

Except for Natalie Bond. I found her in her hotel room, already dressed for rehearsal and running over the script.

"Come on in, Gayla. Drink?"

"No."

She read my tension as I crouched with my back against the door. "All right, hon. Get it off your chest."

"I will."

I told the bitch what I felt and what I thought and didn't leave anything out. It was quite a speech for no rehearsal, beginning with my teens when I first knew I had to play Blanche, and the years and hard work that made me worthy of it. There wasn't a rep company in the East I hadn't worked, or a major role from Rosalind to Saint Joan I hadn't played. To walk out on the show like she did was pure shit. To crawl back was worse.

"Right," said Nattie. She faced me all through it, let me get it all out. I was crying when I finished. I sank down on a chair, grabbing for one of her Kleenex.

"Now do you want a drink?"

"Yes, what the hell."

She wasn't all rat, Nattie. She could have put me down with the star routine, but she fixed me a stiff gin and soda without a word. I remember her fixing that drink: thick glasses and no makeup, gristly thin. She had endless trouble with her uterus, infection after painful infection and a work schedule that never allowed her to heal properly. A hysterectomy ended the whole thing. Nattie's face was thinner than mine, all the softness gone, mouth and cheeks drawn tight. No matter how sincere, the smile couldn't unclench.

And this, I thought, is what I want to be? Help me, Nick. Take me home. There's gotta be a home somewhere, a little rest.

"Know what we're like?" Nattie mused. "A little fish swimming away from a big, hungry fish who's just about to be eaten by a bigger fish. That's us, honey. And that's me in the middle."

She screwed Ermise but someone shafted her, too. The picture deal was a big fat fake. The producer wanted someone a little bigger and hustled Nattie very plausibly to scare the lady into reaching for a pen.

"I'm broke, Gayla. I owe forty thousand in back taxes, my house is on a second mortgage and my kids' tuition is overdue. Those kids are all I have. I don't know where the hell to go from here, but Ermise needs me and I sure as hell need the job."

While I huddled over my drink, unable to speak, Nattie scribbled something on a memo pad.

"You're too good to waste, you're not commercial and you'll probably die broke. But I saw your rehearsal this morning."

I looked up at her in weepy surprise. The smile wasn't quite so hard just then.

"If I can do it half that well, Gay. Half."

She shoved the paper into my hand. "That's my agent in New York. He's with William Morris. If he can't get you work, no one can. I'll call him myself." She glanced at her dressing-table clock. "Time, gotta run."

Nattie divined the finality in my shoulders as I sagged toward the door. "You going to play Eunice?"

"No. I'm leaving."

Pinning her hair, she shot me a swift, unsmiling appraisal through the mirror. "Good for you. You got a man in New York?"

"Yeah."

"Get married," she mumbled through a mouthful of pins. "It's not worth it." As the door closed, she raised her voice. "But call my agent."

My bags were packed, but I hadn't bothered to change clothes. That's why my permanent costume, I suppose. Who knew then I'd get very tired of black? Bill insisted on driving me to the airport. When he came for me, I must have looked pathetic, curled up on the bed in one more temporary, damp summer room just waiting to eject me. No love lost; I got damned sick of yellow-green wallpaper.

Bill sat on the edge of the bed. "Ready, Gay?"

I didn't move or answer. Done, finished. Bill put aside the old hurt and lay down beside me, bringing me into his arms. I guess something in him had to open in spite of his defenses. He opened my heart gently as a baby's hand clutched around something that might harm it, letting me cry the last of it out against his shoulder. The light faded in the room while we lay together.

We kissed good-bye like lovers at the departure gate. Bill was too much a part of me for anything less. Maybe he knew better than I how little was waiting for me.

"Be good, Gay."

"You too." I fiddled with his collar. "Don't forget to take your vitamins, you need them. Call me when you get back."

He hugged me one last time. "Why don't you marry me sometime?"

For a lot of reasons, Bill. Because I was a fool and something of a coward. The stunting begins in the seed when we learn not to like ourselves. The sad thing about life is that we usually get what we really want. Let it be.

Funny, though: that was my first and last proposal, and I kissed him good-bye, walked out of his life and four hours later I was dead.

There was time on the plane to get some of it together. Natalie was a star, at the top where I wanted to be, and look at her: most of the woman cut out of her, flogged to work not by ambition but need. Driven and used. She reminded me of a legless circus freak propelling herself on huge, overdeveloped arms, the rest of her a pitiful afterthought cared for by an expensive gynecologist. I thought, at least when I get home there'll be Nick. Don't call him from the airport, let it be a surprise. We'll get some coffee and cold cuts from Zabar's, make love and talk half the night. I needed to talk, to see us plain.

Get married, Nattie said. It isn't worth it.

Maybe not the way I chased it for fourteen years. I'd call her agent, keep working, but more New York jobs with time left over to be with Nick, to sit on my balcony and just breathe or read. To make a few friends outside of theater. To see a doctor and find out how tough I really am, and if everything in the baby box is working right, so that maybe—

Like she said, so maybe get married and have kids while I can. A little commitment, Nick, a little tomorrow. If the word sounds strange, I just learned it. Give me this, Nick. I need it.

The light was on in our living room as I hauled my suitcase out of the cab and started up. Hell, I won't even buzz, just turn the key in the lock and reach for him.

I did that.

There was—yes, I remember—one blessed moment of breathing the good, safe air of my own living room as I set down the luggage. I heard a faint stirring from the bedroom. Good, I've surprised him. If Nick was just waking from a nap, we'd have that much more time to touch each other.

"It's me, baby."

I crossed to the bedroom door, groping inside for the light switch. "I'm home."

I didn't need the switch. There was enough light to see them frozen on the torn-up bed. The other one was older, a little flabby. He muttered something to Nick. I stood there, absurd myself, and choked, "Excuse me."

Then, as if someone punched me in the stomach, I stumbled to the bathroom, pushed the door shut and fell back against it.

"Get him out of here, Nick!"

The last word strangled off as I doubled over the john and vomited all the horrible day out of me, with two hours left to live, retching and sobbing, not wanting to hear whatever was said beyond the door. After a short time, the front door closed. I washed my face, dried it with the stiff, clumsy movements of exhaustion and got out to the living room somehow, past the bed where Nick was smoking a cigarette, the sheet pulled up over his lean thighs.

I remember pouring a drink. That was foolish on an empty stomach, the worst thing I could have done. I sat on the sofa, waiting.

"Nick." The silence from the bedroom was the only thing I could feel in my shock. "Nick, please come out. I want to talk to you."

I heard him rustle into his clothes. In a moment Nick came out, bleak and sullen.

"Why are you back so early?"

"No, they—" My reactions were still disjointed, coming out of shock, but the anger was building. "They put Nattie Bond back in the show. I walked out."

That seemed to concern him more than anything else. "You just walked out? They'll get Equity on you."

The delayed reaction exploded. "*Fuck* Equity! Never mind about Equity, what are *we* gonna do?"

"What do you mean?" he asked calmly.

"Oh, man, are you for real?" I pointed at the door. "What was that?"

"That may be a Broadway job." He turned away into the kitchen. "Now get off my back."

"The hell I—"

"Hey look, Gayla. I haven't made any promises to you. You wanted me to move in. Okay, I moved in. We've had it good."

I began to shake. "Promises? Of course there were promises. There's always a promise, nobody has to spell it out. I could have gone to bed with Bill Wrenn plenty of times this summer, but I didn't."

He only shrugged. "So whose fault is that? Not mine."

"You bastard!" I threw my glass at him. He ducked, the thing went a mile wide, then Nick was sopping up whisky and bits of glass while I shook myself apart on the couch, teeth chattering so hard I had to clamp my mouth tight shut. It was all hitting me at once, and I couldn't handle half of it. Nick finished cleaning up without a word, but I could see even then the tight line of his mouth and the angry droop of his eyelids. He had guts of a kind, Nick. He could face anything because it didn't matter. All the important things were outside, to be reached for. Inside I think he was dead.

"The meanest thing Bill ever said to me," I stuttered. "When I left him for you, h-he said you played both sides of the fence. And I c-called him a goddam liar. I couldn't believe he'd be small enough to—Nick, I'm falling apart. They took my show, and I came home to you because I don't know what to do."

Nick came over, sat down and held me in his arms. "I'm not, Gayla."

"Not what?"

"What Bill said."

"Then w-what was this?"

He didn't answer, just kissed me. I clung to Nick like a lost child.

Why do we always try to rewrite what's happened? Even now I see myself pointing to the door and kissing him off with a real Bette

Davis sizzler for a curtain. Bullshit. I needed Nick. The accounting department was already toting up the cost of what I wanted and saying, *I'll change him. It's worth it.*

I only cried wearily in his arms while Nick soothed and stroked me. "I'm not that," he said again. "Just that so many guys are hung up on role-playing and all that shit. Oh, it's been said about me."

I twisted in his lap to look at him. "Nick, why did you come to me?"

The question gave him more trouble than it should. "I like you. You're the greatest girl I ever met."

Something didn't add up. Nothing ever bugged Nick before; he could always handle it, but he was finding this hard.

"That's not enough," I persisted. "Not tonight."

Nick disengaged himself with a bored sigh. "Look, I have to go out."

"Go out? Now?" I couldn't believe he'd leave me like this. "Why?"

He walked away toward the bedroom. I felt the anger grow cold with something I'd never faced before, answers to questions that gnawed at the back of my mind from our first night. "Why, Nick? Is it him? Did that fat queer tell you to come over after you ditched the hag?"

Nick turned on me, lowering. "I don't like that word."

"Queer."

"I said—"

"Queer!"

"All right." He kicked viciously at the bedroom door with all the force he wanted to spend stopping my mouth. "It's a fact in this business. That's why I get in places you don't. It's a business, cut and dried, not an *aht fawm* like you're always preaching."

"Come off it, Nick." I stood up, ready for him now and wanting the fight. "That casting-couch bit went out with Harlow. Is that how you get jobs? That and the cheap, scene-stealing tricks you use when you know and I know I played you against the fucking wall in Lexington, you hypocritical son of a bitch."

Nick threw up a warning hand. "Hey, wait just one damn minute, Bernhardt. I never said I was or ever could be as good as you. But I'll tell you one thing." Nick opened the closet and snaked his jacket off a hanger. "I'll be around and working when nobody remembers you, because I know the business. You've been around fourteen years and still don't know the score. You won't make rounds, you don't want to be bothered waiting for an agent to see you. You're a goddam *ahtist*. You won't wait in New York for something to develop, hell no. You'll take any show going out to Noplaceville, and who the hell ever sees you but some jerkoff writing for a newspaper no one reads. Integrity? Bullshit, lady. You are *afraid* of New York, afraid to take a chance on it."

Nick subsided a little. "That guy who was here, he produces. He's got a big voice where it counts." Again he looked away with that odd, inconsistent embarrassment. "He didn't want to sleep with me, really. He's basically straight."

That was too absurd for anger. "Basically?"

"He only wanted a little affection."

"And you, Nick? Which way do you go basically? I mean was it his idea or yours?"

That was the first totally vulnerable moment I ever saw in Nick. He turned away, leaning against the sink. I could barely hear him. "I don't know. It's never made much difference. So what's the harm? I don't lose anything, and I may gain."

He started for the door, but I stopped him. "Nick, I need you. What's happened to me today—I'm almost sick. Please don't do this to me."

"Do what? Look." He held me a moment without warmth or conviction. "I'll only be gone a little while. We'll talk tomorrow, okay?"

"Don't go, Nick."

He straightened his collar carefully with a sidelong glance at the mirror. "We can't talk when you're like this. There's no point."

I dogged him desperately, needing something to hang on to. "Please don't go. I'm sorry for what I said. Nick, we can work it out, but don't leave me alone."

"I have to." His hand was already on the door, cutting me off like a thread hanging from his sleeve.

"Why!" It ripped up out of the bottom, out of the anger without which we never love or possess anything. "Because that fat faggot with his job means more than I do, right? How low do you crawl to make a buck in this business? Or is it all business? Jesus, you make me sick."

Nick couldn't be insulted. Even at the end, he didn't have that to spare me. Just a look from those cool blue eyes I tried so hard to please, telling me he was a winner in a game he knew, and I just didn't make it.

"It's your apartment. I'll move."

"Nick, don't go."

The door closed.

What did I do then? I should remember, they were the last minutes of my life. The door closed. I heard Nick thumping down the carpeted stairs, and thank God for cold comfort I didn't run after him. I poured a straight shot and finished it in one pull.

A hollow, eye-of-the-storm calm settled on me and then a depression so heavy it was a physical pain. I wandered through the apartment drinking too much and too fast, talking to Nick, to Bill, to Nattie, until I collapsed, clumsy, hiccuping drunk on the floor with half an hour to live.

Another drink. Get blind, drunk enough to reach . . . something, to blot out the Lump. Yeah, she's still with you, the goddam little loser. Don't you ever learn, loser? No, she won't ever learn. Yesterday did this day's madness prepare. What play was that and who cares?

I tried to think but nothing came together. My life was a scattered Tinkertoy, all joints and pieces without meaning or order. A sum of apples and oranges: parts played, meals eaten, clothes worn, he said and I said, old tickets, old programs, newspaper reviews yellowed and fragile as Blanche's love letters. Apples and oranges. Where did I leave anything of myself, who did I love, what did I have? No one. Nothing.

Only Bill Wrenn.

"Christ, Bill, help me!"

I clawed for the phone with the room spinning and managed to call the theater. One of the girl apprentices answered. I struggled to make myself understood with a thickening tongue. "Yeah, Bill Wrenn, 'simportant. Gayla Damon. Yeah, hi, honey. He's not? Goddammit, he's *gotta* be. I *need* him. When'll he be back? Yeah . . . yeah. Tell'm call Gayla, please. Please. Yeah, trouble. Real trouble. I need him."

That's how it happened. I dropped the phone in the general vicinity of the hook and staggered to the pitching sink to make one more huge, suicidal drink, crying and laughing, part drunk, part hysteria. But Bill was going to bail me out like he always had, and, boy, ol' Gay had learned her lesson. I was a fool to leave him. He loved me. Bill loved me and I was afraid of that. Afraid to be loved. How dumb can you get?

"How dumb?" I raged mushily at the Lump in the mirror. "You with the great, soulful eyes. You never knew shit, baby."

I was sweating. The wool sweater oppressed my clammy skin. Some sober molecule said take it off, but no. It's cooler out on my balcony. I will go out on my beautiful, nighted balcony and present my case to the yet unknowing world.

I half fell through the door. The balcony had a low railing, lower than I judged as I stumbled and heaved my drunken weight behind the hand flung out to steady myself and—

Fell. No more time.

That's it, finished. Now I've remembered. It was that sudden, painless, meaningless. No fade-out, no end-title music resolving the conflict themes, only torn film fluttering past the projector light, leaving a white screen.

There's a few answers anyway. I could get a lump in my throat, if I had one, thinking how Bill came and checked me out. God, let's hope they kept me covered. I must have looked awful. Poor Bill; maybe I gave you such a rotten time because I knew you could take it and still hang in. That's one of the faces of love, Mr. Wrenn.

But I'd never have guessed about Lowen. Just imagine: he saw me that long ago and remembered all these years because I showed him he wasn't alone. I still can't add it up. Apples and oranges.

Unless, just maybe . . .

"Lowen!"

The sound track again, the needle dropped on time. The balcony door thunders open and slams shut. Al calls again, but Lowen ignores her, leaning against the door, holding it closed.

"Gayla?"

His eyes move searchingly over the balcony in the darkening winter afternoon. From my name etched in the cement, around the railing, Lowen's whole concentrated being probes the gray light and air, full of purpose and need.

"Gayla, I know you're here."

As he says my name, sound and vision and my own strength treble. I turn to him, wondering if through the sheer power of his need he can see me yet.

Lowen, can you hear me?

"I think I know what this means."

I stretch out my hand, open up, let it touch his face, and as I tingle and hurt with it, Lowen turns his cheek into the caress.

"Yes, I feel you close."

Talk to me, Lowen.

"Isn't it strange, Gayla?"

Not strange at all, not us.

"When I saw you that night, I wanted to reach out and touch you, but I was just too shy. Couldn't even ask for my own autograph."

Why not? I could have used a little touching.

"But I hitched all the way from school next day just to catch a glimpse of you. Hid in the back of the theater and watched you rehearse."

That was Blanche. You saw that?

"It was the same thing all over again. You had something that reached out and showed me how we're all alike. I never saw a lonelier person than you on that stage. Or more beautiful. I cried."

You saw Blanche. She did have a beauty.

"Oh, Gayla, the letters I wrote you and never sent. Forgive me. I forgot the name but not the lesson. If you can hear me: you were the first woman I ever loved, and you taught me right. It's a giving."

I hear Al's urgent knock on the other side of the door. "Lowen, what is it? Are you all right?"

He turns his head and smiles. God, he's beautiful. "Fine, Al. She loves this place, Gayla. Don't drive her away."

I won't, but don't go. Not now when I'm beginning to understand so much.

He shakes his head. "This is our first house. We're new, all kinds of problems. Parents, religion, everything."

Can you hear me?

"We were never loved by anyone before, either of us. That's new, too. You pray for it—"

Like a fire.

"—like a fire to warm yourself."

You *do* hear me.

"But it's scary. What do you do with the fire when it comes?" Lowen's hands reach out, pleading. "Don't take this away from her. Don't hurt my Al. You're stronger than us. You can manage."

I stretch my hand to touch his. With all my will, I press the answer through the contact.

Promise, Lowen.

"Don't make me shut you out. I don't know if I could. Go away and keep our secret? Take a big piece of love with you?"

Yes. Just that I was reaching for something, like you, and I had it all the time. So do you, Lowen. You're a—

I feel again as I did when the star fell across the sky, joyful and new and big as all creation without needing a reason, as Lowen's real fingers close around the memory of mine.

You're a *mensch*, love. Like me.

Lowen murmurs: "I feel your hand. I don't care what anyone says. Your kind of woman doesn't kill herself. I'll never believe it."

Bet on it. And thank you.

So it was a hell of a lot more than apples and oranges. It was a giving, a love. Hear that, Bill? Nattie? What I called life was just the love, the giving, like kisses on the wind, thrown to the audience, to my work, to the casual men, to whom it may concern. I was a giver, and if the little takers like Nick couldn't dig that, tough. That's the way it went down. All the miserable, self-cheating years, something heard a music and went on singing. If Nattie could do it half as well. If she was half as alive as me, she meant. I loved all my life, because they're the same thing. Man, I was beautiful.

That's the part of you that woke me, Lowen. You're green, but you won't go through life like a tourist. You're going to get hurt and do some hurting yourself, but maybe someday . . .

That's it, Lowen. That's the plot. You said it: we all touch, and the touching continues us. All those nights, throwing all of myself at life, and who's to say I did it alone? So when you're full up with life, maybe you'll wake like me to spill it over into some poor, scared kid. You're full of life like me, Lowen. It's a beautiful, rare gift.

It's dark enough now to see stars and the fingernail sliver of moon. A lovely moment for Lowen and me, like the night with Bill a moment before we made love for the first time. Lowen and I holding hands in the evening. Understanding. His eyes move slowly from my hand up toward my face.

"Gayla, I can see you."

Can you, honest?

"Very clear. You're wearing a sweater and jeans. And you're smiling."

Am I ever!

"And very beautiful."

Bet your ass. I feel great, like I finally got it together.

One last painful, lovely current of life as Lowen squeezes my hand. "Good-bye, Gayla."

So long, love.

Lowen yanks open the door. "Al, Mr. Hirajian? Come on out. It's a lovely evening."

Alice peeks out to see Lowen leaning over the railing, enjoying the river and the early stars. His chest swells; he's laughing and he looks marvelous, inviting Al into his arms the way he did on their first day here. She comes unsurely to nestle in beside him, one arm around his waist. "Who were you talking to?"

"She's gone, Al. You've got nothing to be afraid of. Except being afraid."

"Lowen, I'm not going to—"

"This is our house, and nobody's going to take it away from us." He turns Al to him and kisses her. "Nobody wants to, that's a promise. So don't run away from it or yourself."

She shivers a little, still uncertain. "Do you really think we can stay. I can't—"

"Hey, love." Lowen leans into her, cocky and charming but meaning it. "Don't tell a *mensch* what you can't. Hey, Hirajian!"

When the little prune pokes his head out the door, Lowen sweeps his arm out over the river and the whole lit-up West Side. "Sorry for all the trouble, but we've changed our minds. I mean, look at it! Who could give up a balcony with a view like this?"

He's the last thing I see before the lights change: Lowen holding Al and grinning out at the world. I thought the lights were dimming, but it's something else, another cue coming up. The lights cross-fade up, up, more pink and amber, until—my God, it's gorgeous!

I'm not dead, not gone. I feel more alive than ever. I'm Gail and Gayla and Lowen and Bill and Al and all of them magnified, heightened, fully realized, flowing together like bright, silver streams into—

Will you look at that *set*. Fantastic. Who's on the lights?

So that's what You look like. Ri-i-ght. I'm with it now, and I love You, too. Give me a follow-spot, Baby.

I'm on.

THE FIRE WHEN IT COMES

This novella had to be written because Gayla wouldn't stay dead. She began life in 1973 as the central character in an occult novel that bogged down in wrong choices and languished in a file drawer for seven years. But I couldn't get the woman out of my head. Gayla was the kind of character that could fuel and drive any novel, but again I was wandering down side roads and tangents trying to find her story.

In 1976 I wrote a new beginning for her, interred it with the rest of the ashes, and turned to other work with mixed feelings. The damned story mattered painfully to me—scared to commit, unable to forget. Gayla's life in show business was tinged with my own, and the truths she learned about the world and herself were of a piece with mine. She made me feel too naked. I never think of this story by its title, but simply as Gayla. Not a work but a woman. When she won the World Fantasy Award in 1982, I thanked them for both of us—Gayla and me.

THE LADY OF
FINNIGAN'S HEARTH

Isolde, if you remember her story, was the girl Queen of Cornwall in the days of King Arthur, and the sweetheart of a bad-luck knight named Tristram.

Though time and legend left their sugary crust, neither these nor any lute-twanging minstrel ever did her justice. She was a joyous, bouncing Irish hellion who died at nineteen, a bundle of brogue and bad manners, all heart and no head, a thoroughly medieval urchin whose first utterance in Glory was that she had been abducted from the world against her will and demanded immediate return. Her claim was not considered.

Isolde was not happy in Heaven. She felt that she just didn't fit in. Some—the women mostly—whispered of her not uneventful past. Others held she was a nice enough little thing if you liked them unpolished. Troubadours protested they would never have put hand to lute in her behalf if they had known what she was really like. The immortal Wagner said flatly and to her face she was not worthy of the magnificent opera he had written about her. To most of the Romantics she was an artistic embarrassment.

Well, it went this way most of the time. In the beginning there had been Tristram for company, but that was short-lived. Isolde came to realize that chivalry, while it might beautify a short life (the shorter the better), did not wear well in terms of the eternal. They bored each other until, mutually relieved, they finally went their separate ways.

But Paradise hung heavily upon Isolde, and her harp—an Irish model brought from home—lay discarded and mute. She passed her centuries longing for the good green world below. Such a short life; so little lived, so little known. She wanted to go back. At last when the yearning was too strong to keep silent, she planted herself before the Recording Angel and let him know her mind.

"Hear me, Angel: I said it the day I was brought here—against my will and before my time—and I say it again. I want to go home!"

"A very peculiar desire," the Angel acknowledged with some disappointment. "I should think you would have had time to let our place grow on you. Very peculiar." He shook his head. "But not impossible; that is, if you can pass the test. Before you can go back you must tell me what is the secret of life."

"And if I know it, I can go back? I can live again?"

The Angel's eyes were old and kind and sad. "You must know it to live at all, child. Where makes no difference."

Isolde pondered this a moment. "Well now, and where might be a good place to look?"

"I don't want to discourage you, child, but if you didn't find it down there, you probably won't find it here. However"—he had said it so often—"look where the heart is."

Isolde went away and thought for a long time, but it seemed hopeless. In her thoughtless lifetime she had never learned the secret of anything. She was doomed to Paradise, as it were, and it galled her more and more as the centuries passed. The virtuous criticized her for what she had been and the snobbish deplored her for what she was. Isolde walked Heaven alone and found no answer to the question. It was as remote from her as Hell itself.

"Well," she decided firmly, picking up her harp, "why not?"

The Recording Angel paused in his eternal occupation and gazed up at the familiar figure. "Yes, girl?"

"I've searched my heart, Angel, and I've looked Heaven high and low and across for the secret. 'Tis not in either place."

"You must know it, nevertheless," the Angel said. "Everyone wants to go back at first. We afford the chance, but we afford it only to those grown wise enough to use a life properly. They are very few and most of them would rather leave well enough alone."

"I never lived to learn what well enough was. An end to this." Isolde raised her hand impatiently. "Open the gates and point me out the south stairway."

The Angel read her intention. "I admire your spirit, girl, but not your reasoning. They can't tell you anything constructive down *there*. I doubt if they'd even want to."

Isolde was not to be swayed. "The gates, sir!"

"Well, if you're determined." He opened the portals of Paradise, and she skipped through, turning to wave to him. "I'm glad you're taking the harp with you. You do play well and they never get a chance to hear a really good one."

She found the new place better suited to her. The climate was agreeable, the people friendly, if irresponsible, and there was always something going on. Her coming caused some social stir; she was soon entrenched in the very best circle, a small but powerful clique of Salem women, stoutly traditional and privileged beyond belief.

But Hell, fun as it was, taught her no more than Heaven. Whatever the secret was, she must go home to find it, to the world she had left. But how? Her friends were allowed one night on Earth at All Saints' Eve, but she was only a novice. It would be ages before they would trust her with a broom, for all her natural talent. Need sharpened her craft to a fine edge. She evolved her plan and put it to work.

Isolde's closest friend was Prissy O'Gowra, a brilliant Irish witch with the most potent broomstick in the trade. Lately, Prissy's carefree spirit was vexed with a bittersweet sadness—her sudden and hopeless love for the American Secretary of State. He was to appear at an international conference in Paris. When the Prince gave her permission to go there, Prissy was ecstatic. Magic and sabbats were not for her. Their charms were flat beside what loomed in Paris. When begged for the broom, she threw it joyously to the grateful Isolde and whirled away on the west wind, trailing a snatch of *chanson*.

And so, on All Saints' Eve, Isolde flew with her friends to Gallows Hill outside Salem. The night was made for revels—raw, cold and wet with the naked trees bending to the wind against a moonless sky. The Prince himself put in an appearance; there was a quadrille to Isolde's harp accompaniment, and as for spells, their form had never been better. The Washington Senators got another year in the cellar and four gluepots waltzed their way to the Kentucky Derby and a four-way photo finish. It was a glorious night in the finest tradition. When dawn came on, dragging a thick fog behind, they sped homeward on the east wind, conscious of a social success.

But Isolde was missing.

It was sorrowfully reported that she had lost control in the fog over the eastern seaboard and was presumed to have crashed. Too late they insisted Isolde was too inexperienced for the flight. Now she was marooned on a world grown callous to the ancient art of witchcraft, but she had the awful O'Gowra broom in her hands and was free to roam till All Saints' next.

For days there was no laughter in Hell. Isolde had been the gayest and dearest of all the brilliant society of the Vivacious Fallen. Now she was gone and with her went some of the sparkle of damnation.

Well now, wasn't it a simple thing to let them think her lost? When she was rid of them, Isolde veered her broom a point or two to starboard and swooped down on the unsuspecting Earth, landing in a small wood. It was early morning still, and the fog coiled in erratic patterns over the ground, seeking refuge in the low places before the sun could drive it away. Isolde listened: not a soul about nor the sound of one, but through the trees the windows of a drab white house stared bleakly at her, just visible above the fog.

"Didn't I always have the luck?" she congratulated herself. "The castle of some lord, no doubt, and I'm fair in time for breakfast."

It was her first thought to hop the broomstick and *whoosh* up to the house, but it was a grand morning for a walk. She shouldered the broom and in fifteen earthly minutes Isolde found herself in the overgrown front yard of the bald-windowed house.

"What manner of hovel is this?" she wondered. "The paint all peeling and not so much as a candle for light or a fire for warmth. It looked better from afar. An ogre lives here, no doubt—but I'll ask just for surety."

She went up to the mud-splashed door and put her hand on the knob.

> "Castle, castle, now will you tell
> Who within your walls doth dwell?"

As one might suppose, there was no answer.

"I'll burn you for kindling, scoundrel!" Isolde hissed, this time in the faerie tongue. "Now open your gawp and tell me who lives here!"

The house groaned, for it had been silent a long time. "Marty Finnigan lives here," it said mournfully. "Alone."

"Sure then, Marty Finnigan keeps a sorry house."

The house sighed deep in its timbers. "No one cares for me," it said with a tremor of self-pity.

"Oh now, and why's that?"

"It's really quite *simple*," said the house peevishly. "Because no one cares for Marty Finnigan."

"Pile of knotholes, keep your tongue in your head!"

"Well," the house groaned sulkily, "either knock or go away." It settled once more in a manner designed to signify the interview was ended.

Isolde rapped on the door with her broom handle.

Silence.

Rap! Rap! Rap! "Halloooo! MARTY FINNIGAN!"

Isolde heard muffled sounds from the second floor. Someone was up. She knocked again. "Up with your gate, Sir Finnigan, for 'tis a gentlewoman waits on your stoop in the cold and wet—"

A window rumbled up. The next instant, Isolde was drenched from hair to heels with cold water. "All right, you gah-damned kids, Halloween's over. Now *blow!*" A tousled head jutted through the window, and Marty Finnigan stared coldly down at the dampened little queen. "Oh . . . I'm sorry, lady. I thought it was those trick-or-treat punks again."

It was Isolde's hot-tempered impulse to singe him roundly with a fireball, but—*noblesse oblige,* and *noblesse* is all the easier when a man's face is no pain to a woman's eye. She gave him a graceful curtsy and asked, "Did I rouse you from slumber, Sir Finnigan?"

Marty rubbed his weekend growth of beard. "Did she wake me up, she says. No, I was just lying there with my eyes closed. What's your problem?"

"Problem?"

"What do you want?"

"Just a morsel of bread and a place by your fire."

"A mors—" The Finnigan features contorted in disbelief. "Get lost."

"So I can wring out the wet welcome you gave me."

"Well," Marty considered it, "I guess that's fair enough." His head disappeared and she heard him descending the stairs. The door opened. In flannel pajamas and a ratty blue bathrobe, Marty motioned her into his house.

And Isolde moved in. She stood in the middle of the living room and tried on Marty Finnigan's house for size. It was dirty, dark and cold, lonely most of all, with no touch of a woman's hand about it. The logs lay unlit in the fireplace, festooned with trash. The dust of the floor swirled up angrily in protest against the fresh air from the open door. In one corner a battered coffee table displayed a week's run of used cups, a wrinkled necktie, two undershirts and a pile of bills surmounted by a stale cracker, buttered and forgotten some days since.

"Cushnoo!" Isolde clucked. "What a hog-sty."

"So excuse it," Marty shrugged, "it's the maid's day off."

He had been watching her with growing curiosity. She was small —a hair over five feet, no more—and mercurial in her manner and movement. Her hair, impossibly red, was upswept on her head and held precariously in place with two quaint gold stays. He decided quickly that her face was made for laughter, not for looks. Her figure, if she had any, was well hidden beneath what appeared to be Methuselah's nightshirt, bunched in at the waist with the hem trailing behind like the undecided posterior of a hook-and-ladder engine.

Now Marty was many months a grass widower. Since his wife departed, a motley procession of women had left their perfumed trace about his house, but none of them were in the same league with this one for the new and different. Being essentially religious, he concluded that she had been visited upon him as some kind of penance.

"Make yourself comfortable," he mumbled, turning toward the kitchen. He shuffled sleepily out of the room. Her voice seemed to float musically through the separating wall.

"Shall I light your hearth for you? 'Tis dreadful cold."

"No," he grumbled. "The flue's messed up. You couldn't burn gasoline in that thing." He filled the coffee pot with water, chuckling in spite of himself. "Well . . . she *looks* like what I'd get for Halloween, broomstick and all."

The time of year and the thought of the queer old broom summed themselves almost unconsciously in his mind. It *was* Halloween, or the day after. Marty grinned. "Oh, come *on*, Finnigan." But the wry smile softened. *Kind of a nice little thing*, he thought. *I wonder where she's from.*

Isolde strolled to the fireplace, skirts switching behind her, crooning softly—

> "Oh Maeldun, son of Ailill
> Came from Aran in Thomond . . ."

She knelt beside the logs, stretched out her hand, beckoning. "Come, fire: so please you, a little of your best for Marty Finnigan."

And the fire blazed up on Finnigan's hearth.

If Marty Finnigan had any true genius, it was in the brewing of coffee. Sitting by the fire they went through two pots with toast and marmalade. Isolde missed her harp; she would have gladly played for her breakfast, but it was lost in her wild plunge to Earth. She stirred the fire, humming to herself, and studied the master of Finnigan's Hall. He was taller by a head than her Trist had been, and leaner. His face was still young but life had happened to it. The eyes were shadowed and the frank mouth lined and drawn too taut for its fullness. The thick brown hair was fading here and there to early gray.

He'd look younger did he smile once a fortnight.

She liked the way his nose wrinkled up when he lit a cigarette. Suddenly she leaned toward him, fixing him with gray eyes. "Marty Finnigan, 'tis a handsome buck you are. Why is it no woman graces your house?"

There was a strange, faraway quality to her voice. It was inside his head like a song remembered from childhood, calling him down the years to where life could still grow green around the heart. *Stay a little*, he wanted to say . . .

But Marty had been barren soil for the seed of impulse for a long time. He threw his cigarette into the fire. "You *are* an oddball. And you're still soggy from that bath I gave you. Wait, I'll get something you can change into so we can dry out that shroud or whatever it is of yours."

Isolde giggled. "Thank you."

"What's so funny?"

"I just bethought me," she said, "how nice your mouth would be if you let it smile a little now and then."

"You," he said with conviction, "are the *damndest*—"

"Aye," she nodded, taking a piece of toast in three huge bites. As he climbed the stairs, her voice floated after him: "But 'twas not my fault. A tedious long tale it is, and so I'll save it for a winter's night."

Marty returned presently with a faded yellow duster, flapping it vigorously to shake out the wrinkles of long storage. "Here. You're about three sizes smaller than my wife, but it'll do."

She shrank away from it. "Your wife?"

"What's the matter? She doesn't need it anymore." He dropped it in her lap but she only stared at it.

"You said nought of a wife, Marty."

"Well . . ." Marty made quite an operation out of lighting a cigarette. "She isn't here anymore. We're divorced. Her name is Alice," he concluded.

His glance met hers and was held. "Her name was Alice," Marty heard himself saying, "and all the things I wanted, she didn't. Not even this house. Wants me to move out so we can sell it. Maybe it's a good idea." He looked around the room with new awareness. "God, this place is cruddy."

Fortune brought me here, she thought, *and here I'll stay. Plain it is that he needs a woman, and here's as good a place as any to learn what I must learn. If I work my spells right, they won't find me till All Saints' next, and what might I not do for myself and this sorry Marty Finnigan before then?*

Isolde stood up before the fire, seeming taller than she was. She had once been a queen and the stamp never left her. And as she spoke, the flames leaped in time to the queer movements of her fingers. "Marty, have you never heard that a cricket on the hearth brings marvelous good fortune?"

"In this house," said Marty, "a cricket would die of T.B."

"Then I'll be your cricket."

"What—?"

"Let me stay by your hearth and sweep your house with my broom till All Saints' next."

Marty was perplexed. "The dangerous thing about you is you're so believable."

"And, Finnigan," she whispered with mock gravity, "you've grown much too wise to believe in what you see?"

He nodded. "When I found out about Santa Claus." He was vaguely disappointed in her. Only a week before, a dazzling young girl had brightened his threshold for a golden minute till Marty found she had come to sell him a pamphlet on the imminent demise of sinful mankind. This one, alas, was compounded of the same unstable elements. He threw the door open and pointed to infinity. "Good-bye, and take your broom with you." He handed it to her. "Sweep my house . . . You couldn't sweep tennis balls with this thing."

"OOOOOH!" Isolde was breathless at the sacrilege. "*That* be too much! Soulless imp, know that on just such a broom, Prissy O'Gowra flew the length and breadth of Eire till it carried her *whoosh!* straight into the cottage of the man who became her husband, it did. Not to mention, of course, her many and glorious services regarding the heathen English. Well, it's like crystal you don't know a good broom or a bargain when they be thrust in your *snout,* Sir Finnigan!''

He propelled her toward the door. "Yeah. Sure. Good-bye."

"Unhand me, ogre!"

He unhanded her out to the front stoop. "Get lost. Break a leg." Slam!

Yet her voice through the heavy door was as clear as though she were beside him: "Just one leg, Marty?"

"Fine."

He was on his back with a terrible pain in his left leg. The instrument of disaster lay beside him. He had tripped over that damned broom.

"Broken," Isolde crooned over him. "Fair brast below the knee, but it's a clean break and will mend soon."

"How did you—*yikes, quit pawin at it*—how did you get in here?"

"Oh," she said airily, "I forgot my broom. But how *fortunate* you are I happened back, for here's yourself with your pin broken and like to be days in the mending by the look of it, with no one but me to get your supper—"

He saw the awful defeat of it. "Oh, no. No . . ."

"—to mend your socks and tend the fire, and take my old broom to the dust that's on your hearth and heart, Marty Finnigan. Till next All Saints' Eve!"

Isolde stood in the middle of the living room, making little swishing movements with the broom and humming to herself. For the time, at least, she was mistress of Marty's house. This was sufficient Heaven. As for Hell, she had brought fair measure. The sun was well up and it promised to be a roaring good day.

> "In Laighin fair, I met a lad
> Who soon came courting me . . ."

She knelt by the hearth. "Prissy!" she whispered. *"Dia dhuit,* Priss, can you hear me?"

The logs crackled furiously for a moment. She listened.

"Oh, I'm grand, Prissy. Thanks for the asking." Isolde took a ball of flame from the fire. Her dexterous fingers shaped a fiery flower as she listened to the small talk of a friend. "Well, if anyone asks, you've not heard one word of me. Promise, now. What? Oh, your old broom's safe with me, and Priss, it still works superiorly!"

Marty always said it was just magic the way she took that house and made it shine. She took care of him and so well that he put on five pounds before he was out of bed. Now and then he admitted to himself that there was something unworldly about Isolde, but then she would bounce into the room and announce with convincing authority that she would serve him that very evening the grandest stew this side of Hell, and could he spare a drop of the whisky his dear uncle had sent him to bring out the flavor of the meat, of course?

Unworldly? In all his drab, disenchanted days, Marty had never known anything or anyone whose reality was so completely undeniable. She was as real as the luck that came with her; as real as the twenty-pound turkey which she swore on the soul of St. Brigid just traipsed into the kitchen and dropped stone-dead—plucked and dressed—on Thanksgiving Day in the morning; as real as the well-paid job that materialized in a formerly uninterested office; as real as the first paycheck, which Isolde set in a place of honor on the kitchen table, toasting it with a royal flourish of her teacup: "Increase, little bag of gold." Then with a wink at Marty: "And good health to the master of Finnigan's Hall."

Marty warmed to the tea, the excellent dinner, the cozy sound of logs crackling lustily on the hearth. "And praise them angels as brung it, my grandmother used to say."

She took his hands across the teacups, and her eyes held something not so heavy as sorrow nor light as laughter. "It's no angel I am, Marty." Then erect and determined: "As Mistress Marcianetti will discover, does she not keep her dog from howling and snapping at me when I come near."

"That's Poobah," said Marty. "He's six years older than God. Funny, you're the only one he does that to."

Nevertheless, Isolde promised herself that she would inflict the venerable Poobah with fleas enough to make him a Job among canines.

"Mrs. Marcianetti has two interests in life," Marty continued. "Poobah and my welfare. I keep hoping she'll run out of home-canned tomatoes, but she never does. She brings them over about once a week, looks around, shakes her head and leaves."

"Aye, and now you have a housekeeper, and the dear old thing's got a fair crick in her neck from spying out her casement at me."

"Spying?"

"Aye, Marty. Wondering who I am, and what I be to you."

He read her delicate meaning. "Well, I've been thinking about that," he started shyly. "I know this is foolish, but—" He stopped. The old fear of being hurt melted his purpose. "What I meant to say was, it's been nice having you here."

She rose and came round the table to him. "No, Marty, say what you started to say. Life's far too short to be afraid of it!"

Marty took refuge in the complicated business of lighting a cigarette. "I don't know. You just walked into this house and sort of put it on like a glove. It lives, it really lives because you're in it. When you leave—"

"When I leave?"

"If you left, I think the life would go out of it. I think it would fall apart."

"Well now," her long fingers assured themselves needlessly that her hair was in place, "what a prudent concern for your house. And what of yourself?"

Marty blew out a great quantity of smoke. "I guess I go with the house."

Isolde knelt and took his hands. "Listen, Marty: if I knew 'twould all end this night, I'd still say those things you lack the heart to say to me: I love you, and your hearth is mine. That's what I'd say, I would."

"Yes," he smiled, and the fear sloughed from him when he looked at her. "And a little more. Marry me and stay here always."

"I will," she whispered, her head in his lap. "I can make you happy, Finnigan."

"I know you can," he laughed, "and when I'm too old for anything else, you can make me respectable."

"Oh, Marty, what a gallant offer . . ."

Suddenly she twisted away from him. Surprised, Marty saw the shadow of a frown cross her face, erasing the happiness and leaving something alien in its place. Her head was inclined sharply as if she had caught some sound beyond his hearing: a footstep lighter than thought, or perhaps a voice on the damp December wind. He started to speak but she stopped him with two fingers across his lips.

"Not a sound, Marty. There now: your supper's turning cold whilst you gape at me."

Isolde stood up. Resolutely, she reached for the old broom that was rarely out of her sight. "Eat, Marty. I'll not be gone a minute."

"Well, hurry back. If we're getting married, there's buckets of stuff we have to talk about."

"True," she murmured. Straight-backed and firm, she turned away from him.

Out of Marty's sight, her resolution faltered, and she shrank back from the sliding doors that closed off the living room. Beyond the doors, she heard a faint rustle of movement. Isolde clutched at her broom, quailed and retreated a step, the fear a hod of hot bricks on her heart. She took one hesitant step toward the kitchen. Then her head went up; she turned a scornful eye on the panel doors.

You need not fear the like of him, and you a queen, the proudest Leinster could spawn. Hold tight the broom. Head up. Now, in you go—

At her touch, the doors slid apart. Isolde took one sweeping step, then halted. The fear dissolved in her throat, welled up and poured out in a peal of relieved, irreverent laughter. She fell back against the doors, the helpless victim of her own mirth.

"Oh God, no!" she gasped. " 'Tis himself."

Tall, tragic and darkly resplendent in the false ermine and sagging black tights of a stock-company Hamlet, her visitor helped himself once more to the Finnigan whisky, threw back his cape and made a sweeping obeisance before his audience of one. "To Her Majestie, Queen of the Faerie Glen," he declaimed in his best third-balcony register, adding a hint of mockery, "greetings from the Joyous Damned."

"Oh my, oh my," she was still giggling. "Expect the worst and get the best. Give you good evening, Mr. Booth."

The gaunt young man favored her with a brilliant smile. "The same: John Wilkes Booth, your servant. I come as herald from our court; *nay*"— Booth put up his hand in protest of her single word— "let not the fear of intrusion mar our meeting. We shall be secret kept, for the time's out of joint, and we are slipped between two broken ticks. That uninspired lout presently absorbing his supper in the scullery will hear no more of us than the wind that brought me."

"Blather, Booth. Spit it out. My supper's cooling while you hold me here."

"The price of materialization," Booth sighed. "One recalls old appetites—as witness that rather artless embrace of a moment ago."

"Oooooh!" Isolde's complexion darkened a shade. "You be no gentleman, John, or the Prince either, and you can tell him that for me."

"Oh, you wrong us, Isolde. For myself, I wanted you home for our annual festival of the Bard. We do Hamlet again, echoing last year's triumph." Booth gathered the ermine to his ebonied breast, paus-

ing for full effect. "The Prince has again chosen me to interpret the
Dane. Wanton nymph, he is a lover and a critic of the arts, a gentleman and a sportsman. When tidings reached him that you were
gone and, through your broom, immune to recall for the nonce, he
smiled in gracious defeat. Aloud he wished you well and ruled that no
unpleasantness attend your holiday."

"Then why are you—?"

"But when he heard that—that *Finnigan* declare his unpoetic desire, he sent me on the first east wind." Booth smote his temples.
"And I in the middle of a rehearsal."

"Sent you to tell me what, John? Can you not deliver yourself
without suffering so? Tell me what?"

"Say rather to beg, Isolde. Come home now, for come you must,
and it will hurt less now than later." Booth moved toward her.
"Surrender your broom."

"I'll not!" she snapped, falling back. "Away with you. I'll not
return before my time." She swung the broom high, wielding it like
a sword. "One step more, John, and I'll sweep eternity clear of you."

Booth halted. "Listen to us, you fool. We know what life is. Madness, blind madness. What was your own time here but misery and
heartbreak? What else will you find here now?"

"Life!" she hurled it at him. "Life, you wretched wreck of a soul.
Life and its secret, for I left too soon to know what it was. But I'll find
it, Booth. You mark me: I'll find it."

"You stole it. You can't steal life, Isolde."

"Then I'll borrow."

"And at what interest?" Booth asked. "You know the Prince never
takes a loss. Come home before it is too late."

"Too late?" Isolde lowered the broom. "Tell me, John, why is't
I've not been called till now. Why all asudden?"

The pale Booth opened his mouth to speak, then stopped. "It is
late. I must go. My rehearsal . . ." He swirled the ermine around
him with pathetic bravado.

"No!" Isolde demanded. "Tell me why I'm sent for now."

"No more . . ." The image of Booth began to blur, each line of
the fine, sharp figure dissolving into an amorphous haze until only
the magnificent voice remained. "Come home . . . Faerie Queen
. . ."

"Back on the wind, Booth," Isolde cried, angry and afraid. "Tell it
to the Prince, and them Above, if you can: I live! I am! For life's not
borrowed, not stolen, but taken free and shaped at will—"

"Illusion . . ." came the faint whisper.

"No, 'tis real," she sobbed. "The knowing and the loving of it. Hear me, Booth—"

"Heartbreak," said the wind.

The unoiled clock on the mantel roused itself and began to grind away the minutes. Her attention drawn by the sound, Isolde looked at the hands. Even as she watched, they seemed to move faster and faster. But she had found something. *The knowing and the loving of it:* that was something to remember.

To know and to love. That must be the secret.

"Hey, good-lookin," Marty enticed from the kitchen, "come on! I've poured the wine."

Was that the secret? Was it?

"Hey, come on!"

"*Illusion . . .*" murmured the rain, but she did not hear it.

"Aye, Marty," she answered, "I'm coming."

Well, wasn't she a bride of two days and mistress of her own house, and that house to be put straight this Monday morning?

Marty had gone to work. Isolde stood in the middle of the living room and raised her voice. "Wake, House of Finnigan! A word with you."

The house stirred and came alive. The furniture dented and flexed itself as if supporting a body, the curtains rustled, the furnace groaned. Floors and stairs creaked with the memory of a million footsteps, and out of all these came the voice: "What do you want?"

"Obedience," Isolde snapped, "for I'm your mistress now, and you'll bend to my wish and the power of my broom. Hold your roof high and gallant, as if you cost twice the gold he paid, and let no one say that Marty Finnigan's a poor man."

"I hear you," sighed the house, "but it won't work."

"And why not?"

"Because it's not real," said the house. "I need love, not spells. There is no love in you and nothing real."

"He knows I love him."

"Words," said the house. "But the belfry told the wind that the candles broke and the Book burned on the altar where you married him."

"And so can I burn you," she threatened, "if your warped temper runs foul of my will. Mind you'll do as I say!"

The furnace rattled violently. "I will do as you say," and the voice began to fade, "but it will only seem, not be."

"Enough," Isolde commanded. "House—be clean."

There was a rush as of a great vacuum that swept every particle of dust from the floor, a flapping and rustling as the curtains and rugs shook out their lint, the swish of a hundred invisible brushes and dustrags rubbing and slapping the dust from woodwork, books and cranny corners. In the kitchen, the breakfast dishes washed and dried themselves, sailing gracefully from the sink to the cupboard— and the immaculate house was quiet again.

So the happiness began for Marty Finnigan and the world was green again. He fell asleep at night with the slight form of her curled like a kitten in his arms and woke in the morning to the joy of her nearness. Drawn by the amazement of his love, he would lie on his elbow watching her sleep. Most of the time she lay quite still, but now and then she tossed fitfully, whispering aloud in some dream. Sometimes she spoke his name or a word in Irish; sometimes strange words that were like far music at the end of night, like the sound of the day itself breaking in their room.

He loved her and the love made him grow, and if everything about her seemed touched with magic, he reasoned it to this love. She had her moods, though, and when they came over her, she wanted to wander alone in the woods and meadows beyond the house. So it was on a Saturday in March that she rose out of sorts from bed and knew the blackness was on her. Without bothering to take her broom, she kissed him good-bye almost solemnly and went out with a basket to gather herbs for salads and spells.

With herself gone, it was a slow morning for Marty. He drank coffee, read the papers and toyed with the idea of beginning his flower bed, but gave it up before it became serious. Sprawled comfortably on the sofa, he became only gradually aware of the sound of a car turning into their lane.

His brow furrowed in a puzzled frown. He wasn't expecting company, and no one just dropped in on a Saturday morning. The frown deepened to irritation: a salesman—blood brother in Marty's eye to the Japanese beetle, the termite and the housefly. He decided to make short, polite work of it.

The woman on the doorstep was tall, poised and beautiful. "Hello, Martin. I see you still resist shaving on weekends."

"Alice, what—"

They stared at each other for a moment.

"Well," she asked finally, "you do have some manners, don't you? Ask me inside."

Marty followed her into the living room, where she stood alertly in the center of the floor, head turned slightly to one side. In this attitude she reminded Marty of a beagle sniffing out a rabbit.

"Sit down, Alice. How about some coffee?"

She made a little grimace of distaste. "Darling, it's much too early for coffee. Coffee's for evening and regrets, but I will take a martini."

"Sorry, no gin in the house," he said. "We're whisky folks here."

Alice laughed drily. "You never did have any taste, Martin. By the way, where's the new Mrs. Finnigan? I hear she's quite young."

"Isolde's nineteen," said Marty. "She's out for a while, but she'll be back soon."

"Isolde?" Alice took a cigarette from her purse and put a lighter to it. "Makes you think of a fat soprano. But nineteen! My God, Martin, what do you talk about . . . when you talk?"

"So what's wrong with nineteen? Am I an antique?"

"Too old for *that*, anyway."

It burned Marty that she could still get to him. He thrust himself off the sofa. "All right, knock it off, Alice. What do you want?"

"And what has she *done* to this room," Alice ignored him. "With my furniture, too." She was ill at ease in the room. It had a new brightness and charm she could never give it despite her driven search for the Room that was Her. "And that's what I came about," she concluded. "Darling, I *am* in a pinch for money, and since the furniture is mine—now that you're doing so well—I want to sell it."

She pronounced it as if the matter was settled and done; it was her way, the way she'd been from the beginning. Marty felt himself beginning to heat. "Why didn't you do this before, when it didn't matter if there was a rug on the floor or even a floor? Why now?"

"Now just a minute, darling—"

"And dammit, don't call me darling. You're the only woman in the world who can make 'darling' sound like a common noun."

"For that matter, darling, the house itself is half mine, legally. I let you stay here because I was a little sorry for you. I mean you're so helpless, Martin. It didn't matter then, but the broker says the value's gone up with the new expressway finished, and I do need the cash." Her expression softened. "I know it's been tough for you, Martin, but it's been no bed of roses for me, either. I work hard, too, and no matter how it turned out for us, give a girl credit, hmm?"

"Oh, I give you credit, Alice," Marty said quietly. Suddenly, he wanted Isolde very much. Now, when he needed her.

Go make yourself some coffee, the thought told him, and Marty acted without thinking about it. Somehow it seemed a very good idea at the moment. He left Alice so abruptly she was startled.

"Where are you going, Martin?"

"To make coffee."

"Oh, for God's sake!" She stubbed out her cigarette with a vicious jab and threw her eyes impatiently around the room. A slight sound made her turn.

The sliding doors that led to the kitchen were drawing slowly together.

"Martin? Why did you close the doors?"

There was no answer, nor could she hear him moving in the kitchen. A deep silence had settled over the entire house, and as if a cloud had slid over the sun, the room was growing darker and rather chilly.

A storm, she thought. *I'd better finish this up and leave.* She remembered an appointment for the early afternoon and looked at the clock on the mantel: ten thirty-three . . .

As she looked, the clock stopped ticking.

"What . . . ?" Alice stepped to the mantel to look at it, and her eye fell on a queer old broom, the handle worn black with use and the head no more than a bundle of birch switches. She picked it up. "Shades of Halloween," she snickered, "how quaint can you be?"

"Put it down."

Alice froze; it was as though the very sound were a pair of hands laid on her will to move. The hands loosened and she turned. A slight red-haired girl stood behind her with cold gray eyes belying the voice that softened to a gentle admonishment.

"Never touch my broom," Isolde took it from her. "It is the luck of Finnigan's Hearth."

Alice felt a tiny chill run like a frightened mouse down her spine. "Oh . . . hello, I didn't hear you come in. You must be Isolde."

"Aye."

"Martin and I have been having a talk." Alice attempted a patronizing grace that fell flat. "I want to make some arrangement about the furniture and the house. But excuse me, I didn't introduce myself. I'm—"

"I know," said Isolde. "The late Mistress Finnigan."

Alice managed something like a laugh. It was a weak sound.

"Do seat yourself," Isolde invited, "and tell me your pleasure in refreshment."

Alice composed herself and prepared to do battle. She arranged her hands delicately in her lap and crossed her exquisite legs, reassured since Martin's new wife was neither beautiful nor sophisticated. It was true; Martin must have gotten her out of an unguarded cradle. "Well, Martin said you didn't have martini makings."

"Oh dear," Isolde laughed. "That be just like a man, not able to find a thing in his own house." She busied herself a moment at the sideboard: "For 'tis here in my hand."

She offered Alice the martini, complete to the olive. Alice blinked. There was nothing on the sideboard but a decanter of whisky. She tasted the drink and found it superb, but with a something in its tang she couldn't place. "Perfect! Thanks so much. Whatever do you add to get this taste?"

"Herbs," said Isolde.

Those cold eyes on her; gray, but darker than before, like smoke. With some irritation Alice found herself becoming increasingly nervous under that gaze. She attempted to avert it. "I think your clock has stopped."

"Aye," said Isolde, without looking at the clock, "it has."

Alice glanced at her watch. "About—well, that's queer. My watch has stopped, too."

"So it has." Isolde's smile was ice. "Time out of joint, Mistress Alice." She took the decanter from the sideboard and sat down facing Alice. "And Marty be asleep in the kitchen, but just for a bit." Her left hand carved a curious shape in the air and held a glass.

Alice gasped. "What on earth—!"

"When the clock rouses," Isolde purred, "so will he. Till then we'll pass a womanly word or two."

She opened the decanter and poured. The glass was a tall one, but the liquor swelled steadily toward the brim, and Alice's jaw dropped proportionately lower as she watched it rise. "Surely, you're not going to *drink* that."

"Oh yes," Isolde sipped at the whisky, nodded her pleased approval and casually drank it down. " 'Tis not pure, but only eighty-six proof."

Alice was shaken beyond manners. "You little fool, that's whisky! You'll kill yourself."

She tried to rise, but her will and legs had turned to water.

"Drink up, Mistress Alice." The voice was music, but the eyes were black. Alice raised her glass; the round brim held her gaze as it spun, developing in concentric circles, drawing her in . . .

"Now," Isolde began calmly, "as to the selling of the house . . ."

. . . There was black Limbo, then Alice felt herself grasped by huge hands, and she was dragged up, up over interminable stone steps by two half-naked brutes. The rays from occasional torches glanced off the crude gold ornaments on their arms and gleamed again in their fierce blue eyes. There was no sound in her ears but the wild beating of her own heart as they passed up over hundreds of steps, ending at the entrance of a great hall. At the far end of the hall, raised on a dais, a familiar figure beckoned them forward. Alice was pushed forward to the foot of the dais.

"Kneel," a voice commanded her. "Kneel to Isolde of the blood of Leinster, daughter of a hundred unblemished kings of Eire."

"Please," Alice croaked, "please, God, this isn't real. It's insane." She raised her head to the slight, erect figure on the throne, but flinched again from the searching eyes. "You . . . what have you done to me?"

"Before I judge you," said Isolde, "one small truth out of a lying life to warm my soul upon. For what reason did you bring the pain of yourself to Marty Finnigan? And taking his heart, unworthy as you are, for what reason did you desert him?"

The truth welled out of the bottom of Alice's being. She had no power to silence it, having never known it, and it passed from her heart to her lips like a stranger.

"I was afraid," said the truth in her voice. "I had nothing to give, but I found that Martin needed giving. There was nothing inside . . ."

". . . And what a shame it is," Isolde crooned, refilling her glass, "that you come now to talk of selling Finnigan's Hearth that we love so much and our friends, too. But here! I've forgot my graces. Do let me fill your glass like a good hostess." She leaned toward Alice, stretching out her open hand. The long fingers closed in a beckoning motion. Alice's glass was full.

Alice rubbed her eyes, shivering with unaccountable cold. She had been sitting and talking, sipping at a delicious drink and listening to a melodious voice that spoke of furniture and trifles. And yet she seemed to have wandered out of time in a nightmare, forgotten

already but leaving its chill on her mind. "What did you say? I'm
afraid I . . . it's very strange . . ."

"Drink up, Alice."

. . . And Alice groveled on the stone floor while Isolde's long
finger lifted and pointed at her. "It was harm enough to take him,
even more to leave. Yea, but to come now like a cloud in the middle
of his brightest day." She leaned back, musing a moment. At a sign
of her hand, a giant shadow loomed beside Alice, ready with the
sword. With cold pleasure, Isolde commanded, "Give me her
head."

"Don't!" Alice shrieked, cowering away from the shadow.
"Please, *don't*—"

The sword came down.

"So will you wake now and leave this house," Isolde whispered
over the sleeping woman. "You will leave us in peace, and only in
dreams will you remember the fear of me, nought but the fear—"

There was a sudden whirr of clockwork. The sound jarred Isolde.
She spun around. Unbidden by her, the mantel clock was ticking.

"Name of a black day," she breathed, "who is it?"

Alice woke with a violent start. She stared stupidly at her drink as
if looking for a reality she might have misplaced. Between her fingers, the glass and drink dissolved to a fine smoke. Then she saw
Isolde—and she remembered. She was too frightened to move, but
she could scream. She was still screaming when the panel doors
banged open and Marty burst into the room.

"What happened?" he looked dazedly at both women. "I must
have passed out. I woke up on the floor and—"

Alice bolted out of the chair and cowered against him, her face
white and contorted with fear. "Martin, she tried to kill me. It was in
a dream, a man with a sword . . . there was a glass in my hand and
it just disappeared . . ."

Isolde backed toward the fireplace in confusion and fright. Something had broken her spell, and now she was caught with her world
falling about her head. The fear became a swelling black anger,
hammering harder and faster at her temples.

"I don't know what she is," Alice moaned against Marty's shoulder, "but, Martin, she's not *human!*" She clung to him like a child
sobbing out of a nightmare to the safety of a grown-up, and Marty,
with the answering instinct, put his arms around her.

The last stroke of the hammer fell. Isolde gasped with a pain that bent her almost double. Only her will remained: "Take your hands from her, Marty, or I'll burn the wench in your arms!"

Marty looked up at her. For a long second, there was only the loud ticking of the clock and Alice's ragged sobbing. Then Marty pushed Alice toward the door. "Get out, Alice," he said. "Don't come back."

"Come away with me, Martin. Please, for your own sake."

But he was already closing the door on her. "No, not with you. This is something between Isolde and me, and you're a stranger, Alice. You always were. Good-bye."

He shut the door and leaned his head against it, eyes shut. From the driveway came the sound of the car started, jerked nervously into gear and roaring down the lane.

"Marty?"

He didn't answer.

"Marty, will you turn away from me now?"

"Turn away? Turn away from what? You aren't real, are you?" His voice was quiet and toneless with the knowing. "I know it now. I guess—always—some part of me knew, but I needed someone. Strange. Sometimes when I loved you, it was like you weren't there, and I was alone. Not always, no; only a few times when I needed you so much I reached for *something*, I don't know what. Some part of me knew. I guess that's why I never asked how you came."

"From Heaven and Hell," Isolde sighed, "and all the winds between." She was tired, tired as she had not been in fifteen hundred years. "I was searching for life, and 'twas here by your fire I found it. And if I be not your first love, Marty—well, you be not mine, either. But that was a long time ago, nor was it half the glory of this."

For the first time, there was something in his expression that escaped her. "Are you afraid, Marty?"

"No," Marty said quietly, "not afraid." He took a step toward the panel doors.

"Then why do you turn away?"

"Don't you know?" He wheeled on her, and Isolde began to understand the thing behind his eyes and in his voice. It was hurt. "Can't you see what you've done? Alice gave nothing, but she promised nothing. She was what she was. You promised everything when you had nothing to give that was real."

"And have you lacked since I came?" she asked, with the strange, sick weariness growing in her. "Have I not won your house for you, once and always?"

"Sure, and for what?" The hurt was a hard brightness in the words. "For the years we'll spend in it?"

"The years? No, we haven't got years."

"For the growing old together, when you'll never grow old, never grow up? For the children we won't have?"

She sank into a chair. "I only had a little time and my broom."

"And you knew that, and yet you couldn't know how I'd feel when you—"

"I wanted life, Marty!"

"Life!" he screamed at her, lunging at the broom. "With *that?*"

Her hand shut in a fist. *"Don't touch it!"*

She could have cut out her tongue before the wish was half uttered. Marty froze, paralyzed with the sudden agony. It faded slowly, leaving him white and spent.

"Thanks," he said weakly. "That was a quick death."

"God and yourself forgive me, Marty. 'Twas the last hurt I'll ever do you."

"Yes. It's killed." Marty smiled sadly at her. "Oh, my poor, scared baby, I couldn't hurt you. I couldn't. But you wouldn't take the chance."

He walked out of the living room. Isolde heard his footsteps on the stairs, then in the bedroom above, and the sound of closets and drawers being opened, not in haste but with deliberateness. She rose from the chair and wandered about the living room, unable to think of what might happen. Suddenly she dropped to her knees, a little ball of misery in the middle of the floor.

"Oh, wretched!" she cursed herself, beating futile repentance into the carpet with her fists. "Worthless, white-livered slut! Be you damned twice over for the hurt in his eyes, for the love you took from him, for the life of him you stole, and yourself not fit to kiss his dear, mud-tracking boots."

After a few minutes, Marty came downstairs again, dressed to go out, carrying a small suitcase.

"Where do you go, Marty?"

"Away," he said. "I'll send someone after the rest of my things."

She bowed her head. "And not come back?"

He shook his head. "I don't want to look at this house again. Alice can sell it if she wants, I don't care. But you can work that broom till it wears out; I won't be back."

"No fear, Marty. I said 'twas the last hurt." When she looked at him, the old pride was there but it was gentled. "You've a queen's word for it."

He put his hand on the doorknob, pulled it open. "I guess I just can't take losing again. Good-bye, honey."

"Fare you well, Marty. The best of my heart go with you."

The door closed behind him.

Isolde fell forward, burying her face in her arms. "Heaven and Hell, Heaven and Hell, let me die once more."

"How unutterably tragic," said the cultivated voice behind her. "I really should have brought Booth along. He fairly wallows in this sort of thing."

Isolde raised her head slowly to the well-tailored man in the easy chair, pursing his lips over a tumbler of whisky. Bitterly and without surprise she said, "Well, now's my day complete."

The Prince sipped at his whisky, knitting fine brows. "Wonderful stuff! The woman was mad to pass this up for that drowned-olive affair. No—as a matter of fact, I hadn't intended to come myself, only to send again to ask you to come home." He gave her a charming shrug and smile. "But none of your crowd was available. Nero is throwing a party for some American senator and Booth is still playing Hamlet. Oh! The conceit of that actor! Do you know where he kills the King in the last act? Well, as true as I'm here, whenever the mood strikes him, that unbelievable ham shoots the King with a pistol and gallops off up center bellowing *sic semper tyrannis*. Still, he's in demand. The women, mostly. As for Prissy, her latest passion is Zen, and she doesn't even care about her broom, though you've certainly made free with it." He chuckled with reminiscent delight. "That execution effect was superb. That's why I broke your spell. I wanted to see how well you could manage *a capella*, and, my dear, you fizzled."

Isolde stared at her hands. "What's it matter now? Marty's gone. 'Tis over."

"You can't say you weren't warned. You had every chance."

"Aye, I did." She rose heavily, picked up the broom and held it out to the Prince. " 'Tis over, let's be gone."

He waved it away. "Not for all the world. No, the moment I saw you, I knew the game was changed. There are more interesting considerations now."

Isolde was firm. "Take it. I want no more of this." Another wave of sickness rolled over her. "I said you've won. Must you rack me as well?"

"That's what I meant," said the Prince, "though I must decline the credit. You see, Faerie Queen, you're with child. What a quaint phrase!" He toasted her with his glass. "Congratulations."

"With child." She dropped the broom and sank to her knees, stunned by the wonder of it. "With child! Oh saints, saints, saints, Marty, I have your child!"

"Precisely," the Prince interjected, "and you can hardly blame me for that. Nevertheless, you can see why I won't recall you before your time. I will even extend your visit if need be. There'll be the child."

"Marty's child!" she flared. "It belongs to him."

"Of course, Isolde, but you belong to me." An eloquent shrug of his shoulders. "Though it is an unusual case. First of its kind, actually. The possibilities are infinite. For example—how would you like to be mother of a President?" He leaned back, speculating with pleasure. "I'll make him a man of universal insight and intellectual power, a natural leader of men and irresistible to women. Yet humble, possessing the common touch. A man of the people. The world will be ready for another Kennedy."

"You'll not have the power of one finger over my son!"

"Oh, stop it!" he snapped. "You're as bad as Booth. He warned you that I never operate at a loss." The Prince picked up her broom. "This is your only hold on the world, and yet its greatest power was only your own lunatic thirst for life. Well, you got everything you wanted. Now, by the same easy method, you want to sweep it all away, and still you don't understand. Not my power but your lack of it will stop you. Yet, with my way, you could have him back."

Isolde was very still for a time, seeming to accept what he said. Finally: "Aye, you do win it all . . . all. You know you can hold me here and that I won't live without Marty. But make me the small promise that Marty and his own will never lack."

The Prince was all graciousness. "They will never lack."

"And my son be happy all the days of his life?"

"Fabulously."

She gave him a cold smile. "Thanks for that."

The Prince nodded benignly. "My pleasure entirely. It's all in the family. So, it's done. Now for the last." He held out the broom to her. "Take this and wish your husband back."

She hesitated. "But will he love me?"

"He will want you. Not quite the same, but good enough for the time you have left."

"No, not quite the same."

He held out the broom. "But still . . ."

She took the broom. "But still."

"Now, Isolde: wish."

And Isolde wished. "Broom," she commanded, "from the world and the memory of Marty Finnigan, *sweep me out forever.*"

The Prince gasped. "Wait!"

"And that done"—she raised the broom with both hands, broke it over her knee and hurled the pieces into the fireplace—"be quit of me!" The two ends flashed into unearthly flame and disintegrated. Isolde sucked in one last breath of sweet air and held it, waiting—

A low moan ran through the foundations of the house. The curtains tore loose from every window, the paint and wallpaper peeled, the dust of months swirled in a brown cloud and settled over the furniture and the floor. All that the broom had done for her was undone, for the house had said it would only seem, and the seeming was ended.

But Isolde still stood there—corporeal, uneclipsed. She opened her eyes to the fuming anger of the Prince.

"You treacherous slut. You puling, sentimental, self-sacrificing *cow!*"

Dumbly she waited to be consumed, not hearing or caring. Marty was free of her, and what was done was done.

"Fool!" the Prince screamed at her, his voice a ludicrous falsetto with rage. "No one since that primal wench in Eden could have been so stupid. To writhe through the agony of this blind hog-wallow of a world, not once but twice. To feel limbs wither and love die—*twice*. To know the death of every dream and its disillusionment—*twice*. And for what grubby little reason? Why do you think that men have clung through all time to the need for Heaven and Hell? Not for punishment, not for reward. They are refuge, both of them, from trying to find a meaning for life; the pointless end to the grisly joke. And it *is* a joke. The immense cosmic joke that you, you second-rate Guinevere, will never understand in a thousand lifetimes. Because in Heaven are all rewards for virtue except the earthly hunger for reward, and if Hell is empty after all, at least it holds no pain. Why shouldn't they be sought after and prayed for by the brave and cowardly alike, the saints and the greedy, the men who knew they walked alone and the petty bargainers who mortgaged their souls to have them loved for five minutes; why shouldn't they be refuge, these two endings that you've tossed out like an old pair of shoes? Neither gives a meaning, but both make an end to *this!*"

Something was dawning on Isolde, something so immense she dared grasp only the littlest piece of it. "Well, take me if you will. Why do you rage so?" She grinned at him. "You've lost your power over me, haven't you, Prince?"

"I wouldn't say that." But he made no move toward her.

"Yes," the thing grew in her, "that's it: the meaning. The Secret. That's why you sent Booth when I was about to give of myself to Marty. Afraid you were that I'd learn the secret and be quit of you." She laughed in his face. "Come, try and take me. Here's my hand, Prince. Try!"

The Prince backed away from the contact. "Now, don't be hasty. Keep away from me. Don't touch me, you grimy little human!"

She pursued him around the room, hooting with laughter. "I've won! I'm alive, and if I lay hand or foot to you, by the Grail I'll leave a lump for every inch. *There!*"

"*Yi!*"

"And there! And there! Now, out of my house, for 'tis mine at last! Oh, Marty, Marty," she sank down on the sofa, weeping and laughing with her joy. "I'm alive. I don't know how, but I'm alive."

"Well," said the Prince nastily, keeping a safe distance from her, "at least I don't have the bother of you anymore. The broom finishes that."

" 'Twas the giving," she said to herself.

"Perhaps," the Prince conceded shortly. "I never have understood that sort of thing."

"The giving. So small a thing."

The Prince snorted his contempt from the doorway. "Even if I were a man, I'd call you a fool."

"Aye, Prince," she answered, and she was no longer a girl. "But if you were a fool, you'd be a man."

He inclined his head with an old-fashioned courtesy. "Well, Faerie Queen: your world and welcome to it. Oh, don't get up. I'll let myself out."

The house was drab and dirty as the day she had come to it, unchanged in any way except that Marty was gone. But she was alive, and it was her house, and she knew what to do with it now.

His house in my hands, she thought, and his son beneath my heart. Well now! A new broom and a bucket, a brush and paint, and new curtains to be made and the kitchen to be cleaned and the lawn mowed and his garden started, and what sit you here for, Mistress Finnigan, when there's your toil waiting. Just you wait, Marty, and *then* say I can give you nothing that's real—and, oh saints, saints, saints, I'm about to be sick again!

She swept and she scrubbed. She chipped and painted. She measured and she sewed. She mowed and raked until, little by little, under blistered hands that now wove no magic but her love, Finnigan's Hearth began to shine once more. She was sick in the mornings with depressing regularity but weathered it with choking curses and went about her work. The spring wind was a bouquet of Moselle in her nostrils, and ancient Poobah no longer growled when she passed.

But the days went by and she found what it was to be lonely.

One afternoon as she was rooting weeds out of the new flower bed, she heard someone call her name. Looking up, she saw a tall, white-haired man standing near the front steps. He seemed familiar but the name escaped her.

"Well, top of the morning, Mrs. Finnigan."

"And the rest of the day for yourself," she responded cordially. "What be you? An insurance peddler?"

"Good heavens, no," he laughed gently. "There's nothing sure in this world. I was in the area and just thought I'd look in. I wondered if you'd found what you were looking for?"

Isolde knew him now. She curtsied in deep respect. "Give you good day, Angel. And how be the Blessed?"

"Tolerably well," he nodded. "You too, by your blossoming aspect. Did you find your Secret?"

Isolde wiped the perspiration from her face, leaving it streaked with brown earth. "Not all, but as much as my poor thick skull can hold."

"That's all anyone can do. Tell me, then: what is it?"

"To keep from hurt the heart of Marty Finnigan, to love him with my own and to give to him all the days of my life."

"Well, now," the Angel stepped back, regarding her with his kind, sad eyes. "As nicely as I've ever heard it put. Different hearts, differents words, but it dresses out about the same."

"Aye, but I learned too late. He's forgot me."

"Yes, I know," said the Angel. "Your finest hour, as that Englishman said. Well, as a woman, you're going to learn that men are very forgetful anyway. It's all a question of what they forget." He indicated the flower bed. "What have you planted?"

"Roses," she said with some enthusiasm. "Marty said when the spring came . . ." the sentence trailed off. "They'll grace the look of the house," she finished, hearing the loneliness in her own voice.

"They will," the Angel said. "I wish you could send me one. But then I never sent you a wedding gift, did I? That just shows you. Forgetful, every one of us. Well, let me think. What would be appropriate?" He considered the problem. "How about a new harp?"

And play it to an empty house, she thought.

"Yes," the Angel nodded, pleased with his choice. "A harp. A forgotten art, these days, but you always did have a talent for it." He took her hands in his. "Good-bye for the time, Isolde. We'll meet again, of course."

" 'Twill be my pleasure, Angel."

"Well, next time, *do* plan to stay." He waved to her and disappeared around the corner of the house. Isolde went back to her digging.

A few minutes later a car turned into the lane. It was a police cruiser, manned by two bored officers and bearing a battered passenger in the rear seat. The policemen helped their charge from the car with the care one accords to a cracked Ming vase.

Isolde's heart came up into her throat. She clutched her trowel as if it were the O'Gowra broom.

The officer gave her a weary, patient nod. "This your husband, ma'am?"

"Oh, for sure," she swallowed. "Whatever's happened to him?"

Marty's left eye was swollen shut in a small mound of royal purple. The other was bloodshot. He was unshaven, unwashed and the remains of his suit were only memorials to an epic struggle.

"Who did this?" Isolde snapped. "Who *dast* do this to Martin Finnigan?"

The officer gave Marty a look of professional compassion. "Couldn't tell you all of 'em. Had complaints on him all week. Drunk and disorderly, damage to property, assault, four fights in three days—"

"Oh, dear God! Four?"

"Yes, ma'am. He must've lost them all. Had him down at the station for two days, drying him out. He wouldn't tell us where he lived." He swung away toward the car. Marty sagged down onto the front stoop, bleakly silent as Stonehenge. The second policeman regarded him.

"You know, lady," he said, "I think your husband's one of those people who just can't drink."

The first officer returned with something under his arm. He proffered it to Marty, puzzled. "This yours, Mr. Finnigan?"

Marty's one good eye appraised the object, an ancient harp. "Hell no," he concluded gloomily. "What would I do with it?"

The policeman handed it to Isolde. Her arms and fingers remembered its curve. "Well, it ain't ours either, so you take it. All right, ma'am, I guess that's all. Keep him home for a while."

"My thanks, sir."

The police car rumbled out of the lane, leaving them alone in their world. Isolde took a deep, tired breath. There were so many things to tell him, about the house and the missing of himself for days, about the lonely expanse of bed at night. About the child.

But no, a little at a time. I'll not tell him; I'll show him a little at a time that what we have is real.

"Well, Marty?"

"Well, what?" he muttered. "Don't think I wanted to come back here. They made me come back."

Isolde fought against the anger, but it rose in her throat. "And—and so you'll be walking off again."

"Yes." Marty's voice was hoarse with fatigue. "But I wouldn't mind an aspirin or two, if we have any."

" 'We,' Finnigan? 'We' have nothing. *I* might have a draught to soothe your head." *There's nothing but to fight him. A little of him must be fought and beaten so all of him can win.* "But when you walk down that road, Finnigan, what pill will you take against the next woman that comes your way and loves you, but, pity her soul, isn't good enough, isn't real enough, isn't perfect enough for you?"

"Don't hand me that, dammit!" Marty lunged up at her. "You know what you are," he seethed. "You're a lie, an illusion. Standing there telling me *I* don't have any guts. Telling a real person—"

"*Real!*" She jabbed a finger into his chest. "I am the realest, strongest clout of woman 'twill ever be your good fortune to look on, and, I might add, getting realer by the moment, as time and the sight of your eyes will unfold to your feeble understanding. See!" Isolde spread her hands before his face. "Those be blisters. That be callus. And do you puzzle where I got them? From work. From cleaning and painting the house that's mine now, because I stayed to care for it, whilst you walked away. And this sweat"— she was almost crying now—"is from loving your own dream enough to plant your bloody roses!"

His face cracked in the beginnings of a sardonic grin. "Looks like you used your nose to dig with."

"Does it indeed?" The nose in point was thrust as close as possible to him. "A minute at a glass will tell you you've not exactly the look of a rose yourself, Sir Finnigan. And was I blindfold with only this poor nose to tell me what I was next to, my first thought would not be any kind of flower. God, what a sorry sight you are, and yourself unwashed as a Cornish cowherd. Crawling home after days—"

"I did not crawl home," Marty bawled. "I am not staying."

"Then crawl away!"

"Don't tell me what to do in my own yard."

"*My* yard!" Isolde dropped the trowel, jabbed her fist into his stomach and kicked him in the shin. Marty doubled for a second in surprise, then grabbed at her, tucked her under one arm and spanked her until they swayed and fell onto the grass. She twisted on her back and looked up at him. Marty was very pale but laughing. "Ah-h, hell. You're right, where else is there?"

"Marty," she said with the anger gone out of her, "will you go? Or do you come home to stay?"

"To stay." He seemed to consider it. "I think I came home to die. Honey, *please*, do we have any aspirin?"

She couldn't bear it any longer. Her arms were around him and she was sobbing. "Stay . . . stay. Please stay."

"Sure," he soothed her. "I have to. The world isn't ready for you yet, baby."

"Oh, Marty, that's finished and dead, I swear."

"Now listen," he said painfully as if each word weighed a ton, "that part is over. Let's never, never even think about it. Because people—oh God, my head—because people like Alice . . . and other people . . . well, they're just not very broad-minded."

"It's done and done." She drew him up gently. "And nothing left of it but ourselves. Our house stands tall and gallant, Finnigan. Welcome home."

Isolde led him inside and stretched him out with great care on the sofa, his head sandwiched between an ice bag and the pillow. She knelt beside him and drew soft chords from the harp.

Marty stirred. "Lovely," he murmured, and then he was asleep. Isolde played softly. Now and then, when he moved, she would replace the ice bag gently, as if it were a crown.

(1956–61)

THE LADY OF FINNIGAN'S HEARTH

Old-home week for the Kid, my official Opus One from an era so distant it's camp now. The story lay in a drawer for years and would have vanished into the maw of the round file but for the pleadings and threats of Marvin Kaye. He said to send it to Ted White at *Fantastic,* and Ted published it. For me, it's very early Rachmaninoff—too fevered, naive and sugared with sentiments I struggle to remember, let alone feel.

The first half was written in 1956 when I was a very married nine-to-fiver yearning out my picture window in suburbia for the bohemian life I imagined to be romantic as hell. It was finished in 1961 when I'd had my wish granted in spades and was yearning out of a rooming-house window for a solid meal. My world had turned upside down and taught me some hard lessons, which may account for the darkening tone toward the end. I still managed to get a few laughs into it; the story would be glutinous without them. Some have said it's that way *with* them. Peace, fellas. Alice doesn't live here anymore.

Interesting to note how the Prince grew between this story and "Teresa Golowitz," written twenty years later. I like him now and want to find another really good story for him someday.

Ted White told me that "Finnigan" won third place for short fiction in 1977 with the British Fantasy Society. I'm happy to say Marvin Kaye won second place with a better story even though he saved this one from limbo. The pure in heart have the strength of ten. And "Finnigan" is the reason why, if not always encouraging, I try to be kind to hopeful new writers.

Hell—they're all me, babe. Every fevered one of 'em.

UNSIGNED ORIGINAL

Renquist's back was presented to me and heaved with eloquent regret as he poured the brandy.

"Murder as a literary art is quite dead, of course," he said. "There remains only refinement of the act itself."

He brought the Martell flanked by our poured snifters on a silver tray to the chess table between us. So we settled for the wet evening in Renquist's quiet house, sixtyish and solitary, given to brandy and reminiscence and precious little else anymore.

"You'll have to stay the night," Renquist told me. "You can't order a cab. My phone's out and there's no bus until morning."

"Why not?" I eased back in the well-upholstered chair. "I've nothing else to do."

"There you have it," Renquist nodded forlornly. "Like our art, we're superfluous—dead, dead, dead. At best, black-veiled mourners at a pulp-paper bier."

It might be said, if not already obvious, that there was always something *de trop* about Renquist. He overpresented himself like someone aspiring to an exclusive club and not altogether secure in his qualifications. "Florid" would describe his complexion and, more often than not, his prose. As his person, so his house. The bookshelves were punctuated with studiedly outré prints and drawings, a few Beardsleys, mostly the renounced monstrosities from *Lysistrata*, an original Bok worth quite a bit now, several of the darker Goyas and what appeared to be a Clarke, though subtly altered.

"There are more murders than ever," I said.

"I said *art*," Renquist grumbled, tugging his vest over an expanding middle. "Not a mere statistic. More murders, yes; more bloody-minded amateurs cluttering the streets with their plebian passions, shooting, cutting—mere ballistic and surgical demonstrations. But where," Renquist deplored, "is the *style*, the originality, the development of the puzzle?"

His gesture of regret sharpened to an index finger jabbed at the rows of books along one wall. "There they lie, all of them. Poe, Conan Doyle, James, Bulwer-Lytton. All the gothics. Christie, Sayers, Rinehart and their trim little tea-with-the-vicar mysteries. The master mechanics: Carr and Gardner. Stout's brilliant obesity issuing *dictums* from the house on Thirty-fifth Street. The less skillful moderns with their banal penchant for hustling a wench into bed rather than an early grave. There you are, Tarking." His hand reverenced my seven slim volumes like funerary urns in a special compartment, then the full, tight-wedged bottom shelf. "And finally myself. This isn't a bookcase, Tarking, it's a damned mortuary. We still live in a murdering world, but to write a superb mystery for its edification today is like serving an exquisitely sautéed shad roe to a redneck raised on grits; like one voice pronouncing 'murder' correctly in a crowd of homicidal harelips!"

I hid my jaded smile. In thirty years, I had written seven mysteries while he'd ground out twenty, all of them direct descendants of mine, varied and—admittedly—developed to their last possible plot ramification, but originality was beyond him. He was a pianist rendering endless variations on a given theme without the ability to pen one honest note of his own. The knowledge made Renquist by turns solicitous and patronizing toward me, as a goldsmith fashioning high art from the element I merely mined. He read my thought as my eye rested on the fat shelf of his books and the handful of my own.

"Yes, I've copied you, Tarking. Say rather improved. You were brilliant but lazy and wasteful. Could have gotten five books from the ideas you poured into one."

"I lose interest." I swirled the brandy in my glass, musing on its color. "The difference between research and development. One is fascinating, the other mere drudgery."

"Touché." Despite the home shot, Renquist was genial. "Still, we've remained friends. In memoriam, then. To a lost art."

I frowned at the amber liquid in my snifter and touched it to my lips.

"There *is* a glimmer of hope." Renquist eased back in the Chippendale. "The Muldauer murder. Surely you've read the papers."

"Yes, the commissioner of police. He won't be missed. Heartwarmingly venal, I hear."

"Passionately. And exquisitely dispatched. Broad daylight, a dozen people near, drilled in his driveway, probably with a silencer."

"Suspects?"

"Thousands!" Renquist hooted. "A neat thousand with as many motives. Needle in a bushel of needles. Result: zero, blank. Immaculate."

"You look as satisfied as if you'd done it yourself."

I was granted a look that only Renquist would have called enigmatic. "No," he admitted, "but I damn well wish I had."

His glance followed mine to the picture on the wall just behind him that I'd thought earlier was a Clarke. There was an alien element in the elongated figures, a vitality that Clarke would have avoided on principle. I leaned forward to it.

"That print; is that . . . ?"

Renquist beamed with pleasure. "I wondered when you'd notice it." He rose and bustled around to the picture. "Not Clarke. My own improvement on him. His figures look as if they'd lived all their two-dimensional lives in that uncomfortable position. Mine have all his macabre aura, but at least they give you the impression they might have gone to the bathroom once in a while."

With a careful fingertip he brushed imaginary dust from the picture. "I should have been a critic, Tarking. Improvement is my ruling passion."

Renquist sighed stagily. "But there are no new plots, no unique methods, the revels ended, the puzzles all undone, charted, catalogued . . . dead. I can no longer create paper mayhem to titillate a world grown numb with crass genocide. *Ergo* . . ."

He turned back to me and picked up the snifter with a flourish. "Therefore, Tarking, I've thought to take up the act itself as an art form, select one prominent person at a time and dispose of him with no clues whatever." He raised his glass. "To a new career."

My laugh hurt him, I think.

"I'm serious, Tarking."

"You're nothing of the sort," I boshed him. "You're fifty-eight and sedentary and, bless you, you couldn't cut your finger without telling the world about it, with a note to your agent to retain the film rights."

Renquist laughed with me, conceding the point. "Well, then: to me."

We drank to him.

"Actually," he said, "the idea was yours to begin with."

"Weren't they all?"

"Oh, don't be pettish, Tarking! What have I stolen that I've not improved a hundredfold? Your second book, *No Darker Art*, held the whole system: murder as a hobby for a retired author of murder mysteries. The goal—"

"Yes, I remember."

"—to accumulate a series of unsolved and unsolvable crimes to stand as a monument of enigma. And for my first," Renquist caressed the phrase with his tongue, "for my auspicious first, I'd choose someone fairly well in the public eye, yet sufficiently reclusive not to be missed for some time. Perhaps someone I know."

He took another satisfied sip of his brandy. We looked at each other across the ticking of the clock.

"The implication is a bit broad-footed."

"A bit," Renquist purred.

"Myself."

"Just so." His smile was sugared Machiavelli. "A night chosen when my telephone decides to take a siesta, the body buried in a pit already yawning in a corner of my large, dark cellar. Police annoyed at widening intervals about my dear friend, who hasn't even called. Think, Tarking: a series of such baroque leave-takings over, say, three years—researched, annotated, published, lauded. My *magnum opus.*"

"A bit sick," I judged, "but not without merit of its kind. And the method?"

"Brandy," he smiled. "An excellent bottle. I wouldn't swing off a friend and connoisseur on rotgut, Tarking. A snifter of Martell envenomed with a swift and painless demise."

I winced. " 'Envenomed,' Renquist?"

"Aye, sirrah. 'Twas my word."

"It reeks of First Folio."

He glared at my breech of decorum. "I *am* serious, damn your *sang-froid*. It's rummaging your vitals right now, very efficiently up to no good. And you, dear Tarking, are my first—perhaps my most poetically original—chapter."

From his expression, I was expected to say something; perhaps to applaud. "Well, Tarking?"

I put down the glass. "Not quite original, not entirely without holes. First: I may have told someone I'd be here tonight."

Renquist chuckled. "Not you; you're gregarious as a clam. What reason would you have?"

"Any number, even casual."

"Your own phone is turned off eight days out of ten. Even your cleaning woman thinks you're a myth. The odds are with me," Renquist concluded happily. "What else?"

"Second: to a connoisseur, a good brandy is too clear to contain any toxin you could procure without clouding even slightly."

"Rot. You drank it."

"Looked like the results of bad plumbing."

"But . . . you drank it!" Renquist's features were a rapidly paling caricature of triumph.

"Did I?"

"I saw you." Renquist tried to rise. The inability surprised him, the high furrows of astonishment on his brow glistening with sudden perspiration. His breathing had accelerated. "I didn't take my eyes off you."

"Except for one moment to admire your improvement on Clarke, to which I directed your egotistical attention. Ample time for the light of hand. If I was wrong, no harm done." I shrugged. "As it is . . ."

He was sinking fast, horror-struck, his hand jittering at his laboring heart. "Tarking . . . a doctor . . ."

"Your phone," I reminded him tactfully. "I really didn't plan it this way. Here you are, my second chapter, and—"

Renquist wheezed hideously and ceased breathing.

—And he was supposed to be number *three*.

STROKE OF MERCY

All Paris knows that Lord Berkeley is notoriously reckless of his life. Since he is also more skilled with a pistol than I, he will doubtless kill me at the appointed hour in defense of what he is pleased to call his honor. The more honor will redound to his name if his adversary is considered sane and not a visionary lunatic.

With the heightened perception of madness, I appreciate the comedy of the situation. We are both from countries in which dueling is outlawed. Burr killed Hamilton two years ago on my native soil, but it cost him his political future. Berkeley's England has frowned on dueling for a century. Paradoxically it is here in Paris, the most civilized city in the world, that we come to this pass.

Berkeley came to play, of course. Arrogant, idle and rich, he has for a year and more indulged himself with the generosity of a ruling class that bequeaths moral restraint to their commons without tax by the peerage. Paris did not corrupt him; its *laissez-faire* only obviated that discretion demanded at home.

For myself, my name is Ethan Flagg. A modest patrimony has allowed me to study literature and philosophy at the Sorbonne, a living I augment in a clerical post at the American Embassy.

Berkeley and I are of an age, three and twenty, but only he is young. I am aged with a sickness of the mind. Or let me pray that I am. At worst, to die at his hand will put a period to those nightmare visions which have tortured me since I was twelve years of age, visions that do not change but evolve, becoming clearer and more detailed until they sear now into my waking as well as sleeping hours with a sharpness of resolution consistent as it is hellish. Denise knows something of these dreams. Though I never speak of them, I sometimes wake her at night crying out in their incomprehensible *patois*. They are not to understand. They are horrors.

Denise—Mlle. Denise Laurenne—is the cause of my quarrel with Berkeley. As an American without class or fortune, I was devastated with happiness when she lavishly returned the attentions I commenced after seeing her perform at L'Opéra-Comique. We are well matched, content together from the first. If she is a few years older and more experienced, if Berkeley's insolent face leers from her recent past, I care not. Most of this infected life I could discard with ease, saving those hours which she inhabits. For her sake I am committed and likely doomed.

Berkeley doesn't care a rap for Denise now. She is *déclassée*, yesterday's diversion, her name to be bandied freely about the Anglo Club to a ripple of stained and cognizant laughter. What I could privately ignore was intolerable when he fronted me with it in the Club billiard room. He chose his time carefully for the largest audience.

"But surely la Laurenne has mentioned me to you?"

I looked about at the ring of his faintly sneering companions who had left off their billiards to enjoy my humiliation, though I still attempted to keep my voice lowered.

"This is not a subject for discussion in a gentlemen's club."

Berkeley took snuff with an air of studied boredom. "Demme, sirrah, are you a gentleman? It seems the definition has broadened."

"Berkeley, as you were once her friend, I urge kindness—"

"Toward whom, sir? Herself—or you?"

"For her sake, if your breeding will not suffice."

He did not expect such a ready riposte. He laughed negligently—or with the appearance of negligence—careful that his friends missed none of our exchange. "Oh come, my dear . . . Flagg, is it? We are men speaking among men. I found her quite amusing."

My retort was the more scathing for its truth. As Denise put it, the well-worn shoe is a good judge of feet. She had mentioned Berkeley, and she is nothing if not candid. "That was her word, my lord: *amusant.* She catalogued you in humorous detail as a clumsy simpleton at *amour.* Clumsy or tedious, I do forget."

Berkeley's smirk faltered. His friends edged closer like a circle of hounds around two of their breed embattled. "You are a demmed liar, Master Flagg."

"Am I so?" With icy precision, then, I proceeded to a probing corroboration of this or that particular, even to the private details of his person, which left no doubt as to the veracity of my account or Berkeley's lamentable lack of finesse with women. Poor man; as I advanced from proof to proof the flush of vicious triumph that colored his inbred features darkened to murderous anger. That he enjoyed Denise before me was to have been his coarse joke on a common clerk. That she found him hopelessly inept was my distilled revenge. The laughter of his friends was of a different timbre now.

Berkeley was in deadly earnest now, perhaps even in pain. "Master Flagg, you will retract every word of this."

"But why?" I sank the dagger to its hilt. "Are we not men speaking among men? It is to laugh, my lord. As she did."

In the moment before he struck me I imagined I perceived something quite alien that peered from behind Berkeley's mask of malicious ennui; as if he were an actor aware of a role, laughing not at me but at us together on a foolish stage. But it was merely my distorted judgment; he has no such sensitivity. His open hand whipped across my cheek.

"You—shop boy!"

Thus the sad comedy begins. These affairs are straitly codified in Paris. Cards of address were exchanged, the Viscount Hampton volunteered as Berkeley's second while I was advised to engage one of my own. If we could not compose our differences, the meeting would take place no later than two mornings hence when a doctor and a suitable place had been found. Someone mentioned the convenient privacy of the St.-Germain district . . .

Denise considers the duel sheer folly and urges me to apologize to Berkeley, as if it were not her honor he derided.

"My honor, Ethan? *Là.*"

How desirable and dear she is, her face framed in dark curls kept very short for the wigs her roles demand. She has seen most of what the world offers women and can no longer be disillusioned by any of it. Those tight *gamine* curls framing the sad warmth of her eyes are a delightful contradiction for me.

"*Mais, bien merci,* I have not such an honor. What I have is a good life with you. That is more important. For Berkeley," her shoulders lift and fall in a gesture only the French can render eloquent, "he is a sad fool, sadder than you guess. Let it go."

"I cannot."

"But why? I do not feel dishonored. *C'est comique.*"

May you never know just how comic, Denise. "But the comedy is not ended."

"Ah, *zut!*" She throws up exasperated hands. "You men. It is not my honor but your own pride."

"He insulted you."

Denise smiles. "France herself has been used to insult since Julius Caesar. Everyone who fancied conquest has found his shortest route through Paris. She has learned to relax in the supine position, as have women. Men take what they want, women what God sends them. So we survive; it is the world."

"And am I just one more conqueror?"

"Non, mon cher." Denise holds out the arms I can never deny. "When God sent you, he was feeling generous. Come: do not talk but love me."

In her all-cleansing embrace I enjoy the only sure sanity I have ever known. Later, as Denise slumbers beside me, I stare wakefully at the moon sinking beyond our window and ponder the shape of time. There are heady new forces abroad in the world. France has built in blood what Jefferson and Paine conceived in noble experiment. The old order, Berkeley's order, is dying, but what will grow in its place? Rousseau eulogizes the perfectible human spirit with no title but Mankind, Beethoven's new symphonies are hammer strokes at the chains of tradition, but what Prometheus do we free?

And so the sickness comes over me as it spreads insensibly over the face of time. I begin to perspire profusely. Thank God Denise is asleep; perhaps this time she can sleep through it. The blood pounds in my ears; I grind my face into the pillow. The sensation of nausea engulfs me. I resist, pray with my whole being. God help me, I am here now in Paris. It is May 15, 1806. May 15. It is—

July 3, 1863. The sun's baked Gettysburg bone-dry for three days. Lieutenant Cushing's tunic is open and the front of his red underwear sticks to his chest. I'm stripped down to drawers with a bandanna around my head and tight over my ears. The sky is made of loud iron, the whistle and scream and boom of shells. Yesterday Lee had eighty guns bearing on this hill. Today there's more than a hundred and twenty. He's tried our flanks for two days and we threw him back. Old Robert E.'s got to fish or cut bait today. First he's got to knock out Cushing's guns.

They're trying. The Southern batteries have shelled us for two straight hours. Not the whole line, just us. We're down to three guns. The rest are junk along with their crews, and every goddamned cannon in the Army of Northern Virginia is pointed across the valley right at me.

Cushing chews a dead see-gar, staring at the trees on the opposite slope. "Why'd Lee wait? He coulda took us yesterday before we dug in."

"Down!" We flatten out as the shell screams over and explodes somewhere near number four gun. Sure enough, someone pipes up, "Number four gun. Short in the crew."

Cush leans his head against the wall, eyes shut, tuckered out. "Flagg, get that gun firing."

I round up three ammunition carriers to fill out the powder-grimy crew. It's just quarter of three. We're loading number four when it happens.

"Here they come."

Across the valley the blue Virginia flag bobs out of the covering trees, flanked by gray ranks, wave after wave of them, moving down the slope like a slow tide.

"That's Pickett."

"Prime . . . ready."

"Stand by to fire."

Pickett's Virginians, part of Dutch Longstreet's command. Old Dutch is a cautious man, but he's held off too long this time. There's all of Hancock's corps behind this wall. We've faced Pickett before; we know his brigadiers.

"There's Kemper."

"And Garnett."

"And that old dandy, Armistead."

My men stop talking. They know what's going to happen. Pickett's men must move across the valley bottom with no cover at all, every inch of it boxed and known to our guns. Nobody talks about that anymore. My mouth is full of cotton watching them come on so slow in such straight marching order. They're leaving wounded like a leaky bucket; you can follow their path by the gray drops.

They halt once to give us a rifle burst. Off to my left, someone screams with a high, gurgly sound like a butchered hog.

"It's the lieutenant. They got Cushing."

Cush is shot through the mouth and crotch, the worst kind of wound. He won't last till night, but I can't think of that now. There's fifteen thousand Johnnys crossing the valley, more people than I ever saw at one time, and Armistead's brigade is running now, straight at me. I pick up Cush's sword—waving a sword in my dirty underwear, that's what I'll remember about Gettysburg—and run hunched over back to number four, while a fat mother-hen staff officer reins up his horse and sits there like someone was going to take one of those glass-plate pictures of him.

"You there! Who's on Mr. Cushing's guns? Who's in command?"

I jam the sword upright in the ground. "Me, Flagg. Stand by, one, two and four."

"Prime . . . ready."

"Fire."

Another shell comes in way too close. "They got Schulz's whole crew. Number one's out."

"Fire!"

My throat is raw with smoke and screaming. We swab, load, prime and fire. The world is all black and red and that one roar tearing out of my lungs. *Fire . . . fire.* There's another roar, dull and far on our left, that I realize is our other batteries as they tear into the remains of Pickett's lost division. The gray ranks are ragged and thin now, no longer anything like lines but still coming. The smoke blossoms out and blows away to show bigger and bigger holes where men ain't anymore, like a boy scooping up lead soldiers from the floor with both hands. But Armistead staggers on toward me with the pitiful remains of his brigade.

"They're too close, Flagg. We're shooting over."

"Battle range! Battle range! Run 'em down!"

The gun is flattened out to point-blank range. We work like maniacs over it, see nothing, know nothing except the gun.

"Fire!"

"Fire!"

"Fire!"

"Number two out."

"Fire!"

Armistead reaches the wall in front of us. He's wounded but he jumps the top and gets as far as the muzzle of number four, waving his damned fool hat on his sword, yelling for his men to follow. He sees me too late as I swing Cush's sword two-handed. Die, you son of a—

He could've got me, but he was slow. And so, for me, the war goes on.

"They're goin' back. They're beat."

"Don't let 'em. Fire!"

We go on tearing up Pickett like old newspaper as he limps home over seven thousand bodies. I want to yell at George Pickett, touch

him, make it personal somehow because it's getting damned hard to
be a person anymore.

"Pickett, you—"

You what? You were a person once, too. They tell me you were
one of those damned daguerreotype-posing fools who loved war.
You could still live like that in '61, but there's no way now. Seven
thousand bodies in the valley down there, divided between a few
cannon. How many are mine? Three, four hundred? I never broke a
law in my life and I've killed more men than the busiest murderer in
history. I thought about that at Bull Run the first time my gun tore
up a line of Johnnys. I can't think of it now, it costs too much. You
used to dream of swords and honor, Pickett. I wonder what you'll
dream tonight.

We swab the gun and let it cool. The war goes on.

Denise makes our morning chocolate and discreetly absents herself on the arrival of Berkeley's second, Viscount Hampton. Son of
the Earl of Albemarle, young Hampton is point-device the blooded
dandy in fitted doeskin breeches and Gieves-tailored coat. He
stands with the distance of my worn carpet between us, as if to tread
on it would soil the soles of his mirror-polished boots.

"Master Flagg: Lord Berkeley has instructed me to accept your
public apology."

"*C'est dommage.* I had hoped you brought his."

"Then, as it is . . ."

"As it is."

Excellent lines for comedy. One can see Kean in my role, though I
hear he loves life.

"The pistols will be Gastinne-Renettes loaded with the fullest
allowable charge," Hampton advises. "There will be heavy recoil
and less accuracy. On the other hand, in the event of a hit . . ." He
elides the thought, searching me for any sign of wavering, finds
none and continues. "He leaves it to you to choose a single dis-
charge at will or exchange of shots until one party is sufficiently
wounded."

"One shot at will."

Our business is concluded, yet some atom of humanity stays
Hampton. "Flagg, I cannot fault you alone in this affair, but Harry
Berkeley has fought before. I urge you to apologize."

"No."

"You are a helpless clerk. He has wagered his life—even foolishly

—more often than I can think of. Have you ever discharged a pistol?"

"Even a cannon, my lord. Indeed, there have been days on end when I did little else."

I did not think Hampton a man for irony, but he surprises me. "You are very like him: a plain brick wall. That the two of you should duel." Hampton shrugs. "Very well. Tomorrow morning at six. The small park beyond St.-Germain." His head chops up and down once and he withdraws.

Shortly afterward my own second arrives: Rijn van den Tronck, a friend from New York City and a fellow student at the Sorbonne. He has been to see Berkeley. Stocky, blond and apple-cheeked, Rijn looks now like a schoolboy fresh from a stiff caning.

"He laughed at me, Ethan. He will accept an apology only if it is public. He will make none himself."

"I expected no grace from Berkeley." We sit down to the remaining chocolate and toast from breakfast. There is another important detail now, the letters I have written.

"This to my father in Washington City. In the event . . ."

"I understand."

"This to Denise."

Rijn shuffles the letters, searching for the right words. "What does she think of this?"

"I would not dwell on that. This last to yourself. It authorizes you to draw on my bank for such arrangements as may be necessary. There is a bequest for your studies. The balance to Denise."

Rijn tucks the letters in a pocket of his waistcoat. "I want no profit from this."

"Have no fear. It is not enough to embarrass your scruples."

"How do you feel, Ethan?"

"Dear Rijn, privately I am terrified for my life—as a miser fears the loss of a false penny. But I am more afraid of my sickness than of dying."

"These dreams you will not speak of: would you confide them to a physician?"

"I dare not. I should be barred up in Charenton for life."

"What are these dreams?"

"Parts of hell."

"And you will not tell even me?"

Tell Rijn? I peer into that stolid *jonker* face, its expression a testament to a sane universe and the ever-improving spirit of man. "How could I? The mercy and justice of God, the application of humanist philosophy, these are a fixed center to the wheel of your life."

"And yours."

"Would it help you to know there is no more God?"

"Don't say that again, Ethan."

"That someday the bare truth of this will permeate the acts, if not the sentience, of the most brutish minds; that a few will accept it, even more flee from it as they have fled down the centuries from every truth worthy of the name—"

"Stop!"

"How stop? Of the most lucid philosophy, how much has the world ever *used*? The great majority, Rijn, unable to endure the reality of God or the reality of *no* God, of personal freedom and sole responsibility, will whirl in futile circles, tearing at each other for the sake of motion. Describe this in detail? For your sanity, no."

"And you will not seek any cure?"

There is Berkeley and tomorrow. "I seek nothing else."

He bends across the table to grip my arm. "You can only seek while you live. Berkeley means to kill you."

"Right on, man. That mother's gonna blow me away."

The table blurs in front of me. My skin sheens with perspiration, my mind expands like a pustulant bubble. Rijn has never seen one of my attacks. He is stunned at the bastard English.

"What—what did you say?"

The demitasse falls from my hand, shattering on the table.

"Number one engine doesn't sound good. Skeet says there's leaves hanging off the tail assembly."

"Denise! Come quickly!"

She is at my side instantly. "It is the speech of his sickness," she says tremulously. "*Bon Dieu,* it comes day and night now. Get him to bed, Rijn. We must hold his arms."

"Hold me tight, Denise . . ."

"I will, my darling."

I feel Rijn's sturdy grip on one arm, the light, loving touch of Denise on the other. "What is today? The sixteenth of May. Say it; that sometimes staves it off. The sixteenth of May in the year of our Blessed Lord 1806. *Say it.*"

"The sixteenth of May—" They repeat it with me, over and over and—

"—over the target in seven minutes."

Lieutenant Saylors, the pilot, sounds shaky on the intercom, like we all feel. This is a bad run. Number one engine isn't turning over right. You can feel when all four engines on a B-24 are copacetic, a deep, steady drone. You get so you hear trouble quick.

"Over the target—shit, we're under it."

Gordini's right. We're coming in at treetop level to stay under the Kraut radar. That's why a screwed-up engine is bad news. No room for error at fifty feet with a full bomb load.

The Kraut phone spotters must have picked us up by now.

Saylors again: "Six minutes to target. Commo check. Copilot."

"Check," says Borowski.

"Bombardier-navigator."

Sweeney in the greenhouse: *"Ding how."*

"Engineer. Hey, Garson."

"Roger, you're five by." In my earphones, Garson sounds worried. "Just listening to number one."

"Sounds bad."

"What's your temp gauge reading?"

"Too high."

"Same here. Can you ease off number one, skip?"

"Negative," Saylors says. "Not now I can't."

"She's gonna go."

"She goes, you're out of a job."

"She goes, you're out of the war."

"Bird-dog it, Garson. I'll feather if we have to. Left waist, talk to me."

I hear the clack-clack, clack-*clack* as Gordini cocks the bolt on his .50. "Left waist, loud and clear."

"Roger. Right waist. Flagg?"

I try not to sound as scared as I am. I'm a short-timer. Five more missions and I rotate. After the fortieth I started praying for milk runs, but it's been Ploesti all month. "Right waist, loud and clear."

"Tail bay, sound off."

In the tail greenhouse, Skeet Mahoney does a Bugs Bunny over the 'com. "Eeeahh—what's up, doc? You're alive and five by five. What's our altitude, skip?"

"Doesn't even read."

Skeet laughs over the 'com. "You won't believe this. We got leaves hanging off the tail assembly. Purple Heart, men! I been goosed by an oak tree."

Saylors again, sharp: "Knock off the chatter. All turrets clear your guns."

I give the .50 two short bursts. Beautiful and smooth, like a Krupa drum riff. "Right waist clear."

"Left waist clear."

"Tail clear."

"Okay, pot right. Four minutes to target. Going upstairs."

I feel it in my stomach as the Liberator pulls up steep to make altitude for the bomb run. The other ships climb with us. The German fighters will be here anytime now. Forty-four missions, this is forty-five, five to go. I won't make it. I was born in this waist bay in a greasy leather flight suit and flak vest, and I'll die in it.

We make bombing altitude, sweating number one engine all the way, but we're formed and ready for the bomb run.

"Five hundred, Sween. Take it."

"Roger."

"Everybody look out for company."

Three minutes to Ploesti, the big Kraut gas station. A lot of oil they won't get to use. In the nose greenhouse Sweeney is the boss now.

"Commencing run."

"You got it. Give me a heading."

"Adjust to course . . . 030."

"030, roger."

"Bomb bay doors open."

"Bandits!" Skeet squeaks with excitement. "ME-109s, six o'clock high!"

"Steady, steady."

"Easy, Skeet," I tell him. "Let 'em break first. Suck 'em in."

Sweeney barks at Saylors, "*Steady* on 030. Give me some trim." What he sees now through the Norden is our whole payoff.

"Correcting to 030."

"Right . . . hold it. Hold it." Sweeney's nothing now but an eye and cross hairs and a thumb on the bomb-release button. "Hold it . . ."

The fighters dive through our formation like a school of sharks. Messerschmitts, long thin wasps, fast and hard to knock down. I watch them wheel away, waiting, saving ammo for when we'll really need it. And then from nowhere two more hit us.

"Going to seven o'clock, Skeet!"

"Bombs away!"

"*Ding how!* Let's go home."

The ship jerks and lifts with the loss of the bomb weight. The burning oil rigs below tilt toward me as Saylors banks her up in a climbing turn. As we level out, the first of the flak hits us. They've got to protect Ploesti, we've been hitting it so much. The antiaircraft cover has doubled in the last month, it's Flak Alley now, the sky is full of sloppy ink blots as the bursts blossom out. There's a flat *boof* and the screech of metal punching through metal. Someone makes an awful sound on the 'com. I twist around to Gordy.

"Hey, who—?"

Gordini's nothing but blood under his helmet. That's it, my personal kiss of death. Gordy and I started out together, one of the first crews in North Africa. If he can get it . . .

"Three o'clock, Flagg!"

I swivel around, swinging the gun. Gordy got it, not me, not yet. "I see him."

The ME turns tight and comes in with the sun behind him. White sky and a black bird getting bigger and bigger. I used to love the sky. Will I ever look at it again without searching, without fear? We all of us have that tight look now, like scared hawks that have no love for the sky but only exist in it as long as they're fast.

I give the Kraut a burst and he veers off, wobbling. The waist bay is full of smoke. "What's burning?"

"Anybody hit?"

"Gordy."

"Six o'clock!"

"I'm on it."

"Way to go, Skeet."

The ship lurches as we take another burst of flak. The drone of the engines strains higher.

"Number four's burning. Fire in number four!"

"Lead 'em, Skeet. Lead 'em!"

"Feathering number four."

We're running on three engines now, and the waist is foggy with smoke. "Waist to pilot, what's burning?"

"Two o'clock! Coming around to you, Flagg."

The ME is turning in, still broadside to me, a good shot. I lead him and get off a solid burst before the .50 jams. My lungs are full of smoke. I go on oxygen as the next blast of flak staggers the ship. Borowski is screaming over the intercom, and for an awful moment I think no one's left in the cockpit.

"Sween!"

That's all I hear before the junk of our nose greenhouse falls below and behind me, Sween twisted up in it. Then number one engine starts to miss. That's bad, that's Sweat City. Two engines gone, we'll fall behind the formation, what's left of it. Two MEs, sensing us for a loser, turn in at five o'clock. Skeet's gun bud-dud-duts in a short burst and then quits. The fighters come on, eight guns wide open, tracers streaming into our tail.

"Skeet? Hey, tail! Sound off."

Skeet chokes something into the 'com.

"Pilot to waist. Get back to Mahoney when you can."

"Wilco. Where's the fire?"

"Aux wiring, no big deal."

I haul the .50 breech open, pull out the bent shell case that caused the stoppage, then yank back the bolt twice to cock it, glaring out at the white panel of sky where less than half our flight is wavering home. Lot of maydays on the radio. We hope someone's listening, even the Krauts. They crash, they ditch over Rumania, over the Adriatic, over Italy and the Mediterranean. To be captured, to be picked up by air-sea, to drown, to spend a crazy day or two drinking wine with Italians before coming home to fly again. A Purple Heart and two bucks extra on payday.

We've taken a lot of flak, but we're beyond German fighter range. "Waist to pilot. Gonna check out Skeet."

I belly along the crawl space with the medical kit over my shoulder. The tail greenhouse is chewed to ribbons. By the time I wrestle off Skeet's flak vest and leather jacket, I'm working on a corpse. I plug into his 'com set.

"Waist to pilot. Skeet bought it. How're you doing up there?"

"Engineer, how's two and three?"

"Overheating."

"Okay, I'll try to ease her down. Flagg, get back on the waist."

Crawling back to my gun, I feel the familiar jerk and grind of the landing gear. Borowski's trying it out. This time there's more grind than jerk.

"They hit the gear. We can't lock down."

Shit, that's all she wrote. I look at the mess of Gordini behind his gun. I'm not going to make the Big Fifty, but I made this time, and so it goes on while the sky beyond the right waist bay, the curtained window, deepens to morning blue.

I am in bed, Denise sobbing against my cheek.

"The ship's junk. We had to belly in."

Over Denise's thin shoulder, Rijn holds the open Bible, praying in a low, earnest voice.

"They had to cut Skeet out of the greenhouse."

"You see?" Denise raises her tear-streaming eyes to Rijn. "You see what I live with, what I love?"

"Rijn . . . you have been praying?"

"For you, Ethan. God help you."

"I told you, God is gone. Even Satan is obsolete. There are only us."

And I stare past them to the May morning beyond our window with the self-preserving keenness of a frightened hawk. Be swift, tomorrow. Berkeley, be skilled. God has abdicated and his throne is left to the hunting birds.

There will be prisoners at Auschwitz who survive only so long as they clean, weigh and keep accurate tally of the gold parted from the teeth of other, gassed prisoners. Like the camp officials who are more intrigued with the economy of Zyklon B than its ultimate use, they cannot afford to ponder what they do, and blot it out by concentrating on weights and the fluctuating value of gold. All true horror sheaths itself in banality.

On this early morning, the day of my death, Denise concentrates on our chocolate and poached eggs as if their correct preparation is the answer to all conflict. She speaks with studied ease about the coming evening, not about the hours in between. She will not be here for supper; she performs in *Tartuffe*. Her eyes dart again and again to the door. She listens for Rijn's step on the stair. I must pretend with her.

"We will dine in Montmartre after the theater. I fancy venison in wine tonight."

"But it is so expensive, Ethan."

"Oh, just this once. We will make a treat of it."

The footsteps thud on the stair. The napkin crumples in her fist. I rise to admit Rijn.

"The carriage is waiting, Ethan."

I turn to take up my cloak. Denise is holding it ready. She arranges it about my shoulders with a too-bright smile.

"*Bonne chance, cheri.* Rijn, we dine in Montmartre tonight after my performance. Will you join us?"

He takes his cue from my imperative glance. "With pleasure."

"Why do you not both come to the theater?"

"We will be there," I promise.

"*Je t'aime*, Ethan."

I start to embrace her one last time. "You have made me very—"

"No, don't!" Denise's hands carve the shape of helplessness in the air. "Go quickly."

This is our parting. Any other would be unbearable.

Our carriage rolls along the Boulevard St.-Germain as the early sun splashes across doors and windows. The breeze is heavy with the scent of dew and spring flowers. It will be a warm day: good weather at Gettysburg, over Ploesti, north of Da Nang. And one day will come a wind so hot that glass melts and steel itself drips like tallow. Distant, but in three years the man will be born who orders my guns to Gettysburg. It begins.

Our driver turns the horses onto an uncobbled road. We jolt with the ruts, and I catch sight of a bare, dead tree among the greenery. Napalm does things like that.

I lean back against the upholstered seat. I know my symptoms well; it will not be a bad attack this time, more like a light doze. If I keep my eyes closed, Rijn will think I am merely at ease or praying.

We defoliated so much of Vietnam, the whole ecology is shot. Less jungle for Cong to hide in, but I know they mined this trail. Even spaced out on grass, you get a feel for mines.

August 4, 1969. S-2 said the trail is cleared of mines, but Big John steps on a toe-popper and loses half his foot. While they're dragging him off the trail, Barrio gets himself fucked up on a betty mine. The platoon freezes. Radio calls for a dust-off to pull out the wounded. Nobody wants to move. Sergeant Tuck is moving up and down the scared line, chewing ass in pure Tennessee backwoods, making one man move, then another. We go on single file and uptight, putting our feet in the same place as the guy in front until we reach the paddy and slide into nice safe mud.

We don't need those mines, not after a week of search-and-destroy. I've been on uppers most of it and a little hash this morning. I couldn't make it any other way. Lost too many good guys. I'm going into that village flying like the rest of the platoon. All but Tuck.

Tuck's RA, bucking for thirty years. Without the Army he'd be pumping gas back in Trashville. He digs this shit; he goes after Charlies for the fun of it when the rest of us would just stay cool. He gets people wasted, guys who were real short and counting days till they got back to the world.

I don't feel much, but I can still be scared. Big John and Barrio and me were the last of the old squad. My chances have run clean off the slide rule, man. Today, tomorrow I'll get it. With hash it won't hurt so much.

The Navy fighters lay down napalm but they must be smoking themselves, because most of it goes wide. The heat is unbelievable as we move in. Napalm sucks up the air; if you don't burn you can smother.

We hear incoming: Cong 82mm mortars. Somebody in Third Platoon starts popping smoke grenades, figuring the Cong is still in the village. The wind blows the smoke right down on us. Nobody can see anything. We're flushing old men and women and little dinks out of the huts, all of us blind with brown and yellow smoke. A white blur of movement flickers in the corner of my eye. I wheel and fire out of reflex. It's a dink, maybe ten years old. He grabs his arm and runs screaming back into the hut.

Tuck chops his arm at the few lousy huts. "Burn 'em all. This one first if they won't come out."

"It's just a dink in there."

"What're you, Flagg? The fuckin Red Cross? Burn it."

Screw it. For all I know the dink would drop a grenade in the gas tank of someone's jeep tomorrow. I put my lighter to the roof thatch and the hut goes up fast. Tuck lobs a frag grenade inside. It goes off like the end of the world. The roof lifts, then falls through, nothing but fire now.

The black sizzling thing crawls out of the hut and flops over, twisting like bacon on a skillet as the fire fries and splits its skin. Thank God for the hash. Used to be something like that would make me sick. But I'm out of it now, don't feel a thing. Not even when Tuck gets zapped.

One minute he's in front of me, then going over backward with the stray round from shit knows where; maybe someone in our own platoon. Screw Tuck. He got a lot of guys scratched for nothing. The hash high makes it funny. Tuck falls and falls forever like trick photography, and I'm laughing as we pull out of the village. What the hell, I'm splitsville anyway, never gonna make it back to the world. Tuck got it, not me, and so it goes on . . .

"Ethan? We've arrived."

We alight from the carriage. Already the day is turning humid. A hundred paces away among the trees are Berkeley and Hampton, both in black, and two other men.

"Ethan, for the last time, I implore you—"

"Let me thank you for your friendship now, Rijn. I have loved you." I fumble for his square hand, but he embraces me fiercely.

"Then for that love and Denise's, stop this. You are ill. Give him his meaningless apology. This is insanity."

"Come. They are waiting."

We move toward the assignation over wet grass that whistles about our boots, through scarlet azaleas and yellow marigolds. The forest at morning looks new-made, virginal, the sins to come unthinkable. It is a good day to leave it.

"By God, Flagg," Berkeley yawns by way of greeting. "I did not suppose you would be so prompt."

"It is a habit of shop boys, my lord."

Hampton opens the pistol case, murmuring introductions: the bewhiskered doctor, still red-eyed from too little sleep; his hastily recruited assistant, a young medical student. Hampton offers the pistols to Rijn for inspection. He does not take them.

"Lord Berkeley—doctor—my friend is genuinely ill—"

"Rijn, no more."

"He is in no condition to fight."

Hampton remarks gravely, "By coincidence, Lord Berkeley himself is not in the best of health."

Berkeley inclines his head to me. "Nevertheless, sufficient to the time."

Rijn is desperate. "Then compose, reconcile."

Berkeley removes his high, buckled hat. "That consideration is past, is it not, Flagg?"

"As are many things. Give me a pistol, Rijn."

Rijn examines each weapon and offers me one reluctantly. How solid and final it feels in my hand. Hampton draws Rijn and the others to one side. "Master Flagg has stipulated a single exchange of shots. Back to back, gentlemen. Twenty paces to my count, turn on my command. A single shot at will."

Berkeley's shoulders press against mine; he turns his head slightly to me. "*Bonne chance*, shop boy."

"One, two—"

We step out; the last scene of the comedy begins, a historic perfor-

mance. We are burying Man as an individual. Our farce has the
absurd motives of artificial honor, but at least each of us completes
and understands the whole violence as the will of an individual. The
conflicts to come will employ more and more men who understand
less and less of what they do until they are drugged numb by the
very proliferation and banality of horrors.

"Eleven, twelve—"

To us, freedom has an elitist meaning. To that coming mass, it will
be a terror. When men walk stultified through obscenities, the last
thing their atrophied souls will want is to control, to assert, to
understand. As the horror grows they will hurl their missiles from
farther and farther away. As the crime grows, the artificial innocence
must be greater until, one day, there will not be enough distance to
purchase detachment at any price.

"Nineteen, twenty."

Is death so frightening that we must labor to make it meaningless?
We are near extinct, Berkeley, still having shoulders to bear the
burden of being individuals, of declaring ourselves, first and last,
responsible. Neither of us deserves tomorrow.

"Turn!"

We whirl in upon each other like dancers, the last of an age.
Berkeley's arm comes down in mirror movement to mine. He is slim
and erect before me. We are beautiful, two Greek columns, proud
but past. In the wine-sweet morning the two shots merge into one
explosion.

My God. He missed.

The pistol bucked so hard in my hand, surely my shot would have
gone wild. But Berkeley staggers and sinks to his knees. Instantly
Hampton and the doctor are at him, opening the black coat. Rijn
runs to me, tearful with relief.

"God be praised, I need not send those letters. It is over."

But I am hurrying toward Berkeley. There is a spreading stain on
his shirt just under the heart. I kneel beside him feeling that there
has been, somehow, an unimaginable mistake that must be set right.
Berkeley's gaze is fixed somewhere beyond me, his lips moving
silently.

"Hampton, how could he miss?"

"You fool. He meant to."

The doctor opens Berkeley's shirt to reveal the smallish wound
and the larger discoloration around it. "It is very close to the heart.
There is internal hemorrhaging. I am afraid . . ."

Hampton sobs over the head cradled in his arms, strangled with grief and bewilderment. "You have freed him. Harry, is it enough this time? Have you found it? Oh, Flagg, if you knew how he sought this. Let it not be on your conscience. You have shown him mercy."

"Red Fox Leader to Red Fox Four . . ."

"He pursued death as this demon pursued him—"

"Red Fox Four . . ."

"—as if there were no God left in the world."

"Be still!" I bend close to Berkeley as the pattering, fevered whisper rises to an audible voice. His head moves sharply from side to side, not in delirium but searching and alert. I have seen that look before: just before he struck me in the Anglo Club. Saylors had it after a month on the Ploesti run.

The doctor closes his bag. "A matter of moments. It will not help to move him."

"Red Fox Leader!" The voice is clear and unemotional, the accent still recognizably Oxfordian but clipped and subtly shaded with overtones Hampton will not live long enough to hear spoken in London.

"Red Fox Leader to Red Fox Four, do you read me, Richard? Take the flight. No, I can't bail out. Bloody flak got my chute . . . a piece of me, too, I'm afraid. Canopy jammed. I'm burning. Romney air-sea rescue. Romney air-sea, this is Red Fox Leader. Mayday, may-day. Can't make the coast, losing airspeed and altitude rapidly. Course 285, airspeed 220 and falling. Going to belly in if I can. Hope you people arrive first. Mayday, mayday. Approximate position . . ."

His head swivels left and right and up. Even as his eyes close, Berkeley searches a sky I have known, empty white or full of death, with the look of a frightened hawk.

Thus Berkeley's lesson to me: though isolated in my disease, I am not alone. The infection spreads.

Berkeley went down over the Channel. For me the war goes on.

I hear nothing Rijn says to me. Plodding back to the coffin of my carriage, I shred the unsent letters, scattering white blossoms amid the scarlet and yellow. There is always hope. I cannot live forever. The Romantics have toyed with opium and suicide, but theirs is a self-consciously tragic muse. Mine is banality. I will dine with Denise in Montmartre and wait for good flying weather over Washington and Moscow.

STROKE OF MERCY

In musical terms, "Stroke of Mercy" is a series of études. I set myself the task of writing in four distinct styles—circa 1806, 1863, 1943 and 1969. In the case of the first, I wanted to show that one could suggest an antique period without exhibiting the Bulwer-Lytton syndrome; could, in fact, use the language of the period to add sinew to a story.

The trouble is, only about five people in the world, including Gardner Dozois, seemed to have read this piece when it appeared in *Twilight Zone*. I'm grateful for a second run in this volume. After all, look how long it took *Abie's Irish Rose* to catch on . . .

THE LITTLE THINGS

Their neighborhood along East Tenth was beginning to make page three of the *Post* for its peculiar variations on street violence.

"Never saw such a block for trashy, mean people," Esther rattled the paper in disapproval. "Trust you to find the right place."

She dropped the Iowa-twanged remark flatly. Neither the Good Lord nor her husband were given to rash judgments, more than she could say for the home office that plucked him up after fifteen years, not a day missed, and planked him down here where they couldn't even breathe without coughing.

They never really accepted New York. The dirt and violence of the city appalled them, to say nothing of the prices. For what they could pay, with three floors of furniture tenderly preserved and as carefully transported, they found a large, dark apartment just off Avenue C, which Esther scrubbed and lighted to a semblance of Iowa propriety. Their sanitation was stringent; they were offended by garbage cans spilling over the front curb, though better there than in the hall, where some left it to rot.

The neighborhood was dangerous as well as dirty. Within a week of their arrival, Bob was beaten and robbed by three youths. It was their numbers and surprise that cost him the swollen jaw. Lanky and long-muscled, he was stronger and faster than the slight stoop and uneven prairie walk revealed.

"Dirt," Bob judged, thinking of the three. "Trash."

"That's true," Esther murmured over the paper. "By the way, 'dyou take it out?"

"Not yet."

"Be a good time for it." Esther peered more closely at the page. "Well, that is—amazing."

For the second time, Bob Peel lowered *Field and Stream*. "What is?"

"The goins-on." Esther squinted at the newspaper through bifocals colorless as her flat eyes. "Oh-h." She drew out the vowel in soft wonder. "They are smart, these city police. They say all those stranglings were done with a belt. All the victims male . . . yes . . . young. 'Police are looking for a p-s-y-c'—oh yes, 'psychotic,' " she finished with a little nod of affirmation. Spelling was always A's in school.

"Needle in a haystack," Bob grunted. "Ten million of 'em in this town."

Esther giggled. His sense of humor always got to her. Nevertheless it was dangerous for him to be out on the street nights, though Bob Peel knew what he was about. Few men else, she reflected with a surge of possessive warmth, were so coolly set on the right path.

The paper held no recipes worth clipping; she must have ten on meat loaf alone. Esther wandered with afterdinner contentment to the little rosewood cabinet on the sideboard, her pride, its facings inlaid with fluted designs in mother-of-pearl. From the top drawer she took five or six small bundles wrapped in tissue paper and spread them on the dining table, unwrapping each with unhurried reverence: her collection.

Esther had no enthusiasms to speak of, never read beyond the newspaper, and looked away from the lewdness of modern film and television—and what passed for women's clothes, for that matter. She clung to conservative, full-bosomed paisleys that were proper back home. Underwear and certain feminine necessities were purchased in painful embarrassment, lingering shyly at the counter and whispering her needs to the salesgirl when no one was in earshot.

One thing alone spurred her whole interest. Now and then, returning from his solitary walk, Bob would bring her a trinket of some kind, and this small display of affection was largesse to Esther's heart. It might be anything, cloth, copper or brass—there was a lovely watchband of expanding metal links; Esther wore no watch, but *still*. Most of the items were worthless in themselves but showed the value of the strong man who slept by her at night, protected her from the mindless violence of this disturbing city and still had the gentleness of heart to think of the little things.

"Which do you like best?" Bob murmured from his chair.

"Oh, all of them." A fib, of course, her one secret weakness. She liked the gold items best, and he knew it, even if they were only gold-washed. She reveled in the sight and lovingly polished feel of them, all the more sensual since pleasure in adornment, she felt, lay aside from the way of the righteous.

Her lips moved soundlessly as a child telling the story of the dolls she manipulated in small drama. Bob watched her and felt the restlessness taking him, the prairie game hunter's need for the open. He tried again with the article on hand-loaders, then laid the magazine aside, fingers drumming on the slick cover.

Esther recognized the signs. He wanted his walk, like at home. There just wasn't enough in this horrible closed-in town to use up Bob's energy. He rose, frowning vaguely through the window at Tenth Street.

"Getting dark," he announced as usual.

"Feel skittery?"

"Kind of. Might go to the store."

"Bring me back something."

"Try to."

He took the small plastic case from a kitchen shelf and opened it, his red, square-tipped fingers trailing wistfully over the skillfully made flies and lures. No chance to use them any more or the oiled Remington deer rifle. He missed it sorely. He lifted the top tray and extracted from the bottom a clip of neatly folded bills, three tens and two fives, rearranging the tens on top, closed the tray and returned it carefully to the shelf.

Esther knew he was gone only from his footsteps receding on the stair.

He drifted north along Avenue C for about ten blocks, south again, then east to Avenue A. On summer nights, he thought curiously, the city lived in the street, on the sidewalk, the worn stoops, leaning out of dingy windows, lolling against corner lampposts. Now and then Bob approached someone to ask the whereabouts of a certain store. They were new in New York, he explained shyly, and never could remember the location of anything.

He felt a repugnance toward the people crowding the sidewalk. No one seemed inclined to help him at all. In their rapid, broken speech, they said they never heard of such a store. Bob Peel walked on.

The side street was poorly lit and, at first glance, empty of people. As Bob advanced along the sidewalk, he saw the two young men leaning arrogantly against the parked car. Instinct twitched at his vitals and tightened his muscles. It was getting late, though, and Esther wanted something. He took a deep breath.

"Say—you fellas know where this store might be?"

Asking, he drew the store address from his pocket; the money was wrapped inside the note, a habit as old as the grocery errands for his mother. He shoved the bills out of sight, though not quickly enough to hide them from the predatory glances of the two. They looked disinterestedly at the paper.

"No, man," the smaller one said. "We don' know."

His mouth, half open, reminded Bob Peel of a coyote. The other, heavy-set youth slid his dark eyes at Bob, wedging a toothpick languidly between front teeth. It was the teeth that held Bob's attention; the two front uppers, large and even, with bright, identical fillings in each face. The dentist must have drilled out healthy teeth, then painstakingly and expensively molded into the declivities the two, star-shaped fillings. It had to be. Who in the sensible world would have star-shaped cavities?

"Maybe down that way," Star Tooth jerked his head toward Ninth Street. He smiled, his private galaxy gleamed. Bob thought a look passed between the two of them. "Yeah, I think is maybe a store open."

He thanked them and moved away, his nostrils recoiling from the pungent cologne one of them must have bathed in. Again the premonition twinged in the pit of his stomach, the feeling he had many times at dawn on the prairie, sending out the rabbit call, waiting in vain for the coyote to show, then suddenly knowing that the scavenger was coming from behind, almost seeing the animal as it closed the ground between them.

He was alone now in the middle of a block of dingy closed shops. No one lounged in the doorways or at the curb. He looked back once, as if getting his directions.

The instinct had been true. The two of them were walking fast to catch up, coming with all of the coyote's hunger and none of his caution. The heavy one reached for a hip pocket; something in his hand caught the meager light.

"Hey, man." It sounded soft, friendly, urgent. "We forgot to tell you something."

The blood pumped faster through Bob's veins, clearing his head as it always did. His right hand twitched slightly and relaxed. Bob Peel watched them come with eyes the color of still, cold water.

Esther knew as soon as he brushed in past her to the kitchen. He'd been running; he was breathing heavily. She bolted the police lock and came to stand beside him as he replaced the bills in the fly box. The pocket of his shirt hung loose and two buttons were missing. A smudged portion of the front was slightly torn and heavily wrinkled as if wadded tightly in a convulsive grip.

"How many?" she asked.

"Two."

Her thin mouth set in a hard line. "This is a bad city." She watched the rise and fall of his muscled back until it moved more gently. "Maybe I can sew your shirt."

"Maybe."

There was nothing more to say. She went back to her collection rearranged on the table in various patterns while Bob was out. While he showered and changed, she toyed absently with yet another design. Someday she might get a real jeweler's board, like in store windows, and mount the things properly.

He was in the kitchen again. Esther closed her eyes and pictured him there, getting ready. A light tapping, four or five strokes repeated twice. Drawer opened, shut. Small sounds, the whisper of soft tissue. She tingled with anticipation.

Bob came to the table and placed before her the tiny, tight-wrapped square of tissue and went to his chair. She saw his whole body relax as if consciously willed. After a moment he took up his *Field and Stream* again.

Esther unwrapped the present as meticulously as he'd done it up and gazed in silent gratitude for some seconds. Finally, with deep wonder:

"Well, you are a *dear*, Bob Peel."

His mouth barely curved. "Just right?"

"Just."

They sank into their separate occupations for a contented space of minutes, touching in their own way, not really apart.

"I bet you left your old belt in your coat again."

He turned a page, absorbed. "Doesn't matter."

Esther sighed. "Makes the pockets all bulgy."

She really didn't expect him to answer. The clock ticked in its polished walnut case, a page rustled. Esther moved the lamp closer to illuminate her new treasures. They should go . . . yes. There.

Between the lighter with the Puerto Rican flag and the patch of skin with the tattooed heart, Esther placed the two exquisite little gold stars.

UP YOURS, FEDERICO*

At four o'clock in the afternoon, exactly four in the afternoon in Chihuahua in the sun-baked clay of Juarez, the Plaza del Toros.

Hurry: it is time for the brave festival, the festival of bulls. *Ai, los toros perdidos*, the lost bulls. So many, their courage scarlet on the sand. The *afición* rents its cushions and eyes the *toril*, the Gate of the Fright, that will expel a ton of death to the clean-raked sand of the ring.

¡Ai! Listen! Now the clock strikes four. In a strutting thrill of brass, the tinny, booming band strikes up "La Virgen de la Macarena." With the rigid march of the matadors in gold and silk, in the suit of lights, with the *cuadrillas* and mounted picadores behind them, now the *corrida* begins.

It has been said by men who know the Hour of Truth, that *corridas* are a marketplace where men buy courage they can never own. At four o'clock it has been said (by bitter men, thinking men) that the Hour of Truth is known only to the killers on the sand, and that for the briefest moment.

When the cape has made its flight, the banderillas placed, the muleta stilled and when the killing horns are lowered, tired. When the matador's *montera* has been lifted to the judge, permission for the kill received, the dedication mouthed—then it seems there passes, eye to eye, from the killer to the killed, whatever truth or poetry the world can find at four o'clock.

There are those matadors who die from time to time, but not a single bull that lives beyond the Hour of Truth—and this, to the embittered thinking men, falls short of the intent of the tragic play.

*With no apologies whatsoever to Federico García Lorca

This smacks of some disparity, and "Macarena" would turn flat but that such men know the world and how it goes.

Consider the breeder of bulls, Don Esteban de Caliente y Escobar, a man of acrid vision far too clear. His son has studied in Madrid, a surgeon of the delicate brain, a balancer of cells upon a knife. A *brujo-médico*, bearer of a torch, thrusting light into the dark places of the brain where intelligence has not gone before.

The bulls have made their family rich and given them the time to think. But then reflection is a bitter path, seeing the world and how it goes. They know the feel of *corrida* and what it means or what it meant. But Esteban was in Madrid in '37 when dreams and blood did not bray out in a skirl of brass at four of a Sunday afternoon, but were bought and sold the usual way the unpoetic world gets on.

Father and son: they have the Castilian look, the thing called *casta*, though their eyes are chilled with knowledge far more northerly: that death is not nor ever was a thing resembling poetry, but an irrelevance except as end to the pulsing single prize of life. Narrow-eyed in seats of honor, both of them are here today to watch their new idea of a bull. (Look at this bull. It moves too quickly for a bull's weight and with a precise deliberation that wastes no energy.)

This bull's sire, at his *tiente*, the testing of his will to fight, charged the lance but once and stopped. Don Esteban frowned. The watching vaqueros sighed in disappointment. One charge is a pallid showing for a bull calf born to fight. But even as the lancer turned with a shrug to Don Esteban and his son, the bull trotted casually to place himself between the rider and the entrance to the corral. Then it pawed the ground absently, as if reflecting on the most efficient means of killing horse and rider both at once and, satisfied with its equation, charged again, a tutored death that dodged the lance and killed the horse and, with a certain detached flair, the rider as well.

"Father," said Esteban's surgeon of a son, "this is a bull to breed with."

And that they did. The bull was only fair at love—all clumsy passion, perfunctory as a human at times—but much more meticulous at death, though for most of his fighting sons with enzymes planted in their brains, intelligence was far too brief before the fever closed their eyes. But now one son of this reflective bull is making his brave festival today, where courage in the face of death is bought (to watch) for the ticket price. And the crowd comes roaring to its feet—

"¡*Toro!*"

"*¡Torero!*"
"*¡Magnífico!*"
—all but the Escobars, that is, who sip *cerveza* as they wait. Their bull has taken the iron like milk. His hide is spined with ribboned cruelty and blood rivers the lathered hump. But the *picadores* are scared; the ones he's left alive, that is. This devil-bull gets past the lance as easy as a *gringo* cheats upon the tax of income. Three horses are dead with their digestive tracts rearranged artistically in view. Their riders hadn't even time to pray.

The bull has charged and whirled and hooked—"To the left. See, Father? Always to the left"—following the cape and not the matador. It isn't time for the matador. The game's not done.

"The greatest of bulls!" cries the *afición*. "Both ears should the *torero* have, and the tail and a hoof as well!"

"*¡Toro . . . torero . . . magnífico . . .*"
But the Escobars with sharp, sad eyes know magnificence is yet to come: new poetry for a bartered world at just past four in the afternoon from a fighting bull too quick for a bull to be, with odd-lit eyes that never glare but only watch and measure.

The *torero* lifts his little hat and asks permission for the kill—which, to the waiting Escobars, is optimism of a tragic cast. The killer dedicates the kill to the noble son of Escobar, to the *médico* and his science, and never knows how right he is.

A hush—the Hour of Truth has come. *Ai!* Pity the bulls who went before, who always died before they learned that brains can keep a bull alive; that killing bulls requires of men a deal of courage and a sum of skills, but killing a clown in a shiny suit is easy as rutting and twice the fun.

The bull pauses. He considers the matador, that slim objective in the shiny pants. Enzymes planted in his blithely murdering brain retain far more than how to charge. He is not a disparity, no more than the matador was to his lumbering ancestors who charged once from the chute and died and never had the time or brains to remember. This bull remembers everything, and if in his inexorable efficiency he strips the drama from the play, so has the world. The bull only states what is. He is a bull for today.

And now the matrix behind his watchful eyes remembers the object of the nimble game. The bull knows it's time; the rag is short. He reflects, fiddles at the sand, computes the distance and the waiting sword—and charges, hooking to the right. Surprise.

The shiny pants go all red and leak their insides on the sand. The terrified pics lure the bull away, and the bull is pleased to comply. This is part of the play, and insofar as a bull can love, he loves the game on the scarlet sand. He lets them lead him far enough for hurrying peons to lift the matador—then turns too fast for a bull to turn and punches the matador's ticket for good and one of the peons just for the fun.

No doubt the matador dies with a prayer and a sense of drama, however aborted. The peon just knows he's been screwed. *Corrida*, after all, is a tragic poem but not so tragic as the truth known to the Escobars: in the hollow-hearted world, the festival of courage, the spectacle at four in the afternoon, is a sweet fed to children against the aftertaste of a world never won in glory but sold since Judas and Madrid, since Munich, Saigon and Watergate and above all since tomorrow by bloodless men who somehow never lose and have no time for bullfights.

The crowd is hoarse but the Escobars are still. Their bull will have to die of course, but not a virgin like most fighting bulls. This one sired calves of a brilliant breed. Amazing what the younger Escobar can do with a scalpel, an enzyme and a truth. God knows what promoters will promote if future bulls are half this smart. Matadors like being alive much the same as buyers and sellers, and there's just no percentage in going against a bull that remembers or knows the whole game coming out of the chute. Like other men they will be, in the Hour of Truth, less inclined to drama than to flight.

The pics are coming to finish the bull for whom this was never a poem. It will be harder to kill his children and theirs will kill the sport, though not before good money's made by betting on the bull at three and four to one (seeing the world and how it goes).

The picadores close on the bull, and he wonders which of them to cancel first. He knows he can and knows besides, in bull-fashion, the clear, cold truth of the world as seen by the men who bred him. He waits, computes and paws the ground and loves the sudden red of it all.

And insofar as a brave bull can, he grins.

Olé.

UP YOURS, FEDERICO

Written with malice aforethought. I was sitting in a Spanish bar on Twenty-third Street, pondering the obligatory bullfight poster, when the old SF "what if" raised its quizzical head. What if the bull was a lot smarter than the *torero*? What price the Hour of Truth then?

The first draft was written in one sitting on a raw February afternoon and in free verse for no other reason than it came that way and Lorca's poem of Manolete was in my mind. Anyone past the ninth grade knows poetry sells about as well as a case of acne, but Ellie Mavor of *Amazing* asked only that I turn it into prose. This was done with hardly any changes but paragraphing, leaving the rhythms virtually intact.

It was written in a curious, cold anger quite foreign to me. It says what it has to about the smell of the world and then shuts up. I wouldn't change a word.

THE LAST RAINBOW

The legend goes something like this.

Once upon a time a princess caught a faerie, one of the little folk, and demanded his treasure, since it was well known that all faerie had fabulous wealth hidden under some hill and were legend-bound to render it on request. The faerie reluctantly waved his hand, the hill opened up and there was the treasure, its dazzle rivaling the sunlight. But, according to tradition, the little folk always ask something in return . . .

Thus the legend. The truth is more fun.

Once upon a time there was a girl named Brangaene—but "once" is vague; we can be more specific. It was rather well on in the Middle Ages, late enough for dragons and quests to be quite passé, late enough for Brangaene to be literate and even overread in that narrow, romantic field. She was the daughter of a harried baron who held a very small castle in a very small and agriculturally uninspired corner of England. His liege lord was both an earl and a bishop which meant the earl could demand his secular rights and, if not forthcoming, the bishop could close the gates of heaven.

Such was the case one spring when Brangaene was fifteen. The earl had declared war on a neighboring tenant and ordered Brangaene's father to send help or money. Since the baron depended heavily on his neighbor's grain mill, had no money and not enough men to populate a decent garden party, he declined with apologies.

The earl bishop thundered and threatened excommunication. The poor baron was in up to his neck, and since his life had gone much this way for a long time, his temper was understandably short.

Brangaene longed to be of help, but the problem was only periphery to her enchanted world. She hunted for unicorns in the forest beyond their moat, nosed for faerie on moonlit nights, and though she never found either, her faith was undented by failure. As pure and good a man as Lancelot hunted the Grail, and Percival even saw it. More than one historical knight had slain a dragon or a giant; it said so in her books. Unicorns might be scarce and shy, but scarce was not extinct. Faerie might be elusive—

"But so are foxes," she reasoned, turning to canonical precedent. If bushes could burn, seas part, tombstones roll aside and the dead rise, this fortuitous bypass of natural law could not logically be confined to the Middle East. So her catechism and belief. The unicorns would come, white and willing, the little folk would be caught, their treasure demanded. Faith would be rewarded.

"I mean, Father, we only have to look for them."

"Ye gods." The baron brooded over his soup, the bishop's tyranny and his daughter's mind. "What have I done to deserve this?"

Brangaene looked like her mother. This did not endear her to him. That pious woman had departed the world leaving behind an unfinished tapestry on the life of St. Paul and, as his enduring penance for marrying a Celt, this unworldly, star-eyed, faerie-chasing wisp of a girl. Her marriage value declined with his own fortunes. Once he might have bargained for a prince or dukeling, later a baron's son or even a plain knight. Now as he watched Brangaene running through the garden and tripping over her own dainty feet, he longed for a decent kidnapping.

She was forever racing up the steps with the news of (maybe) unicorns sighted across the moat, or (they looked like) faerie-folk peeping from behind trees in the forest. He tolerated this until her twelfth birthday and then announced his incredulity by kicking her down the stairs. As Brangaene persisted in her optimism, his placekick and her agility improved with time. She was even able to gauge her father's temper by the manner and sound of the kick. Mild irritation: side of the foot, a flat *bup!* Genuine wrath: point of the toe and swung from the hip with a resounding *poonk!* And as she became airborne, floating down toward the scullery, Brangaene meditated on the treasures and principles of her own, private, shining and utterly undeniable world. She was an unusual child.

Though her latest idea was truly inspired, Brangaene couldn't have chosen a worse day to break it to the baron. They were at dinner in the hall, the dogs rooting in the rushes for scraps and the baron dipping his bread in the soup and wishing it was the bishop's innards. That worthy had made good his threat. The baron was now excommunicate. The clerk in his soul quailed at the red tape involved: audiences with the archbishop, letters to the King and even to Rome, all for reconciliation with the earl bishop, might he strangle on his own *pallium*. Heaven aside, the reelevation from goat to lamb would cost a bundle.

"But, Father," Brangaene pushed her bowl away and went on earnestly, "that's my plan. We'll give the bishop and the Church the greatest treasure they could wish. No, not the bishop, he's too small. We'll *allow* him to take it to Rome, and the Pope himself will reward you, and the King will make you an earl."

"And what had you in mind to present to His Holiness?" asked the baron with deceptive patience.

"Such a treasure," she bubbled. "I thought of it as I was reading in the garden. The holy Grail, father."

The baron sighed. "Oh yes, the holy Grail." He dropped his bread in the soup, where it sank like the rest of his luck. "You've seen it lately?"

"No one has seen it since Sir Percival."

"Some centuries back, I gather, and somehow mislaid since then."

"All we have to do is find it," she asserted. "The faerie have it without doubt, they steal everything. And today I found little footprints smaller than my own in the woods across the moat. I'll take the dogs and trap them, and say 'caught caught caught' three times for the charm, and—"

Thoughtfully the baron laid aside his spoon. Pensively he rose, tenderly he guided his only-begotten child to the head of the stairs. Brangaene knew what was coming, but she was finished eating anyway.

Poonk! went the baron's full-inspired toe.

But Brangaene dreamed as she flew, and her dreams were not to be denied.

From the forest, the two small men in worn green tunics contemplated the unimpressive castle. Wary, dark and sharp-featured, they were accomplished thieves, and their present disagreement over method was conducted in a dialect ancient when the first druids came to wild Britain.

Malgon, slightly the elder, held that the small keep was poor pickings. Best steal two horses and be gone. Young Drust thought it shrewder to ask for a meal at the scullery door, tell a fortune or two and filch from within. They strolled back into the copse that had sheltered them since yesterday and considered strategy.

"Yon's a starveling lord," Malgon guessed. "If a's got a horse, steal it now before a has to eat it himself."

Drust stretched out on the soft, marshy turf, grinning up at him. "Thee's so fond of sleeping on rock, will pass up soft straw?"

"I want my own bed," Malgon wished disconsolately.

"And I. How many days to home, Malgon?"

"Four, five, an thy mother's not moved our tents."

"Hast counted the time since we left her? A full year."

"The leaving was thy madness, not mine."

Arms behind his head, Drust squinted up at the sunlight filtering through the treetops. "But hast not traveled? Hast not seen armies and great battles and the lords of the tallfolk and learned their speech? Hast not thieved in glorious and honorable fashion for a year?"

Malgon snorted. "Hast not *worked* as well?"

"Aye, true," Drust admitted with a tinge of shame. "Too often hast been reduced to that. We'll not tell my mother."

Their kind did not mingle much with the tallfolk of the valleys and towns. They were upland dwellers, following their cattle and goats where the grazing led them as the first of their kind had tracked the reindeer when the land was half ice. Then the tallfolk came with their bronze swords and their planted fields, taking the best lands, forcing the faerie ever further into the hills and heaths. They never planted grain like the bigger folk; if they had, how could they follow the herds? In hard times—and times were very hard now—they hung about the edges of the towns or hovered like Drust and Malgon about the two-penny barons' wars, and over the ages an unspoken contract grew up between faerie and tallfolk based on mutual distrust and fear. The tallfolk came to Drust's people for their magic and their gaiety, and even married them sometimes, though this was rare.

It was taken for granted that they stole as a way of life, but worked well when necessity drove them to it. Drust and Malgon could mend anything from harness to boots and clothing with a lasting skill denied bigger hands. Knowing their shyness, tallfolk left the work outside at night with a few coins so that the bit of paid work could seem the whim of the little folk and the coins honorably filched. It paid to be on good terms with the faerie. The cattle blight that they could cure, they could bring again. They had the magic.

And they *were* small. They lacked the crossbreeding and the grain diet that lengthened the lowlanders' bones, but already legend and fireside tale were shrinking them further into Lilliputian creatures with shining wings, and "faerie" no longer meant what it had. They were men, but few and fading out, fading into the hills and fanciful stories. There was little left of their magic but the tallfolk's dread of it. If Drust had learned anything in the year away from his mother's tents, it was this.

He turned to face his friend. "Malgon, I think—"

A dry stick cracked nearby; his head swiveled around, and then down into the copse poured a conquering avalanche of three men-at-arms, four huge dogs and a blond girl yipping with delight.

"Caught!" She bounded at them. "Caught—" She tripped over a root and went down spectacularly as a fallen empire in a puddle. Undismayed, she leaped up muddy but victorious.

"Caught! Three times is the charm, and you must yield to me or my men will chop you up and the dogs will eat you."

Drust and Malgon considered; there seemed no future in the vagaries of courage. The guards were shabby but armed, and the lean dogs of uncertain benevolence.

"Yours, lady," Drust acceded in English.

She held on to him, not sure he wouldn't vanish if she let go. "You're faerie folk?"

"Aye, but—"

"And have the magic and yield it to my service?"

Drust glanced at the undernourished dogs. "My God, yes."

"Including all hidden treasures—"

"Well, there's sixpence in my—"

"And the whereabouts of dragons to be slain?"

"What's a dragon?"

"Be large and scaly, I think," Malgon ventured, "and dost fly."

Brangaene's free hand clamped on his arm. "Then you have seen them?"

"Not this far north," Malgon hedged. *Aargh*, snarled the largest dog, and Malgon shut up.

"No," said Brangaene, you must uncover every lair, every trove of treasure and grant me three wishes, or one at least, and if I just get one it's going to be a crusher, and then—" she paused for breath "—you must recommend my good fortune to the Queen of Faerie and bring me the holy Grail."

She released them and waited, as it were, for wonders.

"A's mad," Malgon trembled. "Speak gently, Drust. Thee has the better English."

"Lady," Drust began, "it's true we're faerie and do a bit of trading, but—"

"But you will do magic?" Brangaene prompted.

Some of his composure regained, Drust managed a feeble smile. Even if Brangaene were an inch taller than he, her eyes were not difficult to look into, and he had seen very few blond women.

"Not before dinner, lady."

"Of course, of course." She turned, gesturing to the guards. "To the hall. Our plans are perilous and there's not much time. Away!"

"Truly a sweet lass," Drust whispered as they were trundled toward the bailey bridge over the moat. "Such golden hair. None of our girls have golden hair."

"Dost cleverly hide the shape of her skull," Malgon hissed. "And but for that, would swear a was dropped on her soft little head at birth. Oh, if thy mother could see thee now: taken by a mad girl—"

"And three men."

"—it retches me!"

"And four dogs, very large."

"Aye, four dogs," Malgon glanced apprehensively at the drooling of the nearest hound, "and unreasonable at that."

They were hustled over the bridge, across the bailey and up the steps to the hall, Brangaene urging them on. "Hurry! Hurry!"

If prudence were Brangaene's long suit, she would not have disturbed her father just then. The baron had few good days, but this one was a negative gem. The earl bishop had descended on his delinquent neighbor, seized his lands, including the all-important mill, and now perched only two hours away to chastise the baron for his breach of fealty. Thus, his beleaguered lordship was not only excommunicate, he was technically under siege. Prices were going up.

"I can promise God," the baron moaned to Rainier, his steward, "but the bishop wants cash. Bishop, hell, he's a broker! I've got to buy him off when I couldn't afford his horse."

Rainier tried to be helpful. "Is there a Crusade forming?"

"We lost the last two."

"Perhaps a pilgrimage to the Holy Land."

"Full of sand flies and Arabs selling pieces of the Cross. Rainier, we're sunk."

Voices, thumping feet, a skittering of hounds and then the stair-well erupted with Brangaene and her guards, four baying hounds and two rather stunted strangers. Caught up in the excitement, the dogs careered about, slipping on the rushes, *owoo*-ing in a frantic quartet until Rainier booted them into silence. The baron fixed his daughter with a dangerous eye.

"What is this?"

Brangaene's eyes shone. "Father! Guess what I have!"

"Bad manners and mud in your hair."

"I fell down."

"Again? I ought to put you on wheels."

"But I found them!" She tugged Drust and Malgon forward by their wrists, presenting them with a flourish. "They're ours."

Her father studied the two prisoners. "Indeed?"

Drust assayed a tentative smile. "How do you, sir?"

"Miserably, and shut up. Brangaene, your eye for value seems keener than mine. Found what?"

"The little folk."

"Their lack of height is apparent."

"But they're faerie!"

The baron looked again. They did not improve with definition. "These two . . . rabbit droppings?"

Brangaene nodded, jubilant. "And they've been charged to give up their treasures and three wishes and find the Grail, as I told you."

Her father turned away, suffering. "Ye gods."

"They look like thieves," Rainier judged. "What are they doing so close to the keep?"

Drust spoke up. "Just trying to get home, sir. We stole nothing from you."

"Which I take not as innocence but oversight," said the baron. "I ought to hang you—"

"That would be nice," said Rainier.

"—but I'm at war and very busy. Brangaene, you and your trea-sures will accompany me to the head of the stairs."

She winced. "The *side* of the foot, Father. They're really quite nice."

"Of course," he prodded Drust forward. "Come along now—no, wait. What's this?"

He fingered at the neck of Drust's tunic, opened it and extracted a heavy gold chain. From it, winking in the light, dangled a fair-sized emerald. Drust's hand caught his.

"That's mine. My mother gave it me."

"Where would your mother get a chain like that? Look, Rainier. Worth a war-horse at least."

Brangaene clapped her hands. "I knew it. I knew it."

Drust held on. "My mother gave it me."

"And who's she?" the baron demanded.

"Why, Queen Olwen," said Malgon.

The baron's eyebrows rose. "Who?"

"Queen of Faerie," Malgon struggled imperfectly with English. "Hast not stolen them; did give me one, too." He opened his tunic. "See?"

Rainier examined the rich chains and the undeniably precious stones. "This is not English work, my lord. Nor French or German, nor any I can recognize. Extremely antique."

The baron was a practical man, not given to unexamined belief; practical, but in deep trouble. And he had eyes. He turned to Drust. "I've heard those treasure stories from every passing witch and Gypsy all my life. Are they true, then?"

"Remember my wishes," Brangaene jiggled urgently. "Oh, please, please, we need them so much."

The two little men looked at the floor and were silent. Then Drust spoke quietly. "Take the chains, but let us go."

"Oh no," the baron decided. "No, that was hasty. Rainier, deposit my guests in the tower room, it has a workable lock. Golden geese, you're laying in *my* barnyard now."

Standing tiptoe on a stool, Drust viewed the bustling bailey fifty feet below. The bars were meant to constrain larger men; they might wriggle through, but the drop would be terminal. No way out.

"There must be," said Drust.

Malgon hugged his knees on the straw pallet. "Thee's the fleet mind among us. Tell me how."

"By wit and wile. Am I Olwen's son for nothing?"

"Hast not heard? Thee's the property of that great, scowling man, the golden goose to drop eggs like bread crumbs. And must not forget the mad lass with a's caught-caught-caught and the wishes and the Grails." Malgon threw up his hands. "A thinks we're a mill for magic."

Drust studied him with a slow, thoughtful smile. "Then will be one. The great baron wants treasure—"

Malgon's eyes flashed a stern warning. "Impossible."

"Just so," Drust nodded, "and therefore . . ."

They heard footsteps on the stone steps beyond their cell. A key groaned in the lock, then the door swung back and Brangaene hurried in with a tray. Two guards waited at the door. She placed the tray on a stool and closed the heavy door. The faerie men inspected their dinner: two apples, two slices of black bread, but only one bowl of leek and barley soup.

"There were two," Brangaene explained, "but I dropped one."

"Did guess." Malgon fell hungrily to the bread and apples. Brangaene noticed how he offered the soup first to Drust. Clearly this was Queen Olwen's son, a genuine faerie prince, and her luck was almost as great as her imminent need. The bishop would not be put off.

"You must give me my wishes very soon."

Drust spooned the soup, careful to leave half for Malgon. "Oh yes, the treasure."

"And the Grail."

"That's two."

Brangaene blinked. "Don't I get three?"

"Magic's hard, lady, and treasure's rare. There's the bargaining yet." Drust laid down the spoon and offered the bowl to Malgon without taking his eyes from Brangaene. "For a treasure, I'll ask value in return."

Brangaene gazed back at him and suddenly found it a little hard to breathe. She ascribed it to his magic aura—and let that suffice for an answer. Inexperienced as she was, her glands worked very well, thank you, and Drust was something new. She had never seen hair so black or eyes so dark, or a male figure, though diminutive, so perfectly formed. He was her gleaming opposite, and the attractive force of that juxtaposition is magic of a very palpable cast. No man had ever looked at her quite like that before, especially one who came so close and took both of her hands in his.

"It won't be easy, Brangaene. It will take time."

"We don't have time!" she wailed. "The earl bishop is coming, and he'll want just buckets of money."

"The road itself is hard to find, the road of the gods."

"We're in trouble with God, too. Father's excommunicated." Brangaene fluttered to the door. "There's no time for roads. You must wave your hand and make the hill open. Forget the dragons, Father doesn't hunt much anyway. Just one treasure, just a small one, and the holy Grail. You're bound to do it. The books said."

"What books?" Malgon wondered.

"All of them," she said. "The tales of faerie."

Malgon bit into his apple. "Was't *writ* by faerie?"

"Well, no, but—"

"Did think not. Lies."

Drust frowned. "Peace, Malgon."

"It . . . can't be a lie," Brangaene said in a small voice.

Malgon chewed placidly. "Why not?"

"Because—because I need it so much. Because I've searched for you all my life."

"Yes," said Drust. "I see that."

"It *is* true . . . isn't it, Drust?"

Drust glanced once at Malgon. "Tell your father we will bargain."

The color came back to her cheeks. "Oh yes!"

"And a bargain has two sides."

"Yes, yes," Brangaene flung open the door and plunged out. "And quickly, because the bishop—" She tripped over a guard's pike and went flying. Malgon winced.

The footsteps died away, the unbreakable Brangaene in the van. "Hurry! Hurry!"

Malgon sighed. "Now thee's done it. Nay, don't cock thy brow or frown at me who swore to look after the Queen's only son. A will whip me from her tent! And thee's no better than tallfolk with the mooning at yellow hair and watery blue eyes. 'May leave out the dragons. Just a small treasure and the Grail,' a says. Ha! What'll thee give little Sure-Foot and her greedy da but the lone, lorn sixpence between us?"

But Drust grinned from ear to ear. He threw himself down on the straw, glowing with satisfaction. "An impossible bargain, Mal. What I can't give for what the baron won't give up."

His mother's guess at the high birthrate of fools—one a minute—was rather informed, Drust realized. There were not one but two keys to their freedom, the baron's greed and the girl's belief.

Malgon was skeptical. "What won't a give up?"

"Brangaene."

Drust sadly overestimated the baron's parental devotion. With Adam's innocence, he bit lustily into his apple. As with Adam, it was only the prelude to his enlightenment.

The political axiom of the times was "every man must have a lord"—which is to say that no matter how big you were, someone had your number. Someone very definitely had the bishop's.

"Lord, hear thy servant in his hour of need!"

By the altar of a small roadside chapel, the earl bishop prayed very earnestly. He had attached the goods of one baron; his men waited outside amid the snorting of horses and the clank of mail to do the same thing to Brangaene's father, and all out of necessity. The earl bishop was in the same trouble as the baron, but larger.

By chance he was related to the King; by misfortune he was ambitious, since it led him to accept his bishopric from his royal cousin. The King thought it sound policy, in view of Rome's persuasive power, to have a bishop or two he could count on. Unfortunately, the bishop accepted his *pallium* of office from the Crown and didn't wait, as was customary, to have one blessed and sent from Rome. This political oversight has filled volumes; suffice to say His Holiness took umbrage and a flurry of letters coursed between the Crown, the bishop and the Vatican. When the diplomatic smoke cleared away, the bishop was regarded as unreliable in London, quite temporary in Rome, and had to decide which to placate first.

He prayed now for guidance with honest intensity. Truly conscientious, even dogmatic in his holy office, he was less intelligent than shrewd and above all less fervent than superstitious. He could always feel the heat of hell and was not about to fan the flames. The King was a mere relative; he could wait. To pay Peter, Paul would be cheerfully robbed. The gift must be large and of noble intent, one grand gesture of faith.

He and Brangaene had more in common than either realized.

The earl bishop crossed himself, rose and strode out to take his horse from the groom. He mounted in a rattling of mail and an aura of sanctity.

"Quickly on. We'll raise his keep before vespers."

It was late afternoon and rather warm for April when the baron strode into the hall carrying the two gold chains. Drust waited by the trestle table guarded by one man, all the baron could spare from the gates and watchtowers. The baron dropped the chains on the table, sat and poured wine into a silver cup.

"Brangaene says you're willing to bargain for your freedom."

Drust sat and indicated the wine. "May I?"

"Please do. Tell me, how much are you prepared to pay?"

Drust sampled the wine pleasurably. "How much will you ask?"

"A heap, little man. The lot, the bundle. Where is it?"

"Oh now, now, sir. That's not how it's done. The cup of wine begins the bargaining. Aye, there's treasure, but the way to it is a matter of when, not where."

The baron picked up the gold chains; the emeralds flashed in the light. "Did these come from that hoard?"

Drust sipped his wine dreamily. "Mother always liked those. The stones are like the green of wild Britain when we first found it. And the gold—is there any color goes so well with green as gold? Like sunlight it is. But when you talk wealth to us, you talk of wives and cattle and goats. These we value, these bring children and make food. We love gold only because it's so pretty."

"And yet you steal it."

"A hard word, sir. Very hard. We were the first men in Britain, and the land belongs to us. We only charge you rent."

The baron choked on his wine. "You what?"

"My lord taxes his own tenants, doesn't he, for the use of the land? The earl bishop charges you, the great King takes from him. A clear logic."

"What do you charge the King?" the baron inquired.

"Mother's rates go up for him. For you we will be reasonable."

"That's gracious for a man who has no choice. Now, this treasure. How much is there?"

"Your wine is lovely." Drust settled back in the chair, helping himself to more. "How much? That's hard to say. And the road of the gods . . . not where it is, but when. This is April, a fortnight yet to Beltane-fire—aye, could be soon, could be. But your King strikes his coin in silver, and we don't deal in that."

The baron frowned. "You don't?"

"Oh, a wee bit," Drust shrugged, "the larger pieces. It's not pretty as gold. Must think in silver weight. Let me see. Fifty . . . sixty . . . aye, the chest of pearls, large ones only . . . perhaps eighty—"

His host blinked. "Pearls?"

Drust's brow furrowed in concentration. "Eighty-five . . ."

"Eight-five *what*, dammit!"

"No, there's the rubies. I always forget them."

"You forgot—"

"We don't like red. It's the color of rage. That makes ninety . . . and some trifles, cups, ewers and jeweled plate that mother holds dear for the charm of them. Yes," Drust set down his cup. "Near a hundred thousand marks of silver."

Luckily, the baron's cup was empty, because he dropped it. He gasped. "A—hundred—thousand—"

"Oh, and the Grail," Drust snapped his fingers. "Lady Brangaene asked for it."

The baron was still stunned. "Part of the . . . rent, I take it."

"Collected from Glastonbury church by mother's own ancestor these thousand years gone. The Grail, the Cup of the Last Supper. Mother calls it her Jerusalem Cup. She may not wish to part with that."

The baron found his aplomb. "Quite, quite. Now, as to delivery—"

"But, my lord, there's my bargain."

"Well, what is it? What do you want?" A good question. If the gold chains were only appetizer to a hundred thousand marks of silver, what could he toss in to humor this improbable pixie?

Drust picked up a candlestick, admiring the workmanship. When he spoke his voice was gentle with an old sorrow. "Bronze: we learned from the first tallfolk how to make it, and that gave us swords to match theirs. Then others came with the iron we couldn't make or match. We don't like iron. But gold is beautiful, and beauty is what we love. Will you give me one thing with gold in it, even a little, for trade?"

"Done," said the baron.

"And if you fail me, your fields will blight and your cattle perish."

"Done. And if you cheat me—well, *media vita in morte sumus.* In the midst of life, eh? You're rather young to die."

Drust rose and gravely placed his small hand in the baron's. "Done for the third time and the charm. I want your daughter Brangaene for my wife."

The baron dropped his cup again—full, this time. "What?"

"Just that, sir. Not a jot more, not a hair less."

The baron began to chuckle, then to roar with it. Even the guard chortled. "My daughter marry *you?* I'll die laughing."

"Laughing and poor, alas." Drust rose. "Since there's no bargain—"

"Wait a minute!" The baron pushed him down again. "In the midst of life, remember? Ever see a man hanged, drawn and quartered?"

Drust regarded him imperturbably. "That will leave you with two gold chains and my mother's very long memory for injustice. Thy cattle will be Britain's wonder for their mortality." He tried to rise again; this time the guard quashed him back into the chair.

The baron thought rapidly. The earl bishop was imminent. Two dead faerie and two gold chains would benefit no one. He was still thinking furiously when Brangaene pattered up the stairs into the hall.

"Men, father, a whole line of them on the west road. Good day, Drust, are you working on my wishes? At least five hundred men, father, all in iron. When can I have the Grail, Drust?"

He shook his head. "There's no bargain made, lass. 'Done' my lord says and takes my hand on it, then 'undone' says he when he learns what I want. Alas—no Grail, Brangaene."

She flew to her father, stricken. "Why not? It has to be a bargain. The book said. Give him something."

"Don't tempt me." Her father drew her close with an acerbic smile. "He's asked the single rose among my weeds, the joy of my declining years."

She hopped up and down with the urgency. "So *give* it to him!"

"He wants you."

It caught Brangaene on the upswing of a hop. She came down with a thud. "Huh?"

Drust favored her with what he hoped was a winning smile. "You'll be the only golden-haired girl among my people, a bright star in a midnight sky. No longer dreaming of faerie-folk, but a princess among them, sharing their lives, learning to herd and milk goats—"

Rainier panted up the stairs and rushed across the hall. "My lord! The earl bishop is at the gate with five hundred men, five times what we have on the walls. What defense can we make?"

"Against five hundred? What would you do, Rainier?"

"I'd bloody well let him in, sir."

"Precisely," the baron sighed. "Surrender politely, invite his grace to dinner and hope he chokes on it."

Rainier hurried away, his orders trailing behind him through the air like a ragged banner. "Open the gates. Open the gates . . ."

"Goats?" Brangaene said. "Smelly goats?"

Drust smiled. "The most fragrant in Britain. Will learn to skin cattle and scrape hides—"

Brangaene swallowed. "Scrape hides?"

"And wear them as we do, and pitch and strike our tents when we

follow the herds to graze. But look at you! So pale and startled."
Drust held out his arms. "What do I offer you but your own
dreams?"

"I never dreamed goats. Father—"

"Peace, child. Would I marry you to this?"

"I thought not," Drust rose with confident regret. "So, of course
. . ."

Footsteps again. Rainier burst out of the stairwell, even more
breathless. "Ruin, my lord! Poverty, destruction and the end of all!
His grace is taking the cattle and swine and all that's not nailed or
mortared down—"

There was a growing uproar in Rainier's wake, voices, dogs, doz-
ens of feet tramping up the stairs into the hall. The earl bishop
appeared, out of breath, out of sorts and perfunctory. Hardly an
imposing figure either as noble or man of God, he looked like a tax
collector whose books were not yet balanced. Behind him came his
entourage—soldiers, the almoner, the clerks already listing on
parchment the valuables attached, one of them with a voice like
deep-knelling doom reciting aloud as he scribbled, "Four ivory
chests . . . one oaken *prie-dieu.*"

Brangaene wailed to heaven, "I HATE GOATS!"

The bishop nodded to her. "Then you won't mind that I've re-
moved yours."

"Eight goats," verified the clerk. "Seventeen hens . . ."

"I can't stay supper, Baron. I'm dispossessing you. Look to that
table, you men. And the chairs, all of them."

Drust was picked up by two brawny soldiers and the chair swept
out from under him.

"Five chairs . . ."

"Sorry about this, Baron, but you wouldn't help when I needed,
so I must foreclose."

The baron mopped his brow. "Your Grace is known to be just.
Can't we negotiate?"

"Your troubles are miniscule to mine." The bishop swept up the
candlesticks. "That's it, men, all of it. Everything."

The hall was growing quite crowded with soldiers lugging out
furniture and chests, and since it was near suppertime, the quartet
of dogs elected to charge musically through the procession, eddying
about the fringes of the activity. "Four . . . dogs," noted the clerk,
but the bishop kicked him.

"Not them, you idiot!"

"Blot . . . four dogs."

"Not my goldware," moaned the baron. "It belonged to the baroness."

"One chest goldware."

"I'm ruined. I'm a poor man."

"I HATE TENTS!" Brangaene screamed.

"Tent?" The clerk paused, looking up. "Did I miss a tent?"

"KEEP YOUR GRAIL!"

The baron muttered brokenly. "At a time like this—Grails." Instantly the bishop was at his side. "What is this? What Grail?"

"Grails," the baron echoed in feeble despair. Then, slowly he said it again. "Grail!" A dawning purpose lit his eye already tinged with the madness to match a desperate hour. "Grails! Yes, look!" He thrust the two gold chains with their emerald pendants before the bishop. "Treasure, Your Grace. Gold, silver, pearls, a hundred thousand marks of it. Look at these!"

The earl bishop looked, but he had heard something that faded emeralds to green clay. "The holy Grail, did you say?"

It was to the baron's credit he could think on his feet, and he knew how to play a trump. "*The* holy Grail." His arm swept out to point triumphantly at the bewildered Drust. "He has it all and promised it to me."

"The Grail," whispered the bishop, sepulchral as his subject.

"But my *own* goods," the baron reminded him delicately.

The earl bishop hesitated only a moment. "Bring it all back! Everything!" And far down the stairs the order coursed and echoed. *Bring it back. Bring it back . . .* The trudging feet paused, turned and started back up the stairs, the dogs dodging around and among them, baying for supper. One of them nibbled at the clerk.

"Brangaene," said her father tenderly, "I'm a man of my word. Prepare yourself."

"Wait!" Drust looked hopelessly from father to weeping child. "You mean—"

"I HATE COWS!"

"So don't drink milk." The baron took her hand and placed it in Drust's, the world once again in place and revolving nicely. "I mean you made a bargain, you demented elf. You're getting married."

Malgon understood none of it as he waited by the saddled horse watching the approach of Drust and the great bishop. The world had turned turvy. The bishop's men peered from every casement and cranny of the small keep while their lord loped about, muttering feverishly of Grails. The baron looked doubtful. Drust and Brangaene were betrothed and miserable.

But Queen Olwen—he shuddered to think of *her* when he broke the news. Her merest displeasure could blister paint, but her rage was lethal as it was silent and patient. Malgon shivered a little with the memory.

Drust seemed different, too. His open good nature was heavied with sober purpose and a kind of sorrow. It wasn't right for faerie to be so serious.

Drust halted by him, the earl bishop hovering over them both like a thundercloud.

"Malgon, hast the message clear, what to ask the Queen?"

"Clear, Drust."

"Her leave to follow the road of the gods."

"And the Grail," said the earl bishop. "That above all. Her son's life in exchange."

Drust favored him with an inscrutable look. "And the Jerusalem Cup," he verified. "Tell Olwen I would drink from it."

The bishop's mouth dropped open. "*Drink* from it? You would profane—are you serious?"

"Most gravely so," Drust assured him. "It is old custom, almost law. The Queen would demand it if I didn't. Faerie are innocent—as the world goes—and when we travel out among tallfolk, we drink from the Grail on our return to show we are still God's first children. There are dangers . . . Your Grace is a man of learning. Surely you know the legend of this holy vessel?"

The troubled bishop knew only too well. The most sacred relic in Christendom could not be touched or even approached by the impure without instant death. To drink from it as this vagrant pixie proposed was not only sacrilege but madness that beggared adjectives.

And yet the thought came unbidden—he would make confession of the pride if he himself could be allowed . . .

He shelved the thought. Devout he was, but the product of a suspicious world. Faerie were notorious deceivers. He knew not only the legends but the factual history of the relic. A few subtle questions would show the truth of it.

"Where was this stolen?" he demanded.

"Acquired," Drust amended tactfully. "At Glastonbury."

"The abbey, of course?"

"No, the old wattle church. No more than a mud hut it was then."

The bishop felt himself begin to sweat. "Where hidden? Behind the altar? Under the floor?"

"In a well, my mother said."

The earl bishop swallowed hard. His heart skipped a beat. "Wh-why should it be brought to Britain at all?"

Drust answered easily. "The merchant had friends here."

"What friends? What friends would a poor Jew have in Britain?"

Drust smiled at Malgon. "Mark how dost try to catch me out. Your Grace knows Joseph was a friend of the governor of Judea and a merchant in tin. Who needs hearsay when common knowledge will do? Every port in the Middle Sea, from Rome to Thebes on the Nile, shipped its tin from Cornwall. Is not Joseph still remembered and sung about there? Belike he made the journey more than once."

The earl bishop hid his trembling hands in the folds of his robe. "You have seen the Grail?"

"Olwen told me of it. 'Tis kept masked."

"Describe the jewels set in the vessel."

"There be no jewels," Drust shook his head. "No, *those* stories were writ in French, and not even Your Grace would trust a Frank. The Christ-man wasn't rich. Bronze it is and plain as truth. Mother wouldn't prize it else." His glance flicked over the bishop's rich mantle filigreed in cloth-of-gold. "Gaudy's not to her taste."

The bishop turned away to hide his excitement. He looked up at his men perched like predatory birds on the walls, the baron and his daughter waiting at the hall entrance. Most of the Grail stories were maundering, allegorical romance, and over the centuries a thousand liars claimed to have seen it. They all described a cup or bowl too rich for most kings, let alone the simple inn that housed the yet obscure band of the Nazarene on the night of the Last Supper.

Now, the bishop was a religious man—as those things went—though he could not believe the Grail had been withdrawn into heaven or simply disappeared from mortal sight. Lost, stolen or strayed, it had to be somewhere.

"Bring it." He turned and bustled away toward the chapel.

Drust embraced Malgon. "Haste thee back. The tower will be lonely."

Malgon studied him closely. "Thee looks sad as death."

"No matter. Go."

But Malgon caught his arm. "Nay, tell. Hast been thy servant. Hast not been thy friend as well?"

Drust's eye twinkled with the ghost of the old merriment—and an elusive something behind it. "And will be when bishop and baron be long forgot. Faerie's dealt with greedy men before, else why our saying that one thing worse than wanting—"

"Is getting," Malgon finished it. "True, they be all stupid and mad. Help me to this stirrup, Drust. 'Twas set for a giant."

Drust watched him across the bridge and onto the north road, then turned back toward the keep. Brangaene left her father and hurried across the bailey toward him. Drust's mouth curved ironically; this wishing business was quite beyond her now. She looked like someone who'd conjured a rose and received a thorn.

"Drust, what happened to the bishop? Runs past us without a word, talking to himself. Not even vespers yet, and he's in chapel praying for all he's worth."

"That won't take long."

"What did he ask of you?"

His expression was strange, but the words were gentle when they came, as if he were teaching a child. "What you all want of faerie: wishes granted, dreams come true, death put off till some far time when the world's lost all of its sweet. He wants magic in a bronze bowl. And what's your pleasure today?"

Brangaene saw the thing he had tried to conceal from Malgon, the pain. She might have missed it a week before, but even unicorn hunters, when they grow up, have to start somewhere.

"Poor Drust. I didn't mean to . . ."

"Ladybug, don't be sad. I was like you once. Because I couldn't see any further than a frog, I thought my lily pad was the world. Then I saw how big the world really was and how little and how few we are. Olwen has less folk to call her Queen than the great bishop brought here with him. Our cattle are scrawny, our children starve and we have no land. What little graze is left the tallfolk's sheep tear away bit by bit, year by year. We move from poor to worse and must keep on moving until there's nothing left. Gold, jewels," he spread his hands helplessly, "these buy *things*, Brangaene. They can't—there's a word in my tongue that means 'what was then,' but more than that. It means the good green time, all the good things that were. My mother will never understand. Malgon will never understand. It's gone, the green time. And it's not in my poor pudding of a heart to tell them." After a moment, Drust took her hand and kissed it. "And *you* want magic?"

"Not anymore," she confessed. "You're *very* nice, Drust. Just
. . ."

"Not entirely what you wished."

"I guess it's the goats."

Drust surveyed her, his manner changing abruptly. "Look, lass,
when you make a gown, you don't just cut and stitch away with no
thought to it. You measure what's needed. Well, it's the same with
wishes: they have to fit *you*. I'll guess you've never done it right.
Would you like to try?"

Brangaene hesitated; the whole phenomenon had proved hazard-
ous. "Should I?"

"You have one left. Close your eyes and think of something you
want so deep you never even whispered it."

Eyelids squeezed tight around the effort, Brangaene concentrated.

"Oh dear." She giggled. "Oh my goodness!"

"You see?"

"I didn't even wish. It was just—there."

"No dragons or Grails?"

"No," Brangaene blushed—rather more with anticipation than
embarrassment. "No indeed."

Two men-at-arms marched out from the hall, halted, flanking
Drust like falcons bracketing a sparrow. "The baron wants a word
with you. Quick *march!* One-two-one-two—step *out*, you horrible
little man. One-two . . ."

Drust tried to keep up with them.

The baron met them, rubbing his hands together nervously. "No
problems? Your servant will return, of course?"

Drust nodded. "Until then, back to jail, I suppose."

"Just to keep things regular. The *cuisine* will not stint. There'll be a
good supper."

"And wine," Brangaene prompted from behind the soldiers.

"Of course, he's our guest." The baron stepped close to Drust,
lowering his voice. "My abbreviated friend, I don't know how you
take to metaphor, but you and I are ripe wheat." He inclined his
head significantly toward the chapel. "And *he* has a very large
scythe."

"Just so, my lord," Drust said expressionlessly. "And what price
wishes now?"

"Eh?"

"The Grail and treasure make two. 'Twas not in the bargain, mind, but if I *could* eke out a third . . ."

In the eloquent silence of understanding, they listened to the interminable Latin braying forth from the chapel, where the bishop, as it were, was covering his bet.

The baron sighed. "If indeed."

"Just a thought." Drust let it hang in the air between them. The guards in his wake, he started up the tower stairs.

A week passed, eight days, nine. Then a morning came when the sun climbed only halfheartedly into the sky, sulked and then hid its face in thick cloud. On the tenth day, the small world of the keep was wrapped in fog, and out of it came Malgon on the same manor horse, leading two of Olwen's ponies. Drust watched him cross the bailey bridge. Within minutes he heard the heavy tread of the soldiers counterpointed with the light patter of Brangaene's feet.

"Drust! To the hall and quickly. Malgon's come with a letter from your mother, and the bishop's angry because no one can read it, and —oh, hurry!"

The guards hustled Drust away in the backwash of her urgency. In the hall were the earl bishop, the baron and Rainier, and in the center of their regard, like a spaniel pup among irritable grey-hounds, the weary Malgon.

"This fool of yours can barely speak English," the bishop growled.

"Here, read." The baron thrust a rolled parchment at Drust. "I didn't think anyone still wrote on sheepskin."

"And a palimpsest at that," Rainier peered at it. "Ancient as those chains they wore. This Queen doesn't write very often."

The heavy parchment was tied with a strip of worn linen. Drust undid it, speaking elliptically to Malgon in faerie. "How did the Queen at this?"

"Cold," Malgon murmured. "So cold and quiet, would swear 'twas winter and not spring in a's tent. Then a smiles like death and sits down to write this."

Drust glanced at the rounded Gaelic script and the scrawled, looping signature. His mother styled herself, as her ancestors did, with a title that had not appeared on any map for a thousand years, if at all. He felt a pang. For Olwen and her people, nothing would ever change.

To the English who hold Drust:

I marvel that so many tallfolk can prize cold metal over the real treasures of this world and yet call themselves wise.

Natheless, my son is precious to me. For his safety, you have my leave to travel the road of the gods and take such fortune as you find there, to the which is added my chiefest possession known as the Jerusalem Cup, excepting only our custom that Drust may try the innocence of his soul by drinking therefrom.

I wish only to see my son safe home.

Olwen, Queen of Prydn

Rainier squinted quizzically. "Queen of what?"

Drust handed him the letter. "It means 'the very old people.'"

The bishop's eyes were fevered. "But the Grail, where is it?"

"Olwen's word is good," said Drust. "'Tis with the treasure. And I will drink from it." He went to the casement and scrutinized the air beyond it. "After this fog will come rain," he told them. "And we need the rain to find the road. We must leave now."

The bishop needed no urging. "To horse!" He whirled and hurried to the stairs, his officers in his wake. *To horse!* The relayed orders echoed after him.

"Well, Brangaene," her father took her arm. "Will you come? It seems only right. This was your inspiration to begin with."

The guards had taken up their parenthetical position around Drust and Malgon. "Yes, ride with us, Brangaene," Drust laughed. "See the end of wishing. Who could miss it?" He shrugged philosophically to the guards. "Come, sirs."

They traveled north all day through a blanketing fog, Drust and Malgon in the lead, the bishop and two guards just behind, then the baron and Brangaene. Behind them in a train came the bishop's entourage.

The road gave way to forest, the great trees looming up and fading again like ghosts behind them. When the last of the gaunt shapes disappeared in the fog, Brangaene missed them. Nothing now but wild gorse and rolling moor and dampness that chilled through her heavy cloak. They pitched their tents in the middle of it before nightfall. The next day was drearier still. Though the fog was gone, heavy clouds lowered over the barren hilltops. Before midday, the rain began, gentle at first, then harder in a steady downpour through which they plodded all afternoon across the monotonous moor in the wake of the faerie men. Before they pitched camp for the night, Brangaene was sneezing with her worst cold in years.

Swathed in blankets, she huddled over a brazier in her small tent, hating quite beyond demure limits the weather, the moor, her father, the bishop and the whole blighted notion of wishes and magic.

"Dab!" she wheezed. "Dabdab*dab!*"

"Odd, your da just said that."

Drust stood in the entrance of the tent with a steaming cup. "Magic's hard work, isn't it? Here." He handed her the cup. "Olwen's own tea. Made from honeycomb and flowers."

She sipped at it. "Oh, it's good."

"Some say it's the rose does the trick, some the pimpernel, but we never have colds."

"Where are we bound, Drust? Will this moor ever end?"

He nodded. "Soon enough. Tomorrow we must be in a certain place."

"Why?"

"Not why, lass. When. When the sun comes out."

Like much of what Drust said, Brangaene understood it not at all. She listened to the rain drumming against the tent sides. "What if it doesn't?"

"Then we wait till it does. Nothing is perfect."

An interesting aside: this logical question and answer just might have been the end of the Age of Faith and the beginning of the Renaissance. Everything starts somewhere, and Brangaene was no longer a child of pure belief.

The rain let up toward midmorning of the next day. Their way ran through uplands now, wave after wave of bare, steepening hills and rocky outcrop. Drust dropped back to ride at the baron's knee and found him red-eyed as his daughter and definitely out of sorts.

"If you know this treasure to the last pound, why must we look for some damned silly road of the gods?"

"Only Olwen knows the way. I've seen it only once." Drust pointed to the hills, alike as wrinkles in a blanket. "Without the road I couldn't find it again."

The baron exploded. "There's no bloody road! Nothing but heath and no end to that."

"Will be soon," Drust soothed him. "We must have passed the treasure an hour ago."

"An *hour*—?"

"Or thereabouts. Must go beyond to see back, like a lifetime. Brangaene, lass, how's your cold?"

She snuffled. "Bedder, thag you."

Up ahead the earl bishop and his guards were paused over something on the ground. The bishop wheeled his horse and cantered back to Drust.

"There are tracks. They might be your people."

Drust urged the pony forward to the indicated spot. A hundred yards beyond, Malgon was halted, observing the lightening sky.

The prints were those of a small pony, at least two days old and nearly obliterated by rain. They seemed to begin and end nowhere, but they pointed south.

"Faerie horse," Drust confirmed.

The bishop pondered. "Should we follow?"

"You'd never find Olwen. She's only brought the Grail for me to drink."

The bishop regarded him solemnly. "You still persist in that madness?"

"The old custom. My mother expects it of me." Drust smiled quickly as if to dispel any personal doubts. "Will be no danger to Your Grace, of course, though it might be wise to stand well back and perhaps not look it straight on."

The earl bishop could no longer choke back the question. "How many men have drunk from the Grail?"

"In a thousand years? Many."

"And died?"

"Only a few," said Drust carelessly. "It must be the Christ-man's more merciful than one thinks."

"Drust!"

It was Malgon up ahead, pointing not to the sky now, but the ground. "Be shadow! The sun!"

Abruptly Malgon kicked the pony into a flat run up a rocky defile. Drust beckoned the others forward in a sweeping wave and galloped after him, the bishop close behind. The whole column rippled forward in the rush up the narrow pass, the bordering rocks now showing in sharp relief the shadows that raced across them as the last clouds parted and the sun burned through. Up and up they clattered until Brangaene felt the ground level out under her horse. She rounded a sharp bend in the trail. There, on the rocky ledge before her, stood Drust and Malgon looking away to the south, while the bishop sat his horse stunned, saying over and over to himself, "I don't believe it. No, I don't believe it. We should have known . . ."

And Brangaene's heart leaped with the last flicker of an old dream. Sad, because it would never come again. The old tales were not magic, no part of magic, only truth—and a kind of map worn faint with time.

"There, Brangaene," Drust's voice rang out over the bishop's. "The road of the gods. *Where it goes down!*"

Across the moist prism of the morning sky, the rainbow bent its glory to earth.

The long mound looked like any other low rise in the rolling hills. Only when Brangaene knew what it was could she see that it rose too smoothly, the length of its hundred-bow-length ridge too even. It had been built of stone like the great circle on Salisbury Plain, Drust said, and sodded over so long it was truly part of the hills around it.

Now she knew why Drust had stressed *when*. The rainbow lasted no more than a quarter hour, fading as the sun clouded over again. Before it went, Drust carefully estimated the exact point at which it would touch the earth, selected a series of references leading to that spot, then led them back along the trail.

Two more hours and the hardest riding of the whole journey, straight up hills, jolting down the other side. The mist rose rapidly, seeping like pale white snakes into the valleys and copses, rising toward the low hilltops. Just after they attained Drust's last reference point, Brangaene spied the figure that might have been a stunted tree or a large bush in the thickening fog, but she thought it moved slightly. Later, she saw it again off to her left, slipping away into whiteness like a ghost-wolf padding their flank. But for a moment Brangaene had seen clearly, if only in silhouette, the pony and its small, hooded rider.

She could hardly see the others now in the mist. Drust must be moving on pure instinct. At last, the wraith-figures of the two faerie men dipped into one last defile and disappeared briefly. When she and her father drew up on them, they were sitting their horses amid the bishop and his guards. Beyond loomed the long, regular shape of the cairn.

Drust slipped out of the saddle and knelt to examine something in the earth. The bishop followed him.

"What is it?"

Drust pointed to the hoofprint. "Olwen."

If no one else believed, Brangaene did.

The baron studied the dimensions of the cairn. "This thing goes back for yards. Is it all hollow?"

"And goes far down," Drust told him.

The bishop was all business now: "Set my tent here at the entrance. This *is* the entrance?"

"Hard by." Drust took several steps to the foot of the mound where a tumbled outcropping of stones rose some six feet above him. He leaned almost casually against one of the stones; with a grinding rumble, the largest boulder rolled back to reveal an aperture large enough for a man to wiggle through.

"Will need a torch," he said.

"Bring a resin torch, bring them all," the bishop commanded. "A fire here quickly. Set my tent."

Brushwood was collected, rubbed with tallow and lit in a large brazier. With a great deal of bustle, the bishop's tent was pitched. Drust dipped his torch into the fire, slipped into the black opening and disappeared. Malgon waited by the rocks. Suddenly he knelt close to the opening. Brangaene heard him mumble something, then he rose and shouted to all of them.

"The Jerusalem Cup be here. All may look. Be covered with a cloth."

Drust's arm jutted out of the hole bearing an object swathed in a long dark cloth. "Take it, Mal, so I can climb out."

Malgon shrank back and fell on his knees, turning his face away. "Nay, cannot. Do not ask it of me. Be not shriven or heard mass this fortnight."

Still the arm protruded from the opening. Like that which caught Arthur's sword in the lake, Brangaene thought. All around her, the men were dismounting, sinking to their knees, the sound of their armor eerie and distorted in the mist. Only the bishop remained upright, rooted in front of his tent, gazing at the masked object.

"I need both hands to climb out," the voice came again. "Let him who is without fear of his soul take the Grail from me."

Head bowed over her hands in reverence, Brangaene felt the awed silence. Then a rustle of movement. Her eyes opened. Slowly, deliberately, the bishop moved toward the Grail. Brangaene swallowed hard. There must be fear in him, but the bishop kept going till he stood within reach of the upthrust arm.

He stretched out both hands and took the covered Grail. An exhalation of fright and wonder sighed through the company of his men. When Drust clambered out of the hole, he regarded the earl bishop with a grave respect.

"Your Grace is the holiest of men—and the bravest. They may go in now. The treasure is there." He raised his hand for the watching men and opened it to reveal the rubies lying on his palm. He let them fall like so many pebbles. The men watched carefully where they rolled, their eyes wide, tongues licking out over dry lips.

"The treasure is there!" Drust raised his voice. "Olwen's word is kept."

"Yes . . ." The bishop's voice cracked slightly. He stared at his men and hardly saw them. "Yes, go in. Take the sacks. Get it all."

A dozen, twenty torches were dipped into the fire. A line of fireflies in the mist, the men squeezed through the opening and vanished into the cairn. The bishop appeared oblivious to it all. With stiff movements, he carried the covered prize to his tent.

Passing Malgon, Drust whispered something, received the other's silent affirmation, then joined Brangaene at the fire, listening with them to the growing clamor of discovery within the cairn.

"Now they're finding it, hear them? Finding out how much there is, how it shines in the light, thinking there's nothing lovelier, not even a fair woman. Feeling it in their hands. Wondering will it all disappear as they've heard tell. You can smell their greed. Don't go in, Baron." Drust smiled up at him. "There *is* that third wish."

In his tent, the earl bishop placed his precious burden on a low chest. He prayed briefly, then contemplated his soul's desire.

The first test was past. He was allowed to approach, to touch it, perceive its solidity. The shape under the woolen cloth was a foot and a half across by perhaps six inches deep. He fingered the edge of the cloth, took hold of it—

"Your Grace."

Drust moved forward to face the bishop across the chest. "I came to drink, and so grave with the thought of it, I forgot to bring wine. May a frightened man beg that favor?"

"You will still do this?"

"I must," Drust said tonelessly. He indicated a wineskin. "May I?"

The bishop's throat tightened.

"God with us." With a quick motion, Drust jerked the cover from the bowl. As he did, the bishop shut his eyes and crossed himself. Nothing happened; the world churned on. When he looked again, the bowl sat quite mundanely on the chest, feeble light from the one candle darting with unusual brightness over the polished surfaces.

He watched in horrified fascination as Drust unstoppered the wine-skin and poured a good measure into the vessel. The red wine swashed and sparkled over the polished bottom.

"Your Grace will send this to the Pope?"

"What? Yes . . . yes, I will."

"Don't tell him of this act. Would not bring on him the sin of envy." Drust laid hands on the bowl.

"Faerie, are you mad?"

The answer, when it came, was faint and weary. "No. Only a man from a small, weak people whose green time is gone, who will not walk Britain much longer. Olwen and I be their strength and their conscience, perhaps their soul. The Christ-man could not escape Gethsemane, neither can I."

Yet he hesitated, hovering over the vessel. The tent flap rustled back, and a beefy sergeant lumbered into view. "Pardon, Your Grace, but—" He saw the bowl and stopped. "God a mercy!"

"What is it?"

The man tried not to look at the vessel, but his agitation had to do with more immediate problems. "Sir, the treasure—"

"It is there?"

The sergeant's eyes seemed slightly glazed. "Th-there?" he stammered. "God, yes. And there and *there! Yards* of it, levels and stairs of it. Ringlets, plate, torques, jewels. We haven't sacks enough for all there is, and not to the bottom yet. The coins spill out of the chests like pebbles." He thrust out a handful. "See!"

The bishop examined the bronze and silver coins, all very ancient but legible. He turned them over, reading the inscriptions. " 'Agricola.' 'Trajanus.' These are Roman."

"For sure," said Drust blandly. "All Roman and writ of in the Saxon books. Some they took away, some they buried should they return. Faerie watched where they dug." He shrugged. "They were here four hundred years. Did owe much rent."

The sergeant glanced nervously out of the tent. "Sir, the men outside. They hear those in the cave. They saw the rubies this madman tossed on the ground. I can't hold them back much longer."

The earl bishop bristled. "If one of them steals so much as one coin—"

"A wise man would let them," Drust observed. "How much can magpies steal from a granary? Let every man fill his pocket before he fills your sacks."

"That bunch?" The sergeant snorted. "They'll steal my lord blind, little man."

"Would do that anyway," Drust countered smoothly. "Your Grace, when generosity comes cheap, buy a reputation. Will need them all to carry. Singing your praises will make light work of it. Let them go in."

It took only a moment for the bishop to see the wisdom. How much gold could one man tuck away in a tunic? "Give that order, sergeant."

"Yes, sir. God bless you, sir!" The sergeant hurried out. They heard his muffled, staccato orders, the answering shout and the rush of feet.

But Drust's attention had returned to the bronze bowl. "Was glad your man came in. It forestalled—" He broke off suddenly. "Pity a poor man. I must drink, but I cannot, not before shriving. You are a man of God and most blessed. Will you guard—it—while I pray?"

"It will be here." The bishop looked down at the bowl; the wine shone dark and red as rubies. He barely heard Drust leave the tent.

He looked at the bowl. After a long time, he bent and picked it up.

Drust joined the baron and Brangaene by the fire, a small island of light in the fog. For some minutes they watched the last of the bishop's men struggle through the small opening to the cairn. Brangaene wondered if there was room inside for all of them.

"And more," Drust told her.

Then the last man vanished into the black mouth. They heard his shout of discovery added to the others that faded as the men ran and stumbled from level to level, finding, filling their pockets. Then quiet. The horses stamped and snuffled. Only Drust noted the slight sound that might have come from the earl bishop's tent.

"This is a strange place," Brangaene shivered. "The eyes on those men when they went in . . ."

"Like their master," the baron growled. "And what's that holy hypocrite up to?"

"At war with conscience and need." Drust warmed his hands over the fire. "Will not be long."

"A moment's too long with such as these." The baron spat. "Greedy pigs, let 'em choke on the damned gold."

Drust favored him with that odd smile—amusement, sadness, more wisdom than the cairn held treasure. "Yes. Your third wish."

He took several quick strides to the rocky outcrop of the cairn entrance. "Mark how Faerie keeps his word. Three wishes. One, the gold. Two, the Cup. And three to choke them on it. One stone to open, another to close." Drust pressed against one of the stones. With a grating sound, the cairn was sealed tight again. His dark head snapped up. "And the third—NOW, MALGON!"

Brangaene looked up with him. On the roof of the cairn, dim with mist, she saw the little figure bend close to the ground, move something, then sprint nimbly down one slope. Before the booming began, before the earth trembled, she saw another, mounted figure race away behind Malgon. Then the shocks came, and the muffled roar that grew as the ground quaked beneath her feet.

Brangaene gasped, clutched her father's arm. Before their eyes, the long roof of the cairn buckled, went sway-backed and sank as five-ton stones toppled from the first interior level, ruptured the second, and the combined deadweight fell on the third . . . the fourth. The sickening concussions rumbled through Brangaene's feet again and again. At length they weakened, the distant roar faded, the shrieking echoes died. From the entrance stone, a small dust-wraith emerged.

"Good Jesus," the baron managed weakly. "What happened?"

"The end of wishing," said Drust.

Brangaene trembled under her father's arm. "All of them. All the b-bishop's men." The thought struck her like ice water. "The bishop!"

"Let him be," Drust held up his hand. "The thing's done. The Queen will be calling me home. Baron, Brangaene, share a cup of wine with me before I go."

The baron stared at him. "But the bishop—?"

"Please," Drust protested mildly. "It is so peaceful now." He cocked an ear. "Aye, they're coming."

"But where is he?" the baron persisted, nervously eyeing the tent. "Is he deaf?"

"Quite."

The soft *clop* of hooves came out of the mist. One horse stopped, the other grew louder until Malgon materialized, leading Drust's pony up to the guttering fire.

"Thy mother wants thee home, Drust."

"Will come." Drust dug in his saddle bag, extracted a plain wooden bowl and gave it to Malgon. "Fetch me wine, Mal. Some of the bishop's best."

Malgon vanished into the tent. Some yards up the defile, barely limned in the fog, the cloaked and hooded rider waited, motionless.

Brangaene wondered. "Drust, is that—?"

"Olwen. Will not come close. Has been hurt too often by tallfolk."

Malgon reappeared with the filled bowl, which he placed in his master's hand.

"The bishop?" Drust asked delicately.

Malgon shook his head.

"Did drink, then?"

"Did."

The baron put his question gingerly, not that it troubled him overmuch. "The earl bishop is dead?"

"Dead as pork," Malgon contemplated. "Not even Caesar be so well deceased."

"He was reaching for this from the first day," Drust mused. "Did only help him along." He chuckled softly. "Olwen burnished the bowl to make it shine, and in the burnish was rubbed foxglove and hemlock. Would kill six bishops."

Brangaene caught her breath. "You—poisoned—the holy Grail?"

"We tempted him with a custom that never was, Brangaene. If that's a sin—well, I think your father will pray for me."

Malgon laughed. Out of the mist came another laugh like a silvery, musical echo. Drust drank from the bowl and passed it to the baron. "Especially when he has five hundred horses and their saddles to sell."

"Faerie," the baron judged, "I never realized, but you command a sterling quartet of talents: philosopher, diplomat, liar and thief. Have you thought of a career at court?"

"Perhaps someday. If must take up a trade." Drust passed the bowl to Brangaene but she struck it out of his hand.

"YOU POISONED THE HOLY—"

"Naynaynay, lass," Drust patiently retrieved the battered bowl. "Not the Grail. Olwen never promised the Grail. Did write of the Jerusalem Cup—"

"B-but—but wasn't that—"

"—which belonged to Joseph's friend, the governor of Judea."

"The gov—" Suddenly the baron saw light. He could believe anything now. "You mean Pilate? *Pontius Pilate?*"

Drust nodded: "Does sound right, yes. 'Twas his washbowl."

Monstrously sacrilegious, but the baron had an irrepressible and quite secular urge to laugh. "Ye bloody gods."

"Brangaene," Drust offered her the old bowl again. "This is no great Jerusalem Cup. This was made for common folk like us. But it holds pease porridge well and doesn't leak, old as it is." He pressed it into her hands. "Take it as a favor to Drust. When you eat or drink from it, remember me." He kissed her lightly, gave her a wink. "And leave a supper at your gate for tired faerie men."

He nodded gravely to the baron, then mounted his pony. "Let's go home, Mal."

They rode away. Once, after the fog had swallowed them up, Brangaene heard Drust's joyful shout and again that other voice, low, melodious, welcoming.

That was all. She and her father were alone.

The baron spent some time stringing stallions into a train the mares would follow. He also inspected the tent. Malgon's assessment was precise. The bishop rivaled Caesar, even the pharoahs, for the finality of his past tense. When the baron returned to his daughter, she was pensively turning the ancient bowl in her hands.

"Father?"

When you eat or drink from it, remember me.

She recalled the text, almost the same words, written so long ago. So worn it was. So *very* old . . .

Her voice was tiny, a whisper. "Father—what kind of wood is this?"

"Hm?" He examined it. "Not oak or ash. Not English at all, I'd say. It's—well, I don't know."

"I do," Brangaene murmured. "Like my chests from Lebanon. This is cedarwood."

So ancient, dark-stained, the rim warped with time. Brangaene held it to her heart and her laugh was tremulous. "That man, that fine, beautiful man. He brought it after all. He brought it." Her eyes glistened with purpose. "Father, do you think the *arch*bishop—"

Her father understood then. "Oh, not again, Brangaene. That? You heard him, it's his porridge bowl."

"Father." There was something rising in Brangaene's voice that the baron should have heeded. "Listen to me. I think we should ask the archbishop—"

But he turned away and spread his arms to the fog. "She's hopeless. Hopeless! Will she never be done wishing?"

He did not see the subtle change of expression leveled at his back.

Just one more, Brangaene thought. Just the one Drust had taught her to realize, the never-even-whispered wish. It was a good day for miracles, and why not one of her own. She sighted coolly on the baron's posterior, wound up with a dainty hop-step and fired from the toe.

POONK!

The baron flew.

As he lacked his daughter's practice, his flight was brief and grace-less. When he sat up, thoroughly stunned, he faced a new Bran-gaene—confident, serene and sure. She held up the bowl.

"On second thought," Brangaene said crisply, "tell the arch-bishop *I* want to see *him.*"

As it turned out, the baron's judgment was suspect on several counts. He thought his arse would never stop aching, but it did. He thought he might come back and dig up the gold, but he never found it. Though after a while as they rode home, the sun came out and Brangaene sang sweetly.

The archbishop sent the bowl to Rome, where it was studied by Church scholars imbued with the new spirit of rationalism. They are studying it yet, as cautious scholars will, though the history-minded may note how suddenly Grail stories went out of vogue. They might have asked Brangaene, but who in the wise new world would credit a girl who told faerie tales and still left a supper by the gate for no one in particular?

THE LAST RAINBOW

An author's "best" is a matter of opinion, rarely his own. Best or not, this is one of my favorites, one of the very few pieces of my own work I can reread with the same enjoyment that went into writing it. I wrote it for pure fun and escape—for *me*, Charlie. Christ knows, I deserved it.

After two years of *Sturm und Drang* writing *The Masters of Solitude*, I wanted a playroom where I could gibber undisturbed. "Rainbow" is pure fluff, pure Kaufman and Hart, fast entrances, pratfalls. Something to make *me* laugh. I sent the first half of it to Ted White: "If you want the rest of this, let me know."

He did.

Still, it provided the germ for some of the background in *Firelord*, so two cents a word from Ted White turned into considerable profit.

We all like dessert once in a while.

THE SECOND DAY OF GENIUS

Life ended for Winthrop Purdy in Dr. Payne's office when the physician, his expression totally consonant with dismal truth, sat him down for the worst.

"There's no doubt, Winthrop."

Pale as a raw scallop, Winthrop husked, "I see."

"I wish there were."

Winthrop always wondered how men dealt with doom. Part of him accepted, had already accepted. The other part screamed for a higher court when there was none.

"The pains only come and go. I thought for a while . . ."

"They'll worsen." Doctor Payne turned up his palm in a helpless gesture. "If there were any other possible diagnosis . . ."

Winthrop Purdy's response was muted but manly. "You have said."

"Yes."

Then the panic. "I'll die!"

"Oh no, Winthrop. Face it."

"Face what?" Winthrop Purdy lunged out of the chair, prowling the white office like the battlements of Elsinore—tragic, informed against by all occasions. "A restaurant critic, a gourmet? The last word on food and dining as an art, one of the few civilized peaks rearing above a desert of junk food gastronomy? You've read my columns, my books."

"Gospel."

"Savored my judgments."

"Lucullan."

"Food is my life." Purdy appealed to the somber medico. "There's no possibility of error?"

"None. You have ulcers."

A broken whisper: "Ulcers."

Dr. Payne hyperbolized. "The lining of your stomach—"

"Ulcers!"

"Like a potholed county road."

"Nevermore . . ."

"Nonsense. You can eat all you want."

The response was leaden with loss. "Merely eat?"

"I have your seven-day diet here." Dr. Payne produced a typed sheet on which milk, cream, custard and tapioca appeared with obscene frequency. "Life can still be full, Winthrop." Payne considered his own feline wife, who, at that precise moment, basked in the country club sauna contemplating adultery with a muscular masseur. "You're not yet fifty. Find a companion. I know you enjoy women."

"Women?" Winthrop Purdy was tragic dignity at the door, the death writ trailing from numb fingers. "You offer limp *hors d'oeuvres* to one who has eaten roast duck within the ancient walls of Peking? You gaze unblushing into the face of the consummate authority on fifteen variations of cherries jubilee and maunder of tapioca?" The artist's agony burst from Winthrop Purdy, the heart unheard until it is laid upon a thorn. "Full? Take from Kandinsky his eyes, from Oistrakh a mere three fingers of the left hand. Take from the poet the few apses of brain that turn mere words into lyric. You speak to genius, Doctor. And a man." An eloquent heave of the shoulders. "Tapioca . . ."

Dr. Payne stared at the empty doorway. Winthrop Purdy was gone —doomed but still master of a mangled fate.

Winthrop slumped on a park bench, annoyed by the cacophony of children and birds who sang for all the world but him.

One last *envoi*, he thought, and then the burial.

In his fine-honed imagination, he envisioned the ultimately accomplished table, sat down in spirit and bade farewell to each cherished masterpiece. The white damask cloth, impeccable as honor, the sparkling crystal, the ruby vintage open and breathing in its tilted basket. The snowy napkin deftly twisted beside Royal Doulton and silver gleaming in soft candlelight. Forever farewell.

Farewell the asparagus vinaigrette, the garlic snails retrieved from their shells through intricate surgery with clamp and tiny, probing fork. Farewell croissants, light as frivolity, steaming as they broke open to receive the benediction of butter; the mustard-rubbed, garlic-imbedded spring lamb friended with fresh, tart mint. The herb-basted sautéed vegetables akin to the nocturnes of Fauré in their blending of nuance. And all, all complemented by superb wines, each a pedigreed pride, their very names a poem of the *ancien régime:* St.-Émilion, Montrachet, Château de Mouton-Rothschild— oh, the crisp Chablis, sunny Chardonnays, Graves, Médocs, Chiantis assertive as a Sicilian laborer, Cabernets velvet and subtle as sunset in Provence. Brandy and port—one could not bear to think on that loss yet. Some deaths were still too near.

And good-bye to the true passion of genius, the research. What purist delights in mere perfection? There was the quest, the hours and days closeted in his laboratory kitchen before one syllable could be graven on the tablets of gastronomy. Instruments laid out in expert sequence, an arcane reference opened to a sorcerous recipe not invoked in centuries. The trying, the failures, the devil over his weary shoulder urging Winthrop Purdy to accept the merely brilliant when he sought the legendary—and found it in the next exhausted effort, still and perfect as Beethoven's last quartet. And like deaf Beethoven, Purdy would henceforth be Tantalus at the feast.

What now? What work, what art, what center to life?

There were the foolish answers born of panic. Suicide was briefly appealing in a romantic way—one last magnificent feast thrown in the face of his malady—but vetoed as far too drastic. Nor would he descend as mad Bertineau did when the ulcers finished *his* career. Bertineau, acknowledged master of sauces and salads, joined the Salvation Army under an assumed name and was last seen dispensing bean soup and Wonder Bread in the Bowery.

Winthrop dabbed a hint of mist from his eyes and firmed his mouth in a straight line of determination. No self-pity; he'd not hang about the table scavenging crumbs from a luminous career. Nothing extenuate. He'd done the state some service . . . no more of that. Over the science, romance and joy of food as a higher art, Winthrop Purdy laid a funeral pall and a last rose.

He gazed with cosmic loathing at a nearby shish kebab and hot dog stand that wafted its corrupt odors to his insulted nostrils.

His ulcers twinged with warning as a gaggle of adolescents engulfed the stand and came away with chili dogs and black-seared hunks of lamb spitted like sinners in hell. They chattered and ate messily as they approached Winthrop. He gave them baleful note. They looked like all their pap-nourished generation: bred on a high-sugar, high-carbohydrate, frozen-TV, quick-food, heats-in-a-minute, Coke-and-Tab, flaked-and-shaped, burn-it-off-quick, mild-poisons-added-for-preservative diet abhorrent to Winthrop as the writings of Luther to a Pope. They ingested with the selectivity of a garbage disposal—munch, nibble, gulp, the little junk-food addicts were always gobbling.

One girl, gesticulating with a damp-laden chili dog, whipped an ample splotch of sauce on Winthrop's jacket. As the ulcers screamed in earnest, the bilious suffering in his eyes darkened to the hard brilliance of revealed destiny. To be mocked at sunset with bad chili . . . it was the blow that freed him.

No, he was the best still, subtle in his art as the reasoning of a Jesuit. So be it.

In the hushed vaults of the Forty-second Street library, Winthrop approached the central reference desk, rapping for the attention of the bored girl assistant who suffered serfdom here only to finish her master's thesis on the Oedipus complex in *Hamlet*.

"I am Dr. Borgia," he intoned, implying that only the retarded had not heard of him. He fanned the call slips in front of her. "I shall require these volumes from your stacks."

The girl squinted at the slips. "Toxi . . ."

"Toxicology. My field," Winthrop informed her with the secure humility of the professional. "Though I miss my own works from your files. Do hurry now."

Abashed, the girl directed him to the reading room, where she assured him the books would arrive with dispatch.

He would not overextend himself. One small cart would do at first, success would expand him later. They would flock to it as to that mundane vendor in the park; he need only be waiting. The cart should be rapidly mobile for escape as well as trade—clean, bright-painted and gleaming with chrome, its steam table wafting to the doomed odors irresistible as an offer of graft to a ward politician. They would gather, they would buy. In paroxysms of delight, they would gulp down Renaissance cuisine with a new name and, an hour later, close their beady little eyes forever without so much as a hiccup or forensic trace. The thought buoyed Winthrop as it grew. He strained no metaphor in the faith that murder and justice stood hand in hand, smiling upon him. Winthrop Purdy strode through the wide arch toward a new career, tomorrows mordantly resplendent as yesterdays were bright, his smile open and guileless, much less like Hamlet than reborn Richard.

THE SECOND DAY OF GENIUS

I'll come flat out, soul bared, nothing sacred, and say that I love to cook and eat. My own kitchen is one of my favorite restaurants, but when I'm traveling it's a bleak thing to realize that there may be nothing between me and a hunger-faint but Howard Johnson's or—pardon the obscenity—McDonald's. And even in places where the lighting is low and the prices high, you may be at the mercy of mediocrity.

Americans by and large do not have much taste for food—but then I'm the sort of oddball who can easily limit himself at conventions or publishers' parties to two potato chips or two pieces of popcorn, and actually prefer my beer at room temperature.

Yeah, I know. Definitely un-Amurrican, but even us freaks got to strike back now and then. This story was written to be read aloud, and I had a great deal of fun performing it for the Philadelphia Science Fiction Society. A cry from the heart—or the stomach, as you will.

INFLUENCING THE HELL
OUT OF TIME
AND TERESA GOLOWITZ

The first conscious shock after the coronary was staring down at my own body huddled on the floor by the piano. The next was the fiftyish, harmless-looking total stranger helping himself to my liquor. His cordial smile matched the Brooks Brothers tailoring. An urbane Cecil Kellaway toasting me with my own scotch.

"Cheers, Mr. Bluestone. Hope you don't mind."

I found what passed for a voice. "The hell I don't. Who are you, and—and what's happened to me?"

For all the portly bulk of obvious good living, he moved lightly, settling in a Danish modern chair to sip at his purloined drink. "Glenmorangie single malt; one doesn't find much of it in the States. One: my friends call me the Prince. Two: you've just had your second and final heart attack."

Right so far: my first was two seasons back just after finishing the score for *Huey*.

"You've made the big league." The alleged Prince gestured with his drink at my inert form; rich gold links gleamed against snowy cuffs. "No more diets, no more pills, backers' auditions or critics. You've crossed over."

I goggled at my corpulent residue. "Dead?"

"As Tutankhamen."

At first blush, there didn't seem much change. My penthouse living room, the East River and Roosevelt Island framed in the picture window with late winter sun. Lead sheets on the piano with Ernie Hammil's new lyrics. My wife Sarah's overpriced and underdesigned furniture, even the records I was listening to after lunch: Pete Rugolo and Stan Kenton, discs on the turntable, jackets on the shelf. For difference—me, very dead at the worst time.

"It couldn't wait? We open in two weeks, the second act needs three new songs, and God gives me this for *tsouris?*" I collapsed on the piano bench as my mind did a double take. "Wait a minute. Prince of what?"

His smile was too benign for the answer. "Darkness—or light, it depends on the translation. We do get deplorable press."

I took his point, not very reassured. "I'm not under arrest or something?"

"Of course not." He seemed to regard the question as gauche. "Will anyone come?"

"Why should they?"

"Well, what do I do? Where do I go?"

The Prince opened his arms to infinite possibilities. "Where would you like to go? Before you answer hastily—" He sipped his scotch, sighing in savory judgment. "Oh, that *is* good. You see, you've cut your spiritual teeth on misconceptions. Good, bad, I'm in heaven, it's pure hell, all of which rather beg the distinction. We're familiarly known as Topside and Below Stairs."

"Below Stairs." I swallowed. "That's hell?"

"Eternity is an attitude. Some say it looks like Queens. You have free choice, Mr. Bluestone; bounded only by imagination and your own will to create—and that, for far too many, is living hell. For you: *carte blanche* to the past, present or future. Though I did have some small personal motive in dropping by."

"I thought so."

"Nonono. Not a collection but a request. We adore your music Below Stairs. Now that you're eligible, we hoped you'd visit for as long as you like. We've quite an art colony, hordes of theater folk. Wilksey Booth would like to do a musical, and this very night there's a grand party at Petronius' house."

Adventure was not my long suit. "Thanks just the same, I'll stay here."

The Prince pursed his lips and frowned. "You never liked unpleasant scenes. You won't be found until Sarah gets back from Miami and by then not even the air-conditioning will help. There's going to be some abysmal Grand Guignol with the mortuary men, a rubber bag and your wife weeping buckets into a handkerchief."

Not likely. Sarah bought them at Bergdorf's, Belgian lace. For me she'd use Kleenex, the story of our marriage. We never even had children. Sarah was a real princess. Her only bedtime activities were fighting and headaches. For grief, she'd be spritzing the place with Airwick before they got the rubber bagful of me down the elevator. On the other hand, my last will and testament might get a Bergdorf hanky. The Actors' Fund would see a windfall. Sarah wouldn't.

The Prince nudged delicately at the elbow of my thoughts. "Pensive, Mr. Blaustein? It was Blaustein once."

"Not for thirty-five years. Didn't look good on a marquee."

"No fibbing."

"Okay: four years in an upper-class Washington high school. I used to dream I was a tall, blond WASP. On bad days even an Arab." Memories and reasons dissolved to another dusty but undimmed image. My Holy of Holies. Mary Ellen Cosgrove, super-*shiksa*. Wheat blond hair brushed thick and shining in a long pageboy, good legs, tight little boobs succinctly defined by an expensive sweater, sorority pin bobbling provocatively over the left one like Fay Wray hanging from the Empire State Building. I think my eyes really went from following the undulations of her *tush*. She was my first lust, aridly unrequited, but I played the piano well enough to be invited to all her Lambda Pi parties. Oscar Levant among the Goldwyn Girls with weak, horn-rimmed eyes, pimples and factory-reject teeth. Not much hope against jocks like Bob Bolling, who was born in a toothpaste ad.

But I could dream; beside me, Portnoy was a eunuch. My lust burned eternal in the secrecy of my bedroom as near nightly I plowed a fistful of ready, willing and totally unliberated Mary Ellen Cosgrove and panted to my pillow, *Why don't you love me?*

Because you're a nebbish, my pillow said.

The Prince apparently read the thought; his response was tinged with sympathy. "Yes. Mary Ellen."

"It's been forty years. I don't even know if she's still alive."

"More or less."

I was surprised to find how important it was. Past, present or future, the man said. Why not? The Prince's brows lifted in elegant question. "A decision?"

"You won't believe this."

"Try me, I'm jaded."

"I want to *shtup* Mary Ellen Cosgrove."

His urbane tolerance palled to disappointment. "That's all?"

"I've missed a lot of things in life. She was the first, we'll start there."

"My talented friend—*Faust,* for all its endurance, is pure propaganda. I should have thought at the very least an introduction to Mozart or Bach—"

"Look, for *bar mitzvah* I got ten bucks and a pen that leaked on white shirts. Now I'm dead; for door prize you want me to *klatsch* with harpsichord players? Later with the music, I want to ball Mary Ellen Cosgrove."

The Prince regarded me with cosmic weariness, steepling manicured fingertips under his chin. "I wonder. If memory serves, you last saw this Nordic nymphet in graduation week, 1945."

The growing eagerness made me tremble. "What happened to her?"

"You really want to know?"

"Maybe she's not a big deal after forty years, bubby. But she was the first. That's entitled."

"Let me think." The Prince leaned back, concentrating. "Cosgrove . . . from high school she wafted to a correct junior college, married a correct young man with a correctly promising future. Bob Bolling."

"I knew it! That horny bastard just wanted to score. Not just her, anybody."

"A fact Mr. Bolling belatedly appreciates; at eighteen he considered himself in love when he only needed to go to the bathroom. He spends less time on his libido now than his gall bladder; nevertheless, for his better days there is a pliant secretary who understands on cue. Mary Ellen has been relatively faithful."

"Relatively?"

The Prince's hands arced in graceful deprecation. "The usual. First affair at forty when her children were grown and no one seemed to need her any more. An aftermath of delicious guilt followed by anticlimax when no one found out, and one expensive face-lift. The last liaison, predictably, just after her younger daughter's wedding. Relatively, I say. She doesn't care that much now. Ennui is always safer than principles; it locks from the inside. Currently into vodka, vague malaise about the passage of time and what she imperfectly recalls as her 'golden, best years.' There are millions like her, Mr. Bluestone, perhaps billions. She never found much in herself beyond what men expected of her. For such people youth ought to be bright. It's their end."

His voice, cultivated with overtones of Harvard and Westminster, carried all the ineffable sadness of being alive, growing up, growing older. But I knew what I wanted.

"Not Mary Ellen now, but *then*. A night in October 1944, the start of our senior year. There was a party at her house."

The Prince's eyes flickered with new interest. "Oh yes. A fateful evening."

"I kissed her. The first and only time."

Memories like that stay with you. Somehow she was in my arms, fabulous boobs and all, Fay Wray enfolded by Kong Blaustein, and all futures were possible. But I retreated into embarrassment; in the middle of paradise, I thought of my bad teeth and wondered if she noticed. "I blew it."

"By an odd coincidence, the merest chance," the Prince said, "Teresa Golowitz was there that night."

"Who?"

"You don't remember her? Nobody does. Sad child, always faded into the wallpaper. Won't you say hello for me?"

Golowitz . . . no, not a clue for memory. Old acquaintance was definitely forgot. She would have paled under the beacon of Mary Ellen in any case. "Will I be able to make it with her, change the way things happened?"

"I certainly hope so," the Prince purred, making for the whisky again. "If not change, a definite influence."

"Then I'm going to influence the hell out of her."

"I'm counting on it, Mr. Bluestone." For an instant I sensed more in his eyes than weary omniscience. "Remember, you'll be sixteen years old with fifty-odd years of experience. That's not a blessing. Perhaps you can make it one."

Already in a fever to depart, I stopped, agonized by a detail. "I don't remember the exact date."

The Prince flourished like a banner headline. "October 3, 1944! Paris liberated! Allied armies roll across France! Binky Blaustein encircles *la belle* Cosgrove! Why not take the bus for old times' sake?"

"It'll be packed."

"Weren't they all then?" He raised his glass to me. "Good hunting, Binky. And say hello to Teresa."

Again with Golowitz when my soaring purpose strained at the bit. "Who the hell is—?"

But the Prince, the room and the year were gone.

Sixteen feels so different from fifty-five. An unsettling mix of fear and intoxication. A well of nervous energy, health and trembling insecurity based on the hard certainty that you're the homeliest, most unworthy and unwanted, least redeemable *schlemiel* in the universe. God may love you but girls don't, and life is measured to that painful priority.

Even after forty years I knew the route in my sleep. From my father's jewelry store down Fourteenth Street to Eleventh and E. Catch the Walker Chapel bus through Georgetown over Key Bridge into Virginia, up Lee Highway to Cherrydale and Mary Ellen's house on Military Road.

The bus pulled out at 7:10; I'd be there at 7:45. Just a little more than half an hour! Dropping my real-silver Columbia dime into the paybox, I quivered despite the double exposure of age/youth, glowing with the joyful pain that always churned my blood whenever I was going to see her. It was beginning, would be as it was *then* before time turned it into nostalgia and faded both of us to what passed for maturity.

The ancient bus was wartime-jammed with tired government workers and young soldiers in olive drab with shoulder patches no one remembers now: ASTP, Washington Command, the Wolverine Division, 7th Expeditionary Force. Baby-faced sailors with fruit salad on their winter blues, patient and stoic Negroes in the still–Jim Crowed backseats. Two working housewives from the Government Printing Office in upswept hairdos and square-shouldered jackets, bitching about their supervisors and the outlandish price of beef: you wouldn't need ration stamps soon, but *sixty* cents a pound, who could pay that? Bad enough you couldn't get cigarettes now even if you ran a drugstore.

The bus lumbered up the spottily repaired blacktop of Lee Highway toward Cherrydale. Grimy windows and the outside dark made a passable mirror to show me Richard Blaustein—Binky—in his rumpled reversible box coat from Woodward & Lothrop. Bushy brown hair neither efficiently combed nor recently cut, unformed mouth and chin still blurred with baby fat. Not Caliban, not even homely, merely embryonic. I winked at him from forty years of forgiveness. *Hey kid, I fixed the teeth.*

Next to me in the crowded aisle, two sailors compared the proven charms of Veronica Lake with an upstart pinup newcomer named Bacall. I felt dizzy, godlike. It's October 1944. Veronica Lake is box office in four starring Paramount vehicles beside spawning the peekaboo hairstyle that gave eyestrain to a million American girls. *To Have and Have Not* isn't released yet. I might be smoking my hoarded Pinehursts with three fingers along the butt like Bogart, but Lauren Bacall is just a lanky new whosis named Betty Perske.

I looked closer at my mirror-Binky. The liquid brown eyes behind the glasses were not completely naive even then, wary-humorous with an ancient wisdom not yet renamed as Murphy's Law. What can go wrong will, but—a little patience, a little hope. In four years we'll raise our own flag over Jerusalem; for the blacks in the rear of the bus, it'll be longer. Veronica Lake was a waitress before she died. Bacall opened her second Broadway show in 1981. They were both nice girls, but Perske and me, we lasted. Don't ask: there are survivors and others.

Cherrydale: I pulled the buzzer cord and wormed through the press toward the rear door as the bus slowed. It rattled open with a wheeze of fatigued hydraulics, then I was out of the smell of sweat, stale perfume, wool and monoxide, standing on the corner of Military Road under clear October stars.

"Oh, it's you. Come in."

Mary Ellen stood in the open door, one slender hand on the knob, backed by music and chatter. My Grail, the Ark of my libido's own Covenant—and yet different, a subtle gap between my memory and the fact of her.

"Melly?"

"Well, don't stare at me. Come in, hang up your coat. Bo-*ub!*" And she was off paging Bob Bolling. I hung my coat in the familiar closet and stepped into the large living room. Smaller than I remembered it. Gracious, comfortable chairs and sofa, french doors at the rear leading to the yard, Mason & Hamlin grand piano in the far corner. Boys in trousers that seemed baggy and ill-cut to me, girls in pleated skirts and bobby sox. And faces I recalled with a pang: Bill Tait, Frankie Maguerra. And willowy Laura Schuppe, always inches taller than her escorts.

"It's old Blaustein!"

And, of course, Bob Bolling with his unwrinkled Arrow collar and hair that stayed combed. He steered around two girls catting to a record of Tommy Dorsey's "Boogie Woogie," stroking one on the hips—"Shake it but don't break it"—to tower over me with an intimidating sunburst of thirty-two straight teeth.

"Big night, Blaustein," he confided. "Melly's folks are away and I

brought some grade A hooch. Bourbon, Blaustein." He always pronounced it *steen* despite my repeated corrections. He patted me on
my cowlick. "If you got a note from your mother, I might put some
in your Coke. Heh-heh. Come in the kitchen." He disappeared
through the hall arch.

"Skip the bourbon." The unsolicited advice came from an owlish,
bespectacled boy curled in a chair with a thick book. "It's a gift from
Mrs. Bolling's third cousin, a distant relative in the process of re-
treating even further. Try the scotch."

I edged over to him. A great disguise, but there was no hiding
those velvet overtones. "Prince?"

"Even he." He turned a page and giggled. "I love *Paradise Lost.*
Milton gave me such marvelous lines. The scotch is under the sink."

The record ended; couples shuffled about, awkward, faced with
the need for conversation until the music started again. Bill Tait
bummed one of my Pinehursts and I took the first puff. They tasted
awful, but you couldn't find real butts anywhere. I segued to the
kitchen in time to hear Mary Ellen, coy, sibilant and not really angry:

"Bob, now *quit* that. Honest, you're all hands tonight. Grab,
grab."

When they saw me, I felt only a phantom of jealousy. "Scuseme.
Thought I'd get a drink or something."

"Sure, Binky." Mary Ellen switched her pert *tush* to the icebox.
"Coke or Pepsi? Bink, what are you staring at? Coke or Pepsi?"

"Scotch, please."

She made a face at me, strained patience. "You don't drink. Stop
putting on."

Bob whinnied. "Little man had a ha-a-rd day?"

"You wouldn't believe, the death of me."

"Mama and Daddy don't even drink scotch."

"Under the sink."

"See, smarty?" Mary Ellen yanked open the cabinet door. *Voilà:*
Glenmorangie, the bottle collared with a small, handwritten tag:
Against mixed blessings.

"I never saw that," she shrugged. "Anyway, aspirin and Coke are
your speed."

The bottle looked like an oasis. "Ice?"

"Sure, it's your funeral. Just don't get sick on the furniture."

I dropped three ice cubes in a jigger with a decent lack of haste,
christened them with three fat fingers of whisky and inhaled half of it
in a gulp. "Jesus, that's good!"

"Don't curse, Binky. And stop showing off."

I winced in spite of myself at the sound of that thin, plaintive voice. Once it must have been aphrodisiac, especially when she sang. Now it merely grated.

"It's good to see you again, Melly."

"You drip, you saw me in school today." She peered closer at me. "But—gee, I don't know—you look different."

"So do you." It came out flat and not too gracious.

"Well, you don't have to be so sad about it. Bob, let's go dance."

That concluded her obligations as a hostess. Abandoned, I leaned against the sink and watched that little *tush*, the centerfold of a thousand steamy fantasies, bounce out of the kitchen with Bolling in tow. Thank God for the drink; the rest of me was deflating fast. Memory was definitely suspect. I remembered her prettier, even beautiful, and much more mature. She was unformed as myself. The eyes, to which I once wrote saccharine verse, merely blue with a patina of intolerance over ignorance. The figure was child-cute, but after thirty-five years of grown women and a regiment of Broadway dancers, it retreated now as the half-realized first draft of an ordinary, mesomorphic female body. So far from a resurgence of passion, I felt more pity and understanding than anything else, like suffering the gauche sophistication of a daughter struggling to be grown-up. The idea of sleeping with Melly was absurd, even faintly incestuous. My overblown lust went flat as a bride's biscuit, and from the shadows of Shubert Alley I heard the mournful laughter of Rick Bluestone, who would never call a spade a heart. Mary Ellen Cosgrove at sixteen was interesting as a clam. But then, so was I.

More kids arrived, conversation got louder, high and giddy on youth alone. Melly and Bob danced with a glum precision. Suffering from total recall, Frankie Maguerra regaled anyone in earshot with Hope-Crosby jokes from *Road to Morocco*. My bookish buddy had vanished, but Laura Schuppe, over at the piano, gave me an X-rated wink and a little beckoning toss of her head. I joined her on the bench.

"Find the scotch?"

"Huh? Yeah. Where's the little guy who was sitting over there?"

"Nelson Baxley, class of '46. Korea, Bronze Star and Purple Heart. Later: television production, five children, one Emmy, one duodenal ulcer."

I might have known. Laura would never even look at me, let alone wink. "Prince?"

"Nelson left, so I borrowed Laura."

"It doesn't bother her having you in residence?"

"No, it's all rather split-screen. On her side she's drooling over that varsity jock in the maroon sweater. Nice girl, somewhat confused, poor self-image. Top model for *Vogue* and *Harpers*, 1949 to 1955. One therapist, two nervous breakdowns, serial affairs with lovers of mixed gender. Cocaine, anorexia, Born Again Christianity. Married a Fundamentalist, currently works for the Moral Majority. Depressing. And Mary Ellen?"

"The booze is better. Thanks."

Laura sighed with a wisdom eons beyond her. "Nostalgia is always myopic. By the way, there's Miss Golowitz, trying to be invisible as usual."

Even as I recognized and remembered the fat, homely girl, my older heart went out to her. Teresa Golowitz—a dark, shapeless smudge among blondish altos in the school choral section. Coarse, frizzy hair, unplucked eyebrows that aspired to meet over her nose, and a faint but discernible mustache line. Thick legs blotched with unshaved hair under laddered nylons, and—insult to injury—a dress that would look better on Aunt Jemima. Among the relatively svelte Lamda Pi girls, she fit in like pork chops at a *seder*. I wondered why she'd been invited.

"That's why," the Prince read my thought casually. "Cast your mind back: Mary Ellen always had a few plain girls around to make her look good. And tonight is Teresa's turn in the barrel."

Memory sharpened to cruel clarity. My own family was conservative enough, but Teresa's old-country parents made mine look like atheists. She came to school in *shmotte* dresses and no makeup. She'd done her face for the party, no doubt on the bus in a bad light. I watched Teresa trying to press herself through the wall, fiddling with her hands, carmined mouth frozen in a stiff smile. I always avoided her in school; she was all the things I wanted to escape. Now I could see how much she might have wanted it, too, but two to one she married the kind of guy who wears his *yarmulke* to the office.

"You're big on futures, Prince. What happened to her?"

"Don't you remember?"

"Memory I'm learning not to trust."

"She committed suicide."

"No! She didn—" But in the breath of denial I knew it was true, a sensation at school for a day or two. When Frankie Maguerra told me, I said something like "Gee!" and briefly pondered the intangibles of life before getting on with adolescence. "When?"

"Tonight."

Yes . . . it was just about this month. The Prince stroked soft chords with Laura's long fingers. "Took the bus back to town reflecting on accumulated griefs and loneliness, and the fact that no one at this golden gathering even said hello to her, not even Blaustein. She got off the bus and waited at the curb—as she is now, tearing at her cuticles, multiplying this night by so many others and so many more to come. She didn't like the product. When the next bus came along—behind schedule and traveling too fast—she stepped in front of it."

I shook my head, foggily mournful. "What a sad waste."

"Sad but academic." The Prince stood up. "Excuse me. Laura has to go to the little girls' room. Had the immortal embrace yet?"

"No. Who needs it?"

Dismally true. The whole purpose of my flashback was on the cutting room floor. I was pondering whether to talk to Teresa or just leave now when Bill Tait roared away from a dirty-joke session to drape himself over the piano. "Bink! Give us 'Boogie Woogie.' "

"No!" Someone else demanded. " 'Blue Lights.' "

"Hey, Bink's gonna play."

"Yay!"

I swung into "House of Blue Lights" to a chorus of squealed approval. It sounded fantastic, too good, until I realized I was playing with forty-five years of practice behind me and musical ideas still unknown outside of Fifty-second Street: steel rhythm under a velvet touch, block chords out of Monk, Powell and Kenton that wouldn't be heard for years yet. The crowd began to collect around the piano. Mary Ellen got set to sing, her big thing at parties. Teresa Golowitz edged in next to her almost apologetically, pudgy fingers dancing on the piano top. Melly took the vocal on the second verse; not a bad voice, but it wouldn't go past the fifth row without a mike.

And then I heard it, rising over Mary Ellen's whitish soprano like a great big bird, that smoky alto soaring into the obligato release. Yah-duh-dee-duh-DAH-duh-duh-duh-DEE-dah-dah, bouncing twice around the electrified room and sliding back into the lyric like she was born there. The hair rose on my head and arms; everyone stared at Teresa Golowitz, who, perhaps for the first time and on the last night of her life, had decided to leave her mark. I rocked into another coda for her alone, begging.

"Take it, girl!"

Teresa did. Together we worked things on that basic boogie that weren't invented yet. And what a voice—not pure, not classical, but a natural for jazz. Teresa straightened out of her usual slump, closed her eyes and let the good riffs roll. Sixteen years old; you could teach her a little about phrasing and breath control, but the instrument was incredible. She played with the notes, slurring over and under the melodic line with a pitch and rhythm you couldn't break with dynamite. All the greats had this for openers: Lutcher, Fitzgerald, Stafford, June Christy, Sassy Vaughan, all of them. Under the excitement, the Prince's voice whispered into my mind, *Of course she's beautiful. It's her requiem.*

It could well be. When we finished the number, I bounced up and smeared her lipstick with an off-center kiss. "Baby, you're gorgeous. Don't ever think you're not."

"Hey, lookit old Blaustein the wolf."

Mary Ellen snickered; as a vocalist her nose was a little out of joint, say about a mile. "Oh, it's a *love* match."

Teresa blushed crimson. I doubt if she was kissed much at home, let alone at parties. She started to retreat, but I grabbed her hand. "Don't go, I need you. You know 'Opus One'?"

She hesitated, then made her decision. She glared with fierce pride at Mary Ellen and stood even straighter. "Hit it, Blaustein."

I zapped into the machine-gun opening with pure joy. "Opus One" is a real catting number. Most of the kids started to dance, the rest jiggling and beating time on the piano top. From Teresa we hadn't heard anything yet. She vocalized the soprano sax break from the Dorsey orchestration with a scatty-doo riff that wailed like Nellie Lutcher's "Lake Charles." She shouldn't end like this. In four years or less there'd be recording techniques able to put that voice on the moon, and she wants to off herself in an hour or two. The hell with it all, if I could just keep her from that.

We rolled up the wall-shaking finish, both of us out of breath. Teresa parked herself on the bench beside me, guzzling sloppily at her drink. "You are reet, Blaustein. You are definitely a groove."

"Me! Where'd you pick up jazz like that?"

"Who picks up? You feel it. The first time is like remembering."

"Feeling good, Terri?"

"Yeah, kinda." She grinned shyly. "I always wanted to be called that."

"Terri it is. And take advice: tomorrow we start working to-gether."

Her eyes clouded. "Tomorrow . . ."

"Unless you're not around, you know what I mean? Go home, take a *shvitz*. Tomorrow things will look pure gold. And when I call New York about you—"

I talked fast, promising, conning, cajoling, speaking of agents and record producers not even born yet, anything to get her mind off the loser track and that fatal bus. Still talking, I steered her into the kitchen, spiked her a little Pepsi in a lot of bourbon, a new scotch for me. I'd bomb the suicide out of her if I could, sing it out if I couldn't. One hour when she and everybody in range knew Teresa Golowitz was a person, a talent and worth the future.

We were dragged back to the piano. *Play more. Sing, Teresa. Please sing, Teresa.* She didn't know how to handle it all, never opened up like this before. I ruffled a big fanfare chord on the piano.

"Ladies and gentlemen—the fourteen karats of Miss Terri Gold!"

"Yay!"

"Huh?" said Teresa. "What's with 'Gold'?"

"Just like 'Blaustein.' I yell 'Golowitz!' who'd come? Hang on, Terri. We are going to the moon."

I launched into music so far beyond eight-to-the-bar, most of the kids were mystified. Way-out Monk and Shearing riffs, Charlie Ven-tura stuff, bop sounds most of the world hadn't heard yet, like "The Man From Minton's" and the clean, hard-rocking Previn-Manne "I Could Have Danced All Night," still twelve years in the future. Terri's eyes were moons of discovery before she dug it. Like she said, a kind of remembering. On "To Be or Not to Bop," she came in with her own obligato, sure and pure.

"Hey, Bink," Frankie Maguerra wondered. "What *is* that?"

Terri didn't need the name, she knew. I dropped the beat and backed her with light chords in implied time. She was pure gold; with a little grooming she could play clubs now, but she had to live for that. For the other kids, it was too far out; they needed a beat. Teresa yearned visibly after Bob Bolling, who left the living room hand in hand with Mary Ellen. I saw her glow fade back to the one-minute-to-*zotz* look she had before singing. Sadly she glanced at the clock.

"Terri, you want to try a ballad?"

"Gee, I don't know. It's late."

"One ballad. Name it. You got a favorite?"

"Do you know 'I Fall in Love Too Easily'?"

"Does Burns know Allen?" I rippled out a four-bar intro. "Fly, baby. The sky is yours."

Terri closed her eyes, lifted her head and sang. The room grew a little quieter. It's a great old number, an evergreen from an early Sinatra film that you can still hear on FM in New York. All right, critical? Teresa wasn't as sharp on slow ballads, not the best phrasing, a little wobbly on drawn-out vowels, but her feeling for the arc and sense of a lyric was sure and solid. The kids were very quiet now; she had them in the palm of her hand. Then she did something that curled my hair, ended one phrase softly and, on the same breath, swelled into the first word of the next with a gorgeous crescendo I felt down to my socks. I've auditioned a thousand singers. You can hear their technique and training in the first line. What Golowitz had no one can teach. I heard her plain in that short phrase, locked in with a soul full of *schmerz* and one slender lifeline of music. A homely girl, a fat loser in the svelte Rita Hayworth era; anyone could hurt her and everyone would, but when she sang it would all be on the line, bare and beautiful. A voice you listened to because it was your own. A smoky, black-coffee, tapped-out-and-running-on-guts sound you don't hear anymore unless you own some of the old Billie Holiday sides. Or another voice, quite different but as full of life and pain, that will pack the Palace Theatre twenty years from tonight with the same self-lacerating magic in every song. A miracle called Garland.

We finished the song. The kids drifted away, liking but not really understanding what they'd heard, ready for the record player and more grab-ass to music. Teresa looked again at the mantel clock.

"I gotta go. It's late."

"See me tomorrow, Terri?"

"I don't know . . ."

"Promise."

"Blaustein, don't ask. There's a lot of problems."

"Work with me. There's people in New York—"

"Don't put on," she said hopelessly. "You don't know from New York."

"Promise me, dammit."

"Why?" It was a wail, a cry for help. Already in it you could hear the gray decision, a door closing in Losersville. What I answered wasn't from sixteen. I wondered if sixteen could dig it.

"I know from New York and a lot of things. Don't blow it, Terri.

You got more to give in thirty-two bars than most people find in a lifetime. You want to be loved? So does the world. They'll love you, Terri. They'll beat your goddam door down. But it takes time and paying your dues and maybe a little trust. So see me tomorrow and we start."

Teresa tried to smooth the crushed material of her dress over shapeless hips. "Blaustein—you're such a *noodge.*" She said it like a kiss. "G'night."

I tried to follow her but a rather strong influence glued me to the piano bench. *You've done your best, Mr. B. Now a little trust.*

So I sat there guzzling scotch too fast, which was a mistake. Bluestone could guzzle, Binky couldn't. I took a few deep breaths and watched Frankie Maguerra dance with Laura Schuppe through the wrong end of a telescope, then wobbled upstairs to the bathroom, wondering if I'd be sick. Apparently there was enough Bluestone ballast to hold it down. After a few moments glumly pondering the toilet depths, I scrubbed my face with a washcloth and grinned farewell to Binky. "See you at Sardi's, kid."

Wavering toward the stairs, I heard Mary Ellen's voice from behind a half-closed bedroom door: "*Day*-amn, Bob! I said *stop.*"

"For God's sake, what's the matter now? On, off. You're a real tease, you know that?"

I pushed in the door and leaned against the jam. They didn't see me, sitting stiff and apart on the edge of the bed. Melly looked confused and angry.

"You don't have to be so crude about it."

"Oh . . . shit."

"And don't talk to me like that."

Poor Bob: eighteen, all balls and no finesse. He even rated a twinge of sympathy. "Hey, stud," I said, "why not try a little conversation first?"

Mary Ellen whirled and stiffened. Bob only looked annoyed. "Blaustein, blow. Get out of here."

I felt booze-brave. "Better idea, *shmuck.* Why don't you go get started on your gall bladder?"

"Listen, you—"

"Oh, he's right!" Mary Ellen screeched. "Go home. Go home, you're disgusting."

Confused, outgunned, Bob threw her one classic grimace of exasperation. "All *right.* But I won't be back."

"Bet?" I offered as he pushed past me and clumped down the stairs.

"What a jerk." Melly collapsed in a frustrated bundle. "I don't care if he never comes back. I wouldn't see him again if he was the last man on earth."

"Sure you will." *Because for you, he is.* That was less of a future than an epitaph. The whole thing was vaguely sad. I wanted to go.

"God." Her shoulders began to shake. "I'm surrounded with drips."

I put my arm around the forlorn, half-grown lump of her uncertainty: more experienced than her mother would imagine and a lot less than she thought. Sixteen: the voice of the turtle bellowing in her blood, wanting all the things she couldn't handle yet, and all she had were the cards girls got dealt in 1944. Unless you were a freak genius or something, you got married. You got a man. There wasn't anything else; not for Mommy, not for you. Later it might be easy, now it was hell. Only idiots want to be young again. It's a miserable gauntlet to run, but looking back later, Melly would block out the insecurity and pain until only the glow was left to shimmer in soft focus, and her picture would be no more accurate than mine.

"Take it one day at a time, Melly. It's more fun that way."

She wilted against my shoulder. "Binky, are you my really truly close friend?"

"Guess I am." I pulled her gently to her feet. Her lips found my cheek and then my own mouth. A very split-screen moment: enjoyment, regrets and a fleeting taste of what it would have been to have a daughter. I might have been good at that.

"You're nice, Bink. Just sometimes you're a jerk. You going home?"

"Time to go."

"See you in school."

"S'long, Melly. It was a swell party."

Wrestling into my coat downstairs, I peeked once more into the living room, at the kids I grew up with. A damned fool, happy and sad, high on life more than anything else, I ducked for the front door before they caught me crying. But someone did.

"Hey, Blaustein!"

Teresa Golowitz swayed precariously in the kitchen hallway, flashing a fresh drink and a bleary grin. "Hu-hi!"

"Terri! I thought—"

"Ah, hu-hell," she gulped. "I felt so good from singing, I figured one more for the road. I have just two questions for you."

"You didn't go. You didn't—"

"Don't change the su-subject. First: what c'n I do for hu-hic-cups?"

"Hold your breath and take nine sips of water."

"And the big qu-uk-question," said Teresa Golowitz. "What *time* tomorrow?"

"I'll find you." Gloriously smashed, she couldn't see the tears start. "Come on, how about we take the same bus?"

Terri was still grinning and hiccuping when the scene cut.

My penthouse was still there with a few major changes. On the floor, Rick Bluestone was beginning to wilt like leftover salad. The record jackets near the turntable were different but still classics of their kind. Stan Kenton had metamorphosed to *Kenton Digs Gold*. The Pete Rugolo album was titled simply *Pure Gold and Rugolo*. Beside them lay a third: *Gold Sings Bluestone Plays Gold*. On the wall just above the piano was a photograph of that vulnerable, indestructible head lifted, the mouth parted in a lyric. I remembered it with hiccups and much, much younger.

A lot of change, a lot of years. Some great songs.

Across the back of the album we cut together, she'd scrawled in a looping hand: BLAUSTEIN, YOU'RE SUCH A NOODGE— TERRI GOLD LOVES YOU.

The Prince rose and straightened his Sulka tie. "Whither away, Mr. Bluestone?"

I turned once more to the window. After thirty-five years of look-ing at Manhattan, the river and Queens, I wouldn't miss them all that much. As for Sarah, don't ask. With any luck she'd be out of Airwick. "Topside, I suppose. Papa will expect me."

A nuance of mild discomfort shaded the Prince's savoir faire. "Not just yet, I'm afraid."

"Why not? You said anywhere."

"Of course—in time. And time is what we have perverted, not to say brutalized. You won't be welcome just now, I regret to say." He didn't sound regretful at all, more like a sweepstakes winner. "You've played merry hob with the Grand Scheme. Terri Gold: three husbands, four children, three grandchildren, six million-seller records and a career that threatens never to end—all from a girl who was supposed to be a statistic at sixteen. Where Topside is concerned, it's best we maintain a very low profile until—"

"We?" I rounded on him in a chill of realization. "We?"

"You, me, what's the difference?"

"*That's* why you were all the time with Golowitz. You knew! You bastard, you knew all the time!"

He nodded in modest pleasure. "As the lyric goes, it had to be you. Of all that nebulous crew at the party, you were the first slated to die after Teresa. And the best bet. I field the shots, I don't call them."

The immensity of it collapsed me on the sofa, gaping. "You *gonif.* So you just waited until I packed it in, and—"

"Influenced," the Prince capped it with a satisfied smile. "I'm an artist like yourself, a sculptor of possibilities. What could you change with Mary Ellen, who was cast and immutable by the age of ten?"

I stared at him, unbelieving. "Dead one day and already I need a lawyer."

"And you shall have the best," the Prince conciliated. "For services rendered. Darrow loves cases like this."

"I'll bet. No wonder you get lousy reviews Topside."

"Topside!" he flared in disgust. "Stodgy, pragmatic conservatives. Lizst should die of fever before he's thirty, Schubert before he could write the glorious Ninth? Never! It's not all fun, believe me. Win some, lose some. Lose a Shelley, lose a Byron, a Kapell. Lose a Radiguet before he's twenty-five, a Gershwin at thirty-nine. But a Terri Gold at sixteen? No, the world is threadbare enough. And no one Topside, not even my celestial Brother—the white sheep of an otherwise brilliant family—has ever understood the concept of *creative* history. What in the cosmos does it matter if I make a mess of their records? I create! Like any artist, I need to be recognized. I need to be understood. Most of all," the Prince concluded wearily, "I need another drink."

I didn't understand half of it, but—you know?—I couldn't really stay mad at him. Whatever else, bad press or no, the guy has *chutzpah.* And there are all those years of Terri Gold.

"How long has Terri got?"

"Ages, Mr. Bluestone. Dogs' years. More records, more men, more grandchildren. She'll be roaring drunk when she goes and happy as a bee among flowers. And the last drink will be her best." The Prince polished off his own, neat. "Shall we?"

"Uh . . . where to?"

"As advertised, your choice. But till the heat's off, I'd suggest Petronius' party. There's someone positively seething to meet you, that clever little woman from the Algonquin set. Which reminds me."

The Prince swept up the Glenmorangie in one protective arm, the other through mine. "Dottie said to bring you *and* the scotch. *Allons,* Mr. Bluestone. The night is young!"

INFLUENCING . . . TERESA GOLOWITZ

How Can I Ignore the Girl (Boy) Next Door?

Better you should. This was a lovely song in 1944, a drearier reality when you think of all the high school sweethearts who got married for lack of anything else to do.

Still, you never forget the first girl who ever troubled your rest, and I am no exception. As a matter of fact, as I write this, today is her birthday. I hope she's having a ball and hasn't lost the figure that kept me awake at night. This is a valentine for all of us who now and then wish we could go back and have sense enough not to try. No A. E. Housman, I.

"Golowitz" had to be comedy. If you say sad, true things in a tragedy, they'll call you deep and forget it. If you say the same things and make them laugh, they may just remember.

"Golowitz" is a martini, very dry with a twist.

Cheers, luv. And happy birthday.

Parke Godwin
New York, 1983

PARKE GODWIN has been a radio operator, a research technician, a professional actor, an advertising layout man, a dishwasher and a maître d'hôtel. He is the author of three novels: *Darker Places, A Memory of Lions* and the Arthurian epic *Firelord,* which was nominated for the World Fantasy Award. With Marvin Kaye, he has written *The Masters of Solitude,* its sequel, *Wintermind,* and *A Cold Blue Light,* a novel of the supernatural. His story "The Fire When It Comes" won the World Fantasy Award for Best Novella in 1982. He lives in New York City.